A S H E S
and other stories

ASHES

and other stories

Naomi Shepherd

PETER HALBAN
LONDON

FIRST PUBLISHED IN GREAT BRITAIN BY
PETER HALBAN PUBLISHERS LTD
22 Golden Square
London W1F 9JW
2001

A catalogue record for this book is available from the British Library.

ISBN 1870015 75 4

'In Transit' was first published in *Encounter* in 1978. 'Sabbatical'
appeared under the title 'Post Mortem' in *Commentary* in 1978.

Typeset by Computape (Pickering) Ltd, North Yorkshire
Printed in Great Britain by
MPG Books Ltd, Bodmin, Cornwall

To Molly and Zvi Jagendorf

CONTENTS

ASHES

NAPHTALI LEARNED OF Lewis's death in the middle of a committee meeting. His first reaction was annoyance; any news of Lewis was annoying. After a moment he realised what it meant. He lost the thread of the discussion round the table, staring at the piece of paper his secretary had put in front of him. After the meeting ended, he remained alone at the table with his sheaf of papers, empty tea glasses, and ashtrays filled with the stubs of cigars and sodden teabags. The message had said urgent, but what was urgent about death? The urgency probably meant that Yariv, who had brought the message, wanted to get back to his kibbutz. The whole damn kibbutz shared half a dozen cars, or vans, or whatever they used, and someone else was probably waiting for the one Yariv had taken. What he didn't understand was why Yariv couldn't have phoned with the news – unless, of course, there wasn't a line available. Plenty of kibbutzim had private phones for the members, but not Ramat Ha Galil, as a matter of principle. The things that kept those people busy, the things they thought were important, were amazing.

Naphtali pulled himself out of his chair and went for a piss. There was no problem there, the spurt was all right, the colour normal. Still, as his doctor said, 'every day after fifty's a bonus'. Too many men died before sixty, even those who played games and went to the new health clubs. They took up yoga, or swimming, or tennis, not because they liked it, but like medicine, gritting their teeth at every stroke or every ball they hit. Then they ended up on the stretcher on the tennis court. His contemporaries were dropping one after another while his father's generation went on for ever.

Yariv was waiting in his office, staring out of the window. Naphtali recognised his goatish head, curly overgrown grey hair, plaid shirt, sandalled feet, even before he turned round. He was dressed as if it was the middle of the summer; everything about him announcing that people who lived a healthy life in the open air didn't feel the cold, and also that his personal needs were few. Naphtali pulled off his own jacket, slung it on the chair, and loosened his tie. He couldn't do anything about his aftershave, or the smart shirt.

'What happened?'

'Kidney failure; they got him to the hospital too late.'

Naphtali felt relieved. With kidneys you had fair warning. 'That's what happens when you live alone. He should have stayed on the kibbutz.'

'There was a vote against him. I couldn't do anything. You should have found him another job.'

'For the hundredth time.'

'At least I kept in touch. You wouldn't have even known he was dead.'

They had both stayed on their feet, grim faced. Naphtali felt his ears hum, and guessed his blood pressure must be rising. 'That's enough! When's the funeral?'

'No funeral.'

So that was it. That was why Yariv had come in person. The kibbutz wouldn't give Lewis space in their cemetery, though they found room for everyone else – kibbutz members' parents, Russian immigrants, when the body washers spotted their foreskins in the morgue and the Burial Society wouldn't touch them – but they wouldn't bury Lewis. Bastards. All right. If they were going to be vindictive, he'd fix the whole thing himself. He and Yariv were the only ones left now of the gang, and he'd go through the routine: the Burial Society, National Insurance for the funeral expenses, a small notice in the paper (though Lewis's name would mean nothing to anyone), relatives to console (no relatives that he knew of – that would make it easier), and a tree planted somewhere in his memory (the certificate would join all the others in his study). Naphtali had done it all a dozen times. *You don't leave wounded in the field.* The two of them had brought Lewis in once, and they'd do it again. For the first time he felt regret and grief – for Lewis, for Yariv, for himself. He punched Yariv on the shoulder, reassuringly. 'I'll see to it,' he said. 'Don't worry.'

'That's what you think.' Yariv fumbled around in the army knapsack that went everywhere with him and pulled out a crumpled sheet of paper. Naphtali read it slowly, scowling as he deciphered the handwriting. It was in English. Lewis had never learned to write Hebrew.

'Last Will and Testament. I, Lewis Arthur Goldstein, being of sane mind though frail in body and spirit, hereby bequeath all my books and papers to my dear friend and one-time comrade in arms Yariv Cohen of Kibbutz Ramat Ha Galil. All my other effects at my home in 501 Ha Yarkon Street I leave to my other dear friend and one time commanding officer Naphtali Ben David of Phosphates and Fertilisers, asking that he sell off whatever is necessary to pay my debts, two months' rent and the grocer's bill (Ze'ev on the corner). As a last request I also beg of them to cremate my body and scatter the ashes on the Judean Hills where we fought together. Lewis Arthur Goldstein.' Two signatures were appended in Hebrew.

'That's the doctor and the nurse,' explained Yariv. 'He had it with him.'

'How the hell can we cremate him? He must have known it's impossible. He'd been here long enough.'

'He was never *here*,' said Yariv. 'He was in his own goddam stupid head.'

Lewis had always been mad, whatever you liked to call it: crazy, *meshugga*, eccentric, psycho, and at the time it hadn't seemed to matter. As far as Naphtali was concerned, all the foreign volunteers in that war had been mad. Naphtali had never understood why they came; they weren't refugees. He and Yariv had grown up in the country, after all, had grown into that war, it belonged to them, to Yariv on the kibbutz, to Naphtali in the small town where his father owned orchards. He'd played with Arab kids, then he'd fought them, that was normal. Why Lewis had wanted to join in, he had never fathomed. Lewis had come from South Africa. Naphtali had nothing against South African Jews – they were all Litvaks anyway, like his own parents – and they'd done their bit, fought well, and if some of them went off again to be heroes somewhere else, fighting apartheid and so on, that was their choice.

But Lewis wasn't like that. Lewis hardly knew one end of a Lee Enfield from the other. He had to put his special glasses on before he could even see the target. Yariv had taken him in hand, because given enough ammunition and a dark enough night, he could have wiped out the whole platoon. On the other hand, he had his uses. He actually wrote down what you told him. If you pointed him in the right direction and told him to keep watch, he did just that, even if in the event you forgot where you'd left him, forgot he hadn't made contact for hours. That was how he got left behind. The Arabs had blown up the house he was guarding, and a wall had fallen in, and they'd found Lewis much later, unconscious. In those days you didn't radio for M.O.s with their bags and lines of serum and their stretchers. You just patched Lewis up and got on with it. No use trying to explain that to your grandsons, with their computerised artillery.

Lewis had a head wound they bandaged, and he was on his

feet in no time. Nothing seemed to have changed, he was the same Lewis, with his long face and lugubrious voice, asking for more orders, asking to be told where to go and what to do. Different to your schoolfriends who grumbled over every damn command. Commanding officer, Lewis had called him. Lewis was older than any of them, how old was never clear, but Naphtali had been a kid of eighteen, with acne.

Later, Naphtali and Yariv asked themselves whether it was the head wound that had made Lewis so peculiar, but they always ended by agreeing that he'd been odd from the beginning, *meshugga*, psycho, crazy, the blow to his head hadn't changed anything.

Naphtali couldn't remember, now, how it had started, how he and Yariv had become responsible for Lewis. Perhaps it was because it was they who had found him lying askew, under the wall. If they'd known what a headache he was going to be, they'd have left him there, they joked.

Lewis never managed to learn Hebrew properly. Whether it was the result of the head wound, deafness, or problems with other languages, Naphtali didn't know, but Lewis never learned more than a few basic phrases. He went to immigrants' classes, Naphtali bought him Berlitz records, but Lewis didn't dare open his mouth; or perhaps didn't want to. Both he and Yariv suspected that Lewis knew far more Hebrew than he let on. It was uncomfortable, not knowing quite what was going on behind his eyes, not being sure what you could say in front of him, because they spoke Hebrew in his presence anyway; everyone did. It was up to him to work it out. Or not. It was his problem, they'd done their best.

Naphtali and Yariv decided Lewis would be best off working in English; there were plenty of public relations and translation jobs. Naphtali found Lewis a job writing information brochures for the Foreign Ministry, until there was an efficiency drive and they found that someone was employed full time rewriting

Lewis's compositions. Even the other Anglo-Saxons, it turned out, couldn't stomach Lewis's style. It was like his will, full of pompous phrases and quotations. A phone call to the Ministry of Education got Lewis another job, this time teaching remedial English in a development town in the Negev; but the kids tortured him till he wept. Later, Naphtali bullied someone in the Transport Ministry into letting Lewis into the office where they wrote the English version of roadsigns; Lewis resigned in protest against what he called Polish spelling. By this time Naphtali, who was doing well at work, persuaded Yariv to use his influence as a veteran member of Ramat Ha Galil to get Lewis admitted for a trial period. Until then Yariv hadn't pulled his weight, and Naphtali thought the kibbutz was just the place for Lewis.

Like all the rest of the gang (except for Lewis), Naphtali had spent a year on Yariv's kibbutz doing paramilitary service. In later years he went there regularly at weekends, showing the kids, and afterwards the grandchildren, where he'd found a few shards of pottery that were in the kibbutz museum, where he'd killed a jackal or a scorpion. He still went there occasionally to advise the kibbutz on fertilisers. Secretly, he'd always believed that it was the task of the kibbutz to absorb a certain number of social misfits: single parents, problem children, flotsam like Lewis. To each according to his needs. He was sure they'd find a niche for Lewis.

Naphtali was partly right. The kibbutz solution had lasted several years. Lewis fed the animals in the pets corner – he was afraid of anything larger than himself – catalogued the foreign books in the kibbutz culture house, and earned his keep by dishwashing. His status was uncertain, both in the country and in the kibbutz. He never became either an Israeli or a kibbutz member, and officially he existed only on a Commonwealth passport he had never renewed. It was easier to ignore Lewis than to tackle his problems, and no one discussed him at kibbutz meetings. He was the eternal volunteer, useful during wars when most of the other men were called away to fight. In the Sinai Campaign and the Six Day War he had even worked in the fields.

The trouble started during the Yom Kippur war and its aftermath. That was when he met Jennifer, a Baptist girl who had arrived as a volunteer, and Lewis's woman problem came up. Yariv and Naphtali had tacitly agreed that whatever else they could do for Lewis, they couldn't mate him. When they went out together for reunions with the gang, Lewis, normally so quiet, became wildly obscene. Naphtali preferred not to take Lewis to a restaurant because there were always scenes with the waitress. But on the kibbutz he had made no trouble, though the cracks in the wall of the women's showers had to be filled in.

Jennifer and Lewis were sent to work in the cowsheds during the war. Jennifer had grown up on a farm and soothed Lewis's fear of cows. A big, gawky girl with protruding eyes, she had Messianic fantasies about Israel and its world destiny. Lewis came into that, somehow. He was going to father a new race.

One day Lewis announced to Yariv that he and Jennifer were a couple, and that they wanted a 'room', separate accommodation. (Until then, Lewis had shacked up with the other volunteers, most of them hippy youngsters from America). This was a mistake. Once attention was officially drawn to Lewis, once it had to be recognised that he wasn't just like one of the stray dogs that got fed at the kitchen door, the kibbutz secretariat decided that he had no rights at all, as he had never been a member. Then Jennifer backed out, when she found out that she couldn't, as a Christian (and a believing one at that) legally be married to Lewis in Israel. She could not live in sin, she said, even in a kibbutz. She demanded that Lewis take her to Cyprus and marry her there, like all the other people who didn't qualify for a Jewish marriage. Naphtali was asked to finance the trip, and agreed, but Yariv couldn't persuade the kibbutz to give them membership. It was only a matter of time now before he'd be asked to leave; he made too much trouble.

Lewis became depressed and aggressive. He accused Yariv and Naphtali of betraying him; he said in his chronically poetic English that they had abandoned him in his moment of greatest need, he was at the pinnacle of despair (what was this *pinkul*, Naphtali whispered). Jennifer became hysterical and difficult. The cowherds came back from the army, and Jennifer and Lewis no longer worked with the herd, but in the kitchen, where they struggled with the new automatic dishwasher, which arrived with trays, cutlery and plates on a moving belt. They quarrelled and broke plates.

One morning before dawn, Jennifer left the kibbutz without leaving a forwarding address. A few days later, Lewis deserted the kibbutz, telling only Yariv where he was going. For the first time, he became – so Yariv and Naphtali hoped – independent. He turned up only at the gang's funerals, taciturn, standing apart, and always left before they could talk to him. Yariv assured Naphtali that he was keeping track of him. It was agreed that if Lewis was in trouble, they would know soon enough. And they did.

'So how do we cremate him?'

'I thought you'd suggest something,' said Yariv. 'The hospital wants to know what to do with the body, and we seem to be responsible. There's no one else.'

'Aren't you going to eat?' Naphtali eyed Yariv's pizza. He'd sent out for a snack because he knew Yariv hated restaurants, he always made caustic remarks about the wastefulness of it all, and Naphtali didn't need that.

'You finish it,' Naphtali did. He always had a good appetite.

Naphtali cancelled a string of meetings and drove Yariv to the address Lewis had given the hospital. It was near the sea, one room in an old building with a dark entrance hall and broken letter boxes; the plaster on the walls was flaking from the sea air. The room was clean and orderly, and there were piles of typescripts in English with inked-in corrections on a small table; apparently Lewis had been doing editing work for a learned journal. All his household affairs, the landlord's name, and current bills – most of them upaid – were there.

They agreed that it was better than they had expected, though what there was to sell they couldn't see. Naphtali decided on the spot that he'd pay the bills himself; it would take less time. He'd send their Philippine maid in to do a final clean and take whatever she wanted for herself. The problem was the cremation. Naphtali sighed deeply.

'You mustn't blame yourself,' said Yariv, misunderstanding.

'I don't,' said Naphtali truthfully. 'Look, let's just forget about it. I'll fix it with the Burial Society.'

'What? Ignore what he wrote? Just like that?' Yariv looked – Naphtali later told his wife – as if he'd suggested getting the garbage collectors to take away the body. 'We can't do that. We have to do what he wanted.'

'Have you gone mad? Do you think I can just look up cremation in the Yellow Pages?'

'I thought' – Yariv said hesitantly – 'You remember Eichmann. They cremated him in the cement works at Ramle. They scattered his ashes. They must have facilities.'

'The cement works.' Naphtali stared hard at Yariv.

'You *know* people; it can't be difficult.'

For the next few minutes Naphtali shouted at Yariv, banging on the desk for emphasis. He said he'd dealt with enough dead men in his life and he knew where obligations stopped. He'd helped widows remarry and kids through college, and when he couldn't do any more he stopped thinking about it. He had no obligations to Lewis, didn't Yariv hear, didn't he understand? No obligations whatever. People like Lewis were a liability to society. He was sorry he was dead, but there were limits to everything. What he didn't say, but hoped that Yariv understood, was that Yariv had spent his life happily removed from reality, in the kibbutz world where they still traded in the ideas of a hundred years ago, where you didn't have to worry about a salary or the kids' housing or the need to show a profit to shareholders, where you could waste your time and others' trying to gratify the romantic whim of a crazy, screwball, *meshugga* son of a bitch, even if he *was* dead.

But even as he said this, since he knew how furnaces worked at his own firm's plant down at the Dead Sea, he found himself wondering about the Eichmann story. It had been reported, he remembered, that they had cremated Eichmann at Ramle, after he was hanged, so as not to pollute the soil of the country; and his ashes had been scattered at sea, outside Israel's territorial waters. Unless, of course, the whole thing was a lie. You didn't want to think that because too many people now (his grandchildren, for instance) were saying that so many of the stories about his first war and other wars, too, were lies (or myths, that was the favourite word now) but having lived through it all you knew the stories were true. For that reason alone they had to respect Lewis's wishes. So that when Yariv said nothing but just shook his head and got up, Naphtali said abruptly 'I'll check it out. I'll see if anything can be done,' just to see Yariv's gratified surprise; he even put out his hand, and the two men shook on it.

The next morning his secretary told Naphtali that the hospital had been on the phone asking when the funeral was to take place.

'What's the matter, are they charging for storage?' shouted Naphtali. 'Tell them I'm handling it, there's no family, he wasn't insured, give me a few more days, OK?'

After the morning meeting about haulage, Naphtali took

aside the manager of the phosphates plant at the Dead Sea and told him the whole story, which was only feasible because the man had also fought in the War of Independence. But when Naphtali made his request – interrupted half a dozen times by other managers and secretaries asking for favours, advice and signatures – he refused at first even to take it seriously. He reminded Naphtali of the labour dispute that was compromising his production schedules, of his own problem with low blood pressure and the Dead Sea heat, in and out of air-conditioning all day, and the whims of a pampered Galilee kibbutznik about a corpse on ice didn't interest him.

'Tell him this from me,' he said, mopping his forehead automatically (something he did even in winter). 'We're processing thousands of tons of refined phosphates a day through the furnaces, right? If we throw in your friend, what he'll get as a result is about point five million zero and one gram of friend to a kilo of phosphates, and if he wants to scatter *that* on the hills he's welcome, it's good for the poppies.'

'Help yourself to some more meatballs,' said Yariv to Naphtali, as they shovelled grated vegetables on to the hot, damp plates, just rewashed, at the side of the serving tables in the kibbutz dining hall. Yariv had hurried him straight there when he arrived on Sabbath morning alone, without the family, on Lewis business. Yariv was nervous, he said, of being caught in the 'lunchtime crowd' though all the hungry Naphtali noticed were a couple of despondent octogenarians being fed by their grandchildren. You had to admit, he said to himself, that they looked after the old, though thank God his own parents were in a Golden Age home with twenty-four-hour medical care.

Yariv was proud of the Sabbath spread, but Naphtali turned the mound of food on his plate over with his fork and couldn't touch it. He had always disliked kibbutz food. Chunks of bread, mounds of cheese, spongy meatballs, grated salads, all pap, perhaps, it suddenly occurred to him, because it was right for the toothless at each end of the spectrum.

'Why do we eat so much in this country?' asked Naphtali suddenly, looking up from his plate at Yariv.

'I suppose it's because we don't drink,' said Yariv impatiently. 'So what's the answer?'

'There's no way to cremate him in our furnaces,' Naphtali explained. To his surprise, Yariv was prepared, and already one step ahead.

'We'll have to do it privately, I've been thinking it out.' In the kibbutz, on his home ground, Yariv was far more decisive than he had been in Tel Aviv.

'You can't just cremate a man by yourself, there are laws in this country.'

Yariv smiled an irritating little smile. 'I'll bet there isn't a single law about cremation, because no one has ever dreamed you'd want to do it. You can find a little furnace somewhere.'

'You've gone mad. They'd call the police.'

'You've got the death certificate, and the will. No one will think you've killed him. Listen, my wife's got relations in Jerusalem, she told me when the Hasidim don't want the doctors to do a post mortem, they just whip the body out of the mortuary and bury it themselves. Why can't we do the same?'

Naphtali pushed his plate away. 'That's completely different, they have the Burial Society on their side, it's obvious what they're doing, nobody would interfere. The hospital would never give *us* the body.'

Yariv produced his trump card. 'This time *I*'ve got a contact. I have a cousin in the hospital, an anaesthetist. I told him we're burying Lewis in the kibbutz, no problem. You find a plant with a furnace, we take the body there, stick the ashes in the jar and up to Jerusalem. Then we'll have done just what Lewis wanted.'

Naphtali got up. 'You've gone off your head. We said I'd make the arrangements and now look what you're doing, you'll get us both arrested!'

Yariv was unmoved. He went on calmly munching his grated cabbage, waiting for Naphtali to calm down.

'Fine,' he said, looking up, a strand of cabbage on his chin. 'You haven't the guts. You never cared about Lewis, you never understood him. I lived with him for five years. He admired you, and you never responded.'

'Rubbish,' said Naphtali, but he sat down again. That Yariv and Lewis might have discussed him was something he had never contemplated, a betrayal. How could Yariv have talked about him to Lewis, that misfit, that outsider? This talk about 'responding' was jargon. Even the kibbutzniks were in therapy these days.

'He understood *you*, though,' Yariv went on. 'He said you always did what was expected of you.'

Naphtali was speechless with rage. But Yariv took his silence for assent and penitence.

'Can't you understand why he didn't want to be buried? He hated graveyards and ceremonies, but he wanted to be part of the land, not to lie in a grave where nothing grows. We can't deny him that.'

'No!' Naphtali banged on the table, the plates rattled, the octogenarians missed a spoonful, the children looked round. At that moment he had a new idea. 'We'll take him abroad. Cyprus or somewhere. They'd probably do it there.'

Yariv beamed. 'That's a wonderful idea, better than mine. But where will we get the money?'

'I'll work something out,' said Naphtali.

Naphtali took Chedva, manager of Satellite Tours, to lunch at Bijou. He had to consult her anyway about a Far East trip he was to make soon, and it was the perfect opportunity to discuss Lewis.

Naphtali rationed his meetings with Chedva because he didn't want to encourage her. He thought it would take no more than a hint, a slow-burning look, for Chedva to turn up coincidentally in Rome, Paris or Rio on one of his business trips abroad. She knew his schedule, made his schedule. For about two years now he had been playing comfortably with the idea of dropping that hint. But Chedva, at the critical moment, always managed to remind him of his wife. They were both so prepared, so sexually alert. Too alert. As he watched Chedva settle sideways into her seat at his corner table, he could see her settle her haunches on to a well-sprung bed in a foreign hotel: his bed, booked for him by her. There was something he didn't like about that. If ever he made an assignation with Chedva, he decided, it wouldn't be on a trip booked through her agency.

Now he tried to discourage himself by looking her over for signs of deterioration. There were none. She was wearing better than his wife, thought Naphtali glumly, perhaps because she was a widow.

'What do you recommend?' she asked, startling him. It was a minute until he realised that she meant the menu.

'Jacques says the calamari are good today,' he said.

Chedva pondered over the menu through tortoiseshell-rimmed reading glasses.

'I'll have the vichyssoise, if it's not from a tin,' she said. It was an old joke. Nothing at Bijou came from a tin.

They gave their orders and settled back, exchanged a smile. Old friends, easy, why spoil it? On the other hand, why not?

Naphtali said: 'There's something I want to ask you.'

Chedva's smile was crafty, her eyes shone. Once he told her about Lewis, however, the pleasant part of the meal would be at an end. He could hardly lead from cremation to proposition.

So as he explained the story to her he was conscious of a sacrifice. He could have had Chedva, but instead was recruiting her as Lewis's undertaker. It took him twenty minutes to explain fully. As he finished, the waiter was shovelling fried potatoes on to his plate beside the sirloin steak. Had he asked for steak? He didn't remember ordering it. It wasn't even well done, as he liked it.

'Just salad.'

'The usual dressing?'

'No dressing, lemon juice,' said Naphtali irritably. He didn't know this waiter; why did the waiter pretend to know him?

Chedva was already tackling the last morsel of her veal cutlet; she hadn't been doing the talking. She looked up at Naphtali, her eyes masked.

'I'll tell you what,' she said, laying her fork and knife neatly side by side. She took a small notebook from her handbag. 'If you take the body in the coffin with you, there'll be the air freight charges of course, but I think there's a deduction. Have you any idea what he weighed?'

'None.'

'Well, let's say an average unhealthy male, perhaps seventy kilos, plus the coffin.' She made a rapid calculation in her head, musing, 'return fare to London, bad time of year.'

'No reduction?'

'Reduction if you visit a close relation who's dying. If he's dead already it's no good, unless you're going abroad for medical treatment yourself. . .?'

Naphtali considered this and dismissed it; he didn't want Chedva thinking he was a basket case.

'Well then, you'll have to pay the full fare.' She drew a neat line, added tax, and showed him the figure she had written down. He frowned.

'But that's the maximum, I can do better than that for you.' Naphtali recognised the sales talk. This was the way Chedva had netted her clients in Tel Aviv; not the rich men who flew first class, but businessmen and officials like himself who flew at other people's expense.

'Now, if you took a charter and changed planes in Zurich . . .' Chedva was off. Naphtali stopped listening and wondered at her skills. Chedva would send him away with Lewis on a world tour; they would travel eastwards via Delhi, or west through Copenhagen, saving money all the way, flying under and over the Pole, all on paper, forever in transit, never leaving the airport, 'landing at Heathrow at fourteen zero zero'. She could order a hearse, look up the crematorium, check procedures with the Embassy. 'That's the final figure.' Naphtali stared. She had cut the cost by a third, and the waiter had not yet returned with the fresh strawberries. It was still a lot of money. He couldn't put Lewis down as expenses.

'Wonderful. Only I was thinking in terms of Cyprus, or maybe Greece.'

'Not that much cheaper,' said Chedva briskly, 'No special rates this time of the year. Anyway, you don't want to get involved with the police, do you? Flying to London for cremation isn't that big a deal. Documents for the body are a bit complicated, but I'll do that for you.'

She devoured the strawberries; Naphtali worried about the acid, and barely touched them. Chedva was a sensible woman, he thought. If she would only tell him to bury Lewis. He needed someone to back him up on that.

'Thanks for your help. I—'

Chedva didn't let him finish. She pressed his outstretched hand briefly, then returned it to him. 'Of course, that's what friends are for. Now I must run. Delicious lunch.'

Naphtali arrived at the café in one of the Carmel shopping centres in Haifa, halfway between the kibbutz and Tel Aviv, at exactly two in the afternoon a few days later. Neither man could really spare the time. Naphtali couldn't get to the kibbutz again except in the evening, which would mean returning in the small hours, and his wife wouldn't allow that. She said his nightmares were keeping her awake though he didn't know he had them; he never remembered his dreams. Yariv's wife, a real old gossip, had rung to say that she was sorry if there was bad feeling over Lewis. Yariv was so sensitive, but perhaps he had been lacking in understanding. He was sorry if this was so, because Naphtali was always so efficient, and they both appreciated it very much. Naphtali had grunted assent. Privately he despised Yariv for letting his wife talk for him.

This time a final decision had to be taken. Naphtali skipped lunch and kept up a steady hundred and forty on the coastroad to reach the café exactly on time. But Yariv, of course, was late. Kibbutzniks and Arabs had no sense of time. There were no other men in the café at that time of day. All the other customers were middle-aged women – many speaking German, some wearing hats – eating cream cakes. Naphtali battled with the urge to order one for himself. Since the lunch with Chedva, he had been suffering from heartburn.

Yariv ambled in. Naphtali told him that he couldn't pay the whole amount himself, the kibbutz would have to go halves.

'You know we can't do that. He wasn't even a member. A lot of us have been saying that we spent enough on him as it was, which isn't true, but that's the feeling of the majority.'

'I can't do it,' said Naphtali abruptly.

'Look, you make so many trips abroad, it's part of your job, in and out of the country – I thought you might fit Lewis in somewhere.'

'Fit him in? Where? As export?'

Yariv swallowed a sigh. 'What I meant was – I think we could raise the money for the air freight charges if you'd pay for your own ticket.' He glanced again at the figures Naphtali had put in front of him. 'I mean – the urn or whatever they give you, on the way back, not exactly excess baggage weight, is it?'

I can make jokes like that, thought Naphtali, and it works. When Yariv does it, horrible. But he wasn't going to lose his temper. He thought he might be getting an ulcer, he had an evil tasting lump in his gullet; he couldn't digest his food. It was a bad sign.

'Look, friend. When I go abroad I have a schedule. I leave at a certain time, someone meets me at the airport with a car, I usually go straight to a meeting, my days are carefully planned, they have to be. Can you imagine the export manager in London meeting me, and I say hey, wait a minute, I just have to collect a coffin? Can we go over the sales figures in the hearse? I'm on a salary, you know, I don't own the firm.'

'Yes, I know,' said Yariv. But he doesn't, thought Naphtali, those people don't understand, never will.

'If I did take Lewis it would have to be on a private trip. And I haven't been away with my family for four years.' Yariv made no comment. Why am I apologising? thought Naphtali. I don't have to apologise.

'What about you, Yariv? Don't you people ever go abroad? On behalf of the farm?'

Yariv was plaintive now. 'I've explained already that we can't afford it.'

'I'm not talking money, I'm talking time. I've had another idea. Lewis didn't draw disability payment from the army, did he? He was disabled all right, we can both testify to that. It would more than cover the expense.'

Yariv was as excited as a child. If Naphtali would handle the red tape, he said . . .

If Yariv would accompany the body, said Naphtali . . . Yariv said he would put it to the kibbutz secretary. He never failed to remind Naphtali that he didn't make decisions on his own.

The man to talk to this time was Yosske, a lawyer at the Ministry of Defence. The restaurant to take him to was Shmiel's, the kosher place, because Yosske was observant. An old army friend, Yosske was for Naphtali a convenient authority both on defence and religion – separately and in conjunction. If a key man in the plant was called up for reserve duty at the wrong time for the firm; if there was a problem with Sabbath observance in the company, when an inspector was due from the Rabbinate – Yosske was the man to consult. Naphtali had sought his advice about Jennifer and conversion. From Yosske, he was always ready to take instruction.

Naphtali didn't mind going to Shmiel's for a good traditional Jewish meal, either. The chicken soup would be good for his digestion. Meeting Yosske always put things in order, like lighting candles on Friday night for the kids' sake or for the grandchildren, so often parked on them now at weekends – or like fasting on Yom Kippur to give your stomach a rest. They discussed Lewis's last request over the *cholent*.

Naphtali's portion grew cold as he explained the problem, watching Yosske carefully for his reaction, which he hoped would not be so negative (cremation, which he mentioned only to condemn the idea) as to prevent him responding on the disability payment (finance). Yosske wasn't one of those religious people who reminded you of their beliefs all the time. It was only when Yosske bent his head forward for another forkful of food that you noticed his knitted skullcap, fastened with a hairpin to the back of his head, where most of his remaining hair was collected. Naphtali reflected that the skullcap was like the wedding ring he himself wore, a necessary sign, so that people (in his own case, women) should know the boundaries of his tolerance.

Yosske wiped his mouth with the heavy, old-fashioned cloth

napkin that Shmiel's provided.

'I don't say that there's no hope of getting the money, but it's going to take weeks if not months. What are you going to do with the body meanwhile?'

Naphtali sighed. He should have thought of that, he now reflected.

'If people can will their bodies to science, why can't they be cremated?' he asked of no one in particular.

'There are no facilities,' said Yosske primly.

'But—'

'There is no dignity in cremation, but that's not the point. Nor is the Holocaust, though your friend seems not to have thought of that, very strange for a Jew to want cremation. But again, not the point. If Lewis were burned, he would lose the hope of resurrection at the End of Days.' Yosske said this as dryly as if he were talking about Lewis's pension rights.

'But we sometimes bury ashes, if that's what remains . . .'

'That a heap of ashes should be all that remains of a man, a terrible tragedy in war, but not our doing.' Yosske however was briefly shaken. He crumbled a stray crust between his fingers. 'Noodle pudding, compote, strudel,' announced the waiter, sweeping the crumbs from the tablecloth with a flourish of his napkin.

'Nothing, just lemon tea.'

'You've eaten nothing,' said Yosske. 'Noodle pudding for me.'

'Some kind of stomach trouble,' said Naphtali. 'You see, we feel we have a duty to Lewis. It was his last wish, after all, and it seems so little to ask.'

'A great deal to ask,' said Yosske. 'You really have a different duty – to protect him from the consequences of his request. You'd have tried to prevent him committing suicide, wouldn't you?'

'What's the connection?'

'You have an equal obligation to protect him from this request. It wasn't exactly the act of a friend to ask that of you, was it? Surely he must have known that it was impossible?' Yosske looked at Naphtali shrewdly. Naphtali looked away. Not for the first time, he wondered whether Lewis had not anticipated all that would happen, had not known, however vague he was, what he was asking, had not acted, in the last resort, out of malice. The will, they said, had been ready. Yosske noticed Naphtali's hesitation.

'Of course,' Yosske added, 'If he weren't Jewish, the problem wouldn't arise.'

Startled, Naphtali stared at Yosske, whose cool, grey eyes, behind square spectacles, gave no indication of whether or not he was serious. But Yosske was always serious.

'How do you know he was Jewish?' he insisted.

'Of course he was Jewish!' Naphtali protested. 'As Jewish as you or I. Don't you remember when we discussed him getting married? You never suggested then that he mightn't be Jewish.'

'We never reached the stage of checking his credentials,' said Yosske, imperturbable. 'We would have got to that sooner or later. After all, what proof do we have?'

'But he came here to fight!' Naphtali had raised his voice. 'He was wounded! He suffered for the rest of his life from that wound!'

'There are crazy *goyim* too', said Yosske. 'You told me yourself that he wasn't in a hurry to take Israeli citizenship. That was strange, wasn't it?'

Bastard, thought Naphtali. Lawyer. He remembers every detail.

'He was as Jewish as we are,' said Naphtali firmly. 'I know he was. Everything I know about him proves it.'

'All right. Then you have to bury him just like any other Jew.'

Naphtali felt uneasy. An idea was forming in his mind, a good idea, but he didn't like it. The only answer.

'Why do *you* think he wasn't Jewish?' he asked.

'Maybe the will was meant to tell you something. Maybe he repented of the lies he'd told, before he died, and he was trying to tell you he wasn't worthy of Jewish burial, that he wanted to be cremated like the goy he was. It's a *goyishke* will. Don't you think so?'

Naphtali watched Yosske eating his noodle pudding. He felt sick.

'You mean – if we cremate him, then we're treating him as if he wasn't one of us at all? As if we knew he'd lied?'

'*Exactly*,' said Yosske, well pleased. 'So you see you have to ask yourself whether or not it's right to have him cremated, even if it's possible abroad.'

'I don't understand,' said Yariv, at the other end of the line, in the kibbutz office. 'Of course Lewis was Jewish; what nonsense.'

'I'll tell you what I think.' Naphtali spelled it out slowly, stressing every point. 'Lewis didn't know what he was asking. He couldn't have known. We agreed that at the beginning, don't you remember? And it's the spirit of the request that matters, not the letter. He wanted to be one of us, part of the land, like you said. Maybe he never thought the kibbutz would bury him, but you've agreed to that, all honour to you. So if he was Jewish, we ought to bury him, and if he wasn't and didn't know he couldn't be cremated under Israeli law, we still ought to bury him. He wanted to be buried in the soil of the country he fought for, so what's the difference between south and north?'

'Scattered.'

'Scattered, buried, what does it matter?'

'You've been brainwashed. Yosske's brainwashed you.'

'Nonsense. I'm just sure Lewis wouldn't have wanted us carting him off to England. Do you really think he'd have wanted us to have all this trouble and worry and expense? Was that how he wanted to pay us back, after all we'd done for him?'

'Is that what you think?'

'No, it's not what I think. I'm sure he wanted to do the right thing. That's why I think we ought to bury him.'

There was a long, a very long, a very thoughtful silence at the other end.

'Maybe you're right,' said Yariv.

It was a beautiful little cemetery, rather inconvenient for the old people, as it was on the top of the hill. The kibbutz founders had all been young when they came to live there, and had buried their comrades young, so it was only now that the problem of the old burying the old had arisen. Yariv scaled the path up the hill easily, and Naphtali tried not to pant. There were just enough men present from the kibbutz to make up a *minyan* with the rabbi from a nearby town. They might have disposed with his services, but both Naphtali and Yariv thought Lewis deserved a Jewish burial.

Personally, Naphtali understood why Lewis had wanted to be scattered to the winds, not locked into the earth. It was the one thing about Lewis that he could understand. But this too had been the desire of a living man; it was irrelevant now. As the kibbutzniks lowered Lewis's shrouded body into the grave, Naphtali shifted the chewing gum to the other side of his mouth. He didn't like gum, hadn't chewed gum since adolescence, but it was the only sure palliative for heartburn when you were on the move.

Yariv was delivering the eulogy. He was talking about that war, about comrades-in-arms, and he talked well. A couple of kids who had tailed along were listening, probably working on a school project assigned by their teacher, all the kibbutz knew about the burial though few had come. Yariv was wearing a handkerchief on his head knotted at the corners, Naphtali the skullcap he kept in the glove compartment of the car for *briths*, barmitzvahs and funerals. They all said Kaddish and Naphtali was the last to pick up a pebble and place it on the earth heaped over Lewis. He was paying for the headstone, anyway.

Lewis had done it on purpose, he was sure now. He had always been a trouble maker, ever since they had found him lying under the wall. Now he and Yariv would always feel in the wrong. But if Lewis had meant to make trouble, he would be terribly punished, because Naphtali and Yariv would never talk about him again. And that, surely, was the worst thing that could happen to a dead man.

THE HOUSE ON THE FRONTIER

LASZLO COULD NOT admit to anyone that he had preferred Jerusalem the divided city to Jerusalem 'reunited', where they were always building, planting, and hanging out flags. He was anxious, after the Six Day War, to share the mood of those around him, to feel as they felt. If they believed that Jerusalem was now united, liberated, rehabilitated, who was he to feel otherwise?

But his yearning for the embattled, scarred city persisted. He went looking for shell-pocked walls and bricked-up windows in the few abandoned houses on the old frontier which were not yet demolished. Sometimes he chatted to tourists entering the Jaffa Gate, and told them that they had just crossed what was once no man's land, had walked straight through what was once a blank wall sealing Mamilla Road, showed them where the Arab frontier guards had been positioned on the Old City walls. They thought he was proud of the new Jerusalem, this old man with the rifle on his shoulder.

But what Laszlo wanted was to dig in and give warning, as he had done in the days before they tore down the barbed wire, demolished the blank wall, and took away his occupation. That was why he longed guiltily for the divided Jerusalem, because in this clean new open city, with its thundering traffic and hurrying crowds, there was so little left for him to do.

Laszlo had always been out of touch with popular feeling. When he arrived in Israel in 1956 he found that the Russians were popular though the Germans were hated. Laszlo himself made no such distinctions. The Germans had put him to work digging trenches on the eastern frontier to stop the Russian tanks and the Russians punished those who had dug the trenches by sending them to saw wood in Siberia. When Laszlo finally came back to his liberated home town he found that his wife and children had died in the crossfire. His neighbours comforted him with the thought that at least, like him, they had escaped the camps. When the Communists came to power they branded him a capitalist. At the Jewish community centre they said ah, now you remember that you are a Jew, as if he had forgotten. But they gave him a ticket to Israel. They were handing them out like lottery tickets, and even the director of the town's mental hospital received a handful, and declared all his most hopeless patients to be Jews, as well they might have been.

They told Laszlo that in Israel he would be welcome, that he could begin a new life. 'I'm not a farmer,' Laszlo said, 'all I've ever dug is trenches,' but they told him that if he would find a way of getting valuables out, the government would help him set up shop again. Laszlo had been in the furniture business, and knew the value of fine wood, so he made himself crates of the best wood he could buy, nailed cheap plywood to the outside, stuffed bedding and clothes into the crates and handed them in to be shipped out to Haifa.

On the ship going to Israel he met Walter, the only other man in his sixties travelling on his own. Walter was good for Laszlo because when he compared himself with Walter, Laszlo felt energetic. Walter, another assimilated Jew from Budapest, said that his life was at an end, that he was just moving his carcass to another place to die. 'Nonsense,' said Laszlo, 'you'll see how useful you can still be; in Israel they need people badly, look, they even take madmen' – for that contingent was also on the ship.

They were sent to a transit camp near Jerusalem, and for weeks, while Walter languished in the hut they shared and Laszlo looked for a buyer for his wood, the crates stood outside the hut, until the rains began and Laszlo emptied the crates, thinking of dismantling the plywood the following day. But the next morning they were gone. There had been an order to clean up the camp and remove empty crates before they could be turned into kiosks by immigrants who wanted to remain in the camp. Laszlo searched for weeks but never found his crates. 'You see,' said Walter, 'they don't need us; all they can do is to strip us of whatever we have left.' He said he was going on welfare, and advised Laszlo to do the same; 'they owe you that, at least,' he said.

Laszlo volunteered for the regular army. When they told him that he was too old, he was surprised. He still thought of himself as the father of adolescent children, the age they had been when last he had seen them, fifteen years earlier. He went to work as bookkeeper in another Hungarian's shop, a job with no fixed hours, and rented a room in his employer's flat. Then, still searching for his crates, he discovered the frontier. He surveyed it from the old graveyards in the north to the furthest kibbutz at the edge of the hill to the south, tracing it like a geographer, scanning every rusting piece of iron and rotting piece of wood. Twisting and turning in the city's guts, the frontier took different forms – an overgrown field, a patch of rubble between two ruined houses, a wadi between rocky slopes, or a blank wall. He met all the soldiers behind their sandbagged windows, and through them, eventually, he volunteered for Civil Defence. They gave him a room with a stove for the winter on the unoccupied top floor of a house on the frontier, and he left his employer's home. Between the hours of ten at night and six in the morning, he stood guard on the roof, alert to every sound and movement in the sleeping city. Laszlo had found his occupation. The dinginess, the ruins at the city centre, made him feel at home, reminding him of war-torn Europe and his home town.

Laszlo felt that he was doing a service to the country. Even when he was off duty he kept an eye on nearby stretches of frontier, to make sure that nothing changed, to check that there had been no disturbance, no suspicious movements. The regular soldiers who manned the army positions saw Laszlo as comic; they found frontier duty boring, and invented ways of passing the time of which he disapproved, like drawing male and female genitals in every possible conjunction – and some impossible – on the walls of the deserted houses where they stood guard.

Sometimes he visited Walter, who, like him, had found a room in the border kibbutz to the south, keeping watch at night instead of paying rent. To reach Walter's room Laszlo passed through the old, abandoned dining hall, walls pitted with shellholes where birds had made their nests. Walter's room overlooked winding, disused trenches on which Laszlo turned a critical eye. A heavy revolver hung behind Walter's door, next to his thick rubber hot-water bottle. Inspecting it, Laszlo found it was not loaded. 'What would you do,' Laszlo asked Walter, 'if infiltrators came?' 'I'd piss on them,' said Walter. 'Be serious,' said Laszlo, 'you have a responsibility.' But Walter said: 'What has this country done for me, that I should defend it. Let them come, and I'll piss on them, and die pissing.'

Laszlo's 'position' was on the flat roof of the house, a few steps up from his room. The house was on the slope of a hill south of the Old City walls. From his vantage point on the roof he could see, through the binoculars they had given him, the Arab Legion guards on the battlements, the gleam of the Dome of the Rock behind them, and, if he turned, the desert hills cascading towards the Dead Sea. The frontier cut across the valley separating the Old City walls from Laszlo's hill, and ran up beside him, cutting in between his house and the house next door, also an Arab Legion post some ten feet distant. The two houses were identical, the lowest lying buildings of a district sliced in two by fighting at the time of the ceasefire. Both houses were two storeys high, the 'enemy' house slightly lower. The windows of the houses which faced one another had been bricked in. Sandbags were piled high on the parapets of the roof, but there were gaps for observation. The guards on both roofs were invisible to one another most of the time, but it was one of those points where 'incidents' could easily occur, and Laszlo's chief concern was that no 'incident' should ever start from his 'position'.

Laszlo did not spend all his time on the roof. In winter it was too cold. His room, with one corner boarded off as a wash-room, was now his home. The army had provided him with a table, chair and bed, a paraffin heater which warmed him in winter and doubled as a cooker, and some army sheets and blankets. His other belongings were sparse: an alarm clock, a heavy outdoor barometer from Hungary, books and a few items of clothing for excursions into the town centre – the army had lent him some old fatigues. Laszlo's employer, a good-natured fellow, kept his old room empty, 'in case Laszlo should care to return'. But, arguing that he was 'on important national service', Laszlo made out that his 'superior officer' expected him to 'maintain a presence' there except during his daytime working hours. Laszlo described this 'officer' as if he wore jackboots and carried a sabre, but he was in reality a sloppy sergeant called Yosske, who did not realise that Laszlo actually lived at the 'position'. When Yosske came to visit, Laszlo covered his possessions with a blanket. But after some months had passed, and Yosske and Mottele and Arele (Laszlo privately thought it most unprofessional that all his superiors were called by nicknames and that he never learned their real surnames) raised no objections, Laszlo left his belongings openly displayed, evidence of tenancy.

Yosske and the others did not, he thought, realise the importance of keeping the post manned at all times. They often suggested he should take a holiday, but he told them that it would be dangerous. No one knew the details of the position as he did, and if they wanted to replace him, he said, he would have to train his successor. Heaven forbid, said Yosske and the others, rolling their eyes, they wouldn't dream of replacing Laszlo.

Perhaps it would be just as well to explain the terrain to a deputy, Laszlo insisted, in case something should happen to him. This man would have to be told, when a twig snapped underfoot, from which direction someone was approaching. He would have to work out, as Laszlo had done, the visibility of the surrounding area at all times of the year and under all phases of the moon. Laszlo would make him familiar with the voices and footsteps of every member of every family who lived along the ridge of the hill, the habits of the family in the enemy house next door, and the immigrant family who lived in the house he guarded. Most important of all were the habits of the Legion soldiers on the other house, men who, unlike Laszlo, were frequently changed. The rifle, the binoculars and a field telephone to army headquarters – Laszlo's equipment – were all very well, but no help if the guard couldn't interpret correctly what he saw and heard. Wasn't that so? Absolutely, said Yosske and the others, Laszlo was a real pro, no one doubted that. Sometimes Laszlo noticed the winks they exchanged, but he said nothing. One day, he said to himself, when trouble comes, they will see how right I am.

One night a rotten sandbag fell from the parapet on to the roof. The sandbag had rotted slowly, but now it collapsed, the sand leaking out of the torn sacking, and Laszlo could see straight through on to the roof of the other house. It was not quite dark on an autumn evening, and now he saw the Arab soldier on the roof, the man his friends called Abed. He was a tall, thin man of about thirty, with a heavy moustache and a high forehead, oddly dented as if from a childhood accident. It was the first time that Laszlo had seen his counterpart, and Abed saw him almost immediately, and scowled. Laszlo withdrew from the gap in the sandbags. The next day he mended the rent in the sacking and replaced the sandbag, now lighter than before. From then on it was easy to see what was happening next door by moving the sandbag an inch or two to the side. Abed was usually on the roof, cooking on a small brazier, as odours of roasting nuts and coffee drifted across the rooftops. He was noisier than the previous guards had been, played his transistor radio, relaying music from Amman and Cairo, at top volume, sang to himself, and occasionally tossed stones down into the wadi. Once a stone landed on Laszlo's roof; it might have been an accident. So, perhaps, was the solitary shot which rang out one night during a *chamsin*. Laszlo had been sitting on the roof, and he reported the shot, but was told that one shot did not make an incident.

The glimpse of Abed wasn't the only change in Laszlo's life. Walter had moved to one of the ugly new housing development blocks on the western hills, renting a room from a newly arrived Hungarian family. He made no further pretence of being in any way useful to his new country. Laszlo saw him less often, yet what affected him more was the departure of the family downstairs. During the eight years Laszlo had kept watch, the lower part of the house had been occupied by an agreeable Moroccan family, lodged there in the early fifties by the Custodian of Enemy Property. Even before Laszlo had met this family, he noticed how alike were the habits of the neighbours in the two houses on either side of the frontier. Their radios played the same music all day long, their families were the same size, and the odours from their kitchens were indistinguishable. Laszlo had enjoyed the sounds coming from downstairs. They meant that he was not only a lonely lookout, but someone protecting a family. And the family was good to Laszlo; one of the eight children was always tramping upstairs with bowls of fruit, pastries and steaming Turkish coffee. Now they were rehoused. For a few weeks after they left, sitting on their bales of bedding in the back of a lorry, the house was eerily silent.

One night, as Laszlo was on his way upstairs, he heard the sound of an organ — for the first time since leaving Hungary — and recognised church music. For a second he was a child again, passing the open doors of the church near his home, staring at the schoolfriends who became strangers on Sunday. Then, the sound had been both forbidding and seductive. Now it brought tears to his eyes. Alarmed, Laszlo hurried upstairs.

After that he noticed music every evening coming from below him, European music. There were organs and recorders, and choirs. Sometimes the music continued until long after midnight, but in the morning, as Laszlo passed by on his way to work, there was no sound from downstairs. No one came out to greet him, and he missed the shouts of the children who had lived there. He saw no one, save for a young girl scrambling up the slope to the road so quickly one morning that Laszlo had no time to speak to her.

Then Laszlo ran out of matches to light his paraffin stove. It was a cold night at the beginning of winter, and he decided to ask his new neighbours, the music lovers, whoever they were, for help. At his third knock at the door downstairs he heard a burst of young laughter, and the door was thrown open by a dark, slim boy in his early twenties, still smiling from something his friends had said. He stared at Laszlo but, before he could speak, Laszlo said: 'You shouldn't open the door like that to strangers. You are on the frontier.'

The boy burst out laughing, and taking Laszlo by the shoulders, propelled him into the house, and pushed him into the crowded, bright room.

'Hey, listen to this: I open the door to this guy and he tells me I ought to keep it shut.' There was a roar of laughter from the young people gathered there, and even Laszlo, embarrassed, smiled and stammered, 'But I might have been anyone.' Laszlo was pushed into a chair, and a glass of hot wine forced into his hands.

He could only stare at what had been the bare guest room of the house, for it had been transformed. There were Persian carpets and paintings in frames, bookshelves, and musical instruments hanging from the walls. The windows facing on to the wadi were framed with heavy red curtains, and at one side was a huge bed covered with cushions and furry rugs. The front windows, which looked out on to the weed covered slope of the hill, were still veiled with the Moroccans' shabby muslin; that was why Laszlo had not noticed the change. He looked shyly round at the room. All the young people were handsome, he thought, and all were staring at him curiously. Two men and a girl lounged on the bed and another girl, in a chair near a large oil stove, had been reading. The boy who had answered the door sat down on the floor cross-legged, and looked up expectantly at Laszlo. He realised, as he swiftly dismissed the sharp memory of his lost children, that the young were all foreigners to him now.

'Well, we're waiting,' said the boy at his feet. 'Who are you?'

'I have come down from above,' said Laszlo in his slow, careful Hungarian Hebrew. Another shout of laughter, and one of the men said: 'The prophet Elijah in person'—

'But at the wrong time of the year,' said the dark boy.

'Poor man, you're embarrassing him,' said the girl on the bed. 'Maybe he wants something.'

'Maybe he came to read the electric meter?'

'In the middle of the night?'

The boy who had opened the door said; 'Not as unlikely as you think. They don't like coming here in the day, they even collect the garbage at night.'

Untrue, thought Laszlo, they come at five in the morning, but he said nothing. These were students, he guessed, who slept late in the mornings.

'It's perfect,' said one of the boys to Laszlo's host. 'You're lucky, Dan. No neighbours, no interruptions.'

'No man's land is the only place to live, I told you that already,' said Dan. 'Mind you, the place was impossible, it's a beautiful house, look at those alcoves and the way the roof is constructed, but it was wasted on those immigrants, they were just dying to move into one of the horrible boxes they're building now'—

'That's not true,' cried Laszlo. 'They were very civilised people, and they put up with the danger all these years, with small children . . .'

'What danger little father,' said one of the young men. 'Safer than Budapest, I'll bet.'

'This isn't a luxury district,' said Laszlo, his face hot. 'It's a responsibility to live here.'

'Listen to that,' said the young man. 'My father fought here in '48. Were you here then?'

Laszlo shook his head.

'Well then. Don't tell us about the frontiers.'

Offended, Laszlo stood up to go, but Dan was faster, and held him tight with an arm round his shoulders: 'Don't be rude to my guest,' he said. 'You're my neighbour, aren't you?' he said to Laszlo, 'You still haven't told us what you're doing on the roof, and we all want to hear about it.'

Laszlo allowed himself to be calmed and petted and sat down on the bed with all the young people asking him questions. He was made to drink the wine and given toasted cheese to eat when he protested that they would make him drunk.

The truth was that apart from the odd glass of schnapps with Walter and a thimble of local vodka with his employer at festivals, Laszlo hadn't had a real drink in years. Nor had he been asked questions about himself. He said more than he intended to say, and found himself telling them about his routine, and about Abed, and as he talked, he looked only at Dan and the girl on the bed, who had been kind. She leaned her chin on her hand to listen, with a little attentive smile. She had big blue eyes with dark lashes and she seemed to be saying to him, look at me if you wish, no one will mind, you are too old for it to matter. Dan sat on the floor, as Laszlo described how he had heard the music as he passed by on the stairs.

'We'll bring the record player up to you one night,' said the girl.

'Oh no, that's not allowed,' said Laszlo hastily. 'Only I am allowed on the roof.'

'Yessir nosir,' said Dan, saluting smartly, and the others smiled, even the man whose father had fought in '48, and who squeezed his shoulder to show he had meant no offence. Laszlo shook hands all round and marched back upstairs in an elated mood. When the effect of the wine wore off he realised that he had forgotten to ask for matches, and spent the rest of the night shivering.

The next day he went all the way across town to Walter's new room to describe the evening; he had no one else to tell.

'You can't imagine how friendly the young people were, the music and the wine. Dan has made it look so warm down there.' He enjoyed speaking the young man's name – he had caught no other.

Walter made Laszlo tea in his electric heating spoon, packing the tea leaves into the bowl with the perforated cover and dipping it into a teacup full of water.

'And this girl?' asked Walter slyly. 'Is she the one you saw rushing out in the morning?'

'I didn't understand everything they said,' Laszlo replied, not wishing to gossip; 'They speak real, literary Hebrew, not the kind of language we hear.'

'Yes. We're too old to speak the langage properly. We shall always be illiterate.'

Laszlo turned on him angrily. 'I'm determined to speak better. Now that I have the chance of speaking to a real sabra, a young Israeli with real education, culture, I'm sure I shall make progress.'

And Laszlo began to visit Dan frequently. Dan never came up the stairs, which Laszlo thought was tactful and a sign that he had understood that Laszlo's area was official territory, out of bounds to civilians. The Moroccan family had never grasped that. At first Laszlo did not knock on Dan's door, but he would pause to listen to music, hum a little. If Dan heard him, he opened the door and invited Laszlo in for coffee or a drink. He lent Laszlo books, in German and in Hebrew (his parents were German speaking, he said) and Laszlo in return cooked him Hungarian dishes, which, Dan told him, were much appreciated by his friends. Laszlo began to make himself useful in other ways: he ran errands for Dan in town, retrieved shirts which blew on to the barbed wire on windy nights, took messages from callers – he was always on the watch when Dan went out. He noted his return, pleased when Dan returned home, when he heard the door close at night and knew that he was safely inside. At weekends, Dan went to visit his family in Tel Aviv. Laszlo assumed that they were wealthy, as they had bought the house for him, and though he was a student living what Laszlo recognised as a bohemian life, he had no need to earn money. His records were never replaced in their covers, but lay gathering dust, and Laszlo surreptitiously dusted them on his sleeve and fitted them back into place. Dan often allowed him in to listen to music when he was studying. Laszlo even collected Dan's orders from the little grocer shop on the road above the slope; he told himself that otherwise the boy, immersed in his studies, might forget to eat. Dan showed Laszlo all the souvenirs he had picked up on journeys abroad: pottery from Sicily, puppets from Spain. From Greece he had brought three ikons which hung in the entrance, near the front door. Laszlo was faintly disturbed.

'Why do you have Christian symbols on your wall?' he asked one day.

'*Dachilak*, come on Laszlo,' said Dan, 'you're not religious, are you?'

Laszlo tried to explain. As a child, he told Dan, he had wondered whether after all he was not condemned to Christian damnation, a Jew who had rejected and killed Christ, as his teachers taught him.

Though his freethinking father had scorned priests and rabbis equally, the fear remained. As insurance, Laszlo the child had bought a picture postcard of a Madonna and Child, and kept it in the drawer of his desk. He had forgotten this shred of childhood until now.

Dan was sitting with his feet up, listening simultaneously to a Bach Mass on the gramophone and to Laszlo's reminiscences, his hands behind his head. He waited until the cellist finished playing a long, poignant phrase.

'They really screwed you people up in the Diaspora, didn't they?'

One evening, towards the end of the winter, Dan asked Laszlo to prepare him a goulash – with plenty of spice. That night, shortly after midnight, there was an exchange of shots somewhere across the wadi, like applause in an empty theatre. Laszlo hoped it would not spread. Usually, once the commanders on either side noted the incident, the shooting was stopped. Meanwhile, it was important not to give provocation. As Laszlo peered over the wall facing the wadi, he noticed a fan of light spreading over the hillside beneath, coming from the window of Dan's room, where Laszlo inferred that the red curtains had not been drawn.

The lighted window was an invitation to a sniper – not from Abed's position, where it would be invisible – but from the old City Walls some two hundred metres away. The Moroccans had always kept the curtains drawn at night, on Laszlo's advice. Should he remind Dan that the curtains had not been drawn? The sporadic shooting continued.

When Laszlo knocked on the door, Dan appeared, wearing a dressing gown, his feet bare.

'What the hell's going on?' he asked.

'You must draw those curtains,' said Laszlo. He did not want to enter, but Dan pulled him into the room. The blue-eyed girl lay sideways on the bed, propped against a cushion, with a rug pulled over her; her face was flushed and her eyes bright.

Dan drew the thick red curtains together. 'OK chief?' he asked mockingly. 'If you need help, I have a Beretta.' He looked pale and irritable.

'No, it's probably over now,' said Laszlo. They listened, but there were no more shots. 'That is usual,' he added. 'But the first incident since you came. It is unwise to show so much light.'

'You mean it's my fault?'

'No no,' said Laszlo. 'Anything can start them off. You see many of the soldiers on the wall are very young men, and once they begin, they often can't stop, it runs away with them.'

The girl suddenly began laughing. At first Laszlo thought it was relief from tension, but she couldn't stop; she went on shaking with laughter till tears ran down her face. Laszlo smiled too, realising the double meaning in what he had said.

'Shut up!' Dan shouted. Laszlo was amazed by the change in the boy's face, which was completely distorted by anger. The girl subsided, giggling. Dan pulled the rug away with a brutal gesture and the giggling stopped. Laszlo had a brief, reluctant glimpse of the girl's white body before he rushed out of the room and up the stairs, shocked and anguished. Worst of all was the dull stirring of lust in his old loins at the sight of the girl's body, her flushed face as the rug was pulled away, the abrupt end to the giggling.

For weeks, Laszlo crept up the stairs silently. The music continued, the guests came and went. Laszlo missed Dan's company. He couldn't tell Walter what had happened, but Walter was so preoccupied with his own grievances that he did not notice the signs of distress in his friend.

Discreetly, Laszlo began to leave peace offerings at Dan's door. One day it was a bag of biscuits, another a bottle of fruit cordial. For days they remained there, and then they disappeared. Laszlo was afraid to look in the dustbin.

Spring came, and Dan threw his windows wide open and turned the dial on his gramophone up to full volume. Laszlo thought this would annoy Abed, and he could in fact be heard swearing away on the roof next door when Dan put on Stravinsky. Then Abed, too, turned up his radio. The cacophony was bad enough, but Laszlo suspected that the musical duel would end badly. Something had to be done, and one evening Laszlo steeled himself to go down and knock on Dan's door; it was a matter of duty, he told himself.

When Dan opened the door Laszlo felt his heart leap painfully. He gazed hungrily at the boy's sullen, indifferent face and tousled hair. At one time he might have walked straight in, even reproached Dan gently for the disorder, told him a story about the quarrels that day in the furniture shop.

'Well?' Dan leaned against the side of the door, making no move to welcome Laszlo. Laszlo found that he was unable to speak, but, with a gesture, indicated the roof of the next house.

'Let *him* turn his radio down,' said Dan coolly.

'But I can't talk to him,' said Laszlo.

'Why not get your people to contact the Armistice Commission? They've nothing better to do, I'm sure they'll help. Why bother me?'

I must be patient, Laszlo thought, hearing the edge of anger. He was young, he had been hurt, it was up to Laszlo to show understanding.

'If you turn your radio down, I'm sure Abed will do the same. We mustn't provoke them.'

'It's my house and my country. I can play whatever music I want. I bet your nice Moroccan family played their radio as loud as all hell. And I bet you never pestered them about it.'

'But don't you see,' Laszlo pleaded. 'It was the same kind of music, the soldiers didn't even notice. Please, Dan, try to understand.' He touched the boy's shoulder in an affectionate gesture, not daring to look at his face.

'There's nothing to understand,' said Dan coldly. 'I'm busy.'

Laszlo stood on the doorstep for a moment after Dan had closed the door in his face. Then he went back upstairs. Within ten minutes Abed had gone off duty and his replacement turned the volume of the radio higher still. Laszlo was caught in the crossfire, between Radio Cairo and the Sacre du Printemps. He put his hands over his ears, and wept.

The Hungarian daily paper for immigrants said that war was inevitable. The Egyptian troops had moved into Sinai and it could only be a day or two now before all the reserves were mobilised. Every day Laszlo expected the music from downstairs to stop, or to see the big padlock fixed on the front door, as it was when Dan went out of town. He did not know Dan's unit, but he hoped that he would have a chance to wish him luck before he went.

But Dan continued as before. One warm night he gave a party. Laszlo watched from the roof as a crowd of young people stumbled down the hill, the girls squealing as they tripped over stones.

The trouble began shortly after one o'clock. The confused, agreeable sounds from downstairs became startlingly loud as the windows on to the wadi were thrown open. The music tonight was Wagner – which Laszlo had not heard for a long time as it was banned on the radio: it was the Ride of the Valkyries. He had hoped for anodyne dance music – didn't young people dance any more?

Laszlo waited for Abed's response, and soon enough the throaty voice of the Egyptian Umm Kul Tumm throbbed out over the wadi. Laszlo heard the sound of the table on which the gramophone stood dragged over the stone floor to the open window below. The Valkyries were now far more powerful than Umm Kul Tumm, who battled on feebly somewhere in the background.

On the roof next door, Abed was stamping his feet and laughing. He raised his voice and began singing with Umm Kul Tumm, not quite in tune. Downstairs, someone had taken the hunting horn off the wall and was trying to sound it. Shrieks of laughter came from the open window. Lights went on in the houses at the top of the hill in the Israeli sector behind them. People came to the windows. Laszlo knew that at all costs he must stop the noise, even if it meant spoiling Dan's party. He started for the stairs and was met by Dan's guests, merry, boozy, climbing up.

'Please,' he said. 'Please go back. No one is allowed on the roof, it is not permitted.' He tried to bar the way, stretching his arms to close the narrow staircase. The young people, still laughing, stopped.

Dan pushed his way up through the guests. 'Laszlo, brave commander, I'm taking over. I'll make him turn that garbage off. You take cover.' His face was red, his eyes glassy. He pushed Laszlo aside, and, encouraged by the laughter of his friends, he lurched up, pushing Laszlo aside.

'Please,' Laszlo hurried after them. 'Please. No one is allowed.'

'Everyone is allowed,' Dan yelled. 'Not in Hungary now, little father, no Russians, no Germans, just a little concert with our cousins over there. Come on!' An invading comic opera chorus pushed past Laszlo, carrying the hunting horn, recorder, guitar – plucking, banging and tooting.

'Anyone know a tune? Dan appealed. Everyone knew a tune. On the roof Umm Kul Tumm sang on.

'A duet!' shouted Dan, pulling one of the girls towards him.

Laszlo had managed to get past them, and ran across the roof. He knew exactly where Abed must be standing, behind the parapet, facing the weakened sandbag. He turned to face the young people.

'Get down. You're making him angry, I'm responsible. There must be no incident. Please, Dan, take them downstairs.'

'Oh, get down yourself if you're afraid,' said Dan, scowling. 'You're always interfering, spoiling everything. Haven't you had what you wanted from me, free liquor, food, a good look at my girl – what do you think, the roof belongs to you?'

'Dan, leave him alone,' said one of the boys.

'I leave him alone. It's he who doesn't leave me alone. Ya'Allah,' shouted Dan, whirling a girl round by the shoulders. 'Sing, come on now, you can sing better than that fat Egyptian cow,' and staggering back and forth with the half protesting girl, who was trying to put her hand over his mouth, he began to sing in a falsetto 'Ya ha'bi–bi, ha'bi –bi . . .'

The first shot struck the slack sandbag, topping it forward and showering sand into the face of the boy standing nearest the parapet. Laszlo wrenched the rifle off his shoulder and began firing wildly into the air, shouting – in Hungarian, – 'cease fire', but Dan, instantly sobered, had thrown the girl to the ground and was shouting counter orders: 'Down, everyone, close against the wall, that's right, don't try to move, stay where you are.' He snatched the rifle from Laszlo and fired straight in the direction of the shots, through the gap left by the sandbag. There was no further sound from the next roof. But almost instantly, the guards on the Old City walls opened fire, and in seconds the wadi was echoing to shooting from all sides, while Um Kul Tumm sang inexorably on, Wagner boomed below, and Laszlo, lying unarmed against the parapet, nursing a bruised elbow, did not want to turn his head, even when they tried to lift him away.

After the war was over, Laszlo persuaded Walter to share his patrols in Civil Defence, strolling the streets of the centre a few hours a week, skirting the excavations and the building lots, in the shadow of the high swinging cranes. The two of them kept an eye open for suspicious objects; they opened bulky parcels carried by Arab passers-by; they checked handbags at the entrance to cinemas and concert halls. Walter said that it was a farce, that no one took them seriously. The police did the real work, removing bombs and cordoning off dangerous areas. What possible deterrent could he and Laszlo be, he asked, two old men in faded khaki sweaters and armbands, with ancient rifles slung over their shoulders (no smart new machine-guns for them).

Not so, said Laszlo. Who would alert the police if they were not there? Everyone was in too much of a hurry these days, no one would notice the old piece of sacking bundled into the doorway, the discarded ice box which shouldn't have been left there at the corner of the road. Better a thousand false alarms than one real neglected bomb.

One afternoon he persuaded Walter to stray a little from their usual circuit, to stroll down the road and along the ridge of the hill facing the Old City walls. The two houses were still there. But the old path downwards had disappeared, and in its place was an asphalted playground with slides, swings and flower beds; the entire slope had been weeded and landscaped. The houses were accessible, now, from the new road half way down the wadi. Arab and Jewish houses had become neighbours. Both houses had television aerials. The garden of the house Laszlo gazed at most intently was untended, but someone had placed potted geraniums near the door. An expensive-looking but very dirty sports car was parked at the gate. Laszlo stood for a few minutes looking at it. Then he took Walter's arm. 'Let's hurry back,' he said, 'I thought I heard an explosion.'

'What should we care,' answered Walter, shaking his arm free, 'let's take our time, what has this country ever done for us?'

INTIMACY

MENAHEM HELLER, a comfortably married man, awkwardly in love, drove down from Jerusalem to Tel Aviv as he had done every Thursday for the last eighteen years. He was planning to go through the files in the branch office of his lawyers' firm. Then, if they could find a place, and if she was still willing – he felt as unsure as a boy – to make love.

The landscape played tricks with him. The almond trees in fresh bloom looked like puffs of pink smoke on the terraced hillsides, dust raised by shellfire. Though it was spring, there was snow on the pine trees which reared crookedly above him as he steered the car down the wooded gorge; or so he fancied, though he knew from the newspapers that the blanching was the sign of a strange disease. He was still unused to the new stretch of road constructed after the Six Day War. The drive down through wooded hills was familiar, but once beyond the gorge, the road went straight on along what had been the old frontier. Was that what made him uneasy, or was it all part of this new, disturbing state of mind?

Menahem had thought himself immune, emotionally solid, sexually well nourished. Fixed up at the right time in life. That was what people said: fixed up. Everyone he knew was married, had a wife and children. What else was there? Menuha, his wife, and he were sturdily united; but it troubled him that he could not remember ever having yearned for Menuha as he yearned now for Shula. Menuha was his chosen partner. He had rejected others and chosen her. She had been a placid girl with a long thick plait of hair down her back; her round, serene face was still unlined at forty-five. Shula could never have been serene, never reassuring, though she, too, like everyone he knew, had married very young. Her children were still at school.

A passion like this in middle age was like a childhood illness in a grown man, all embarrassment and itching. But if it was an escapade – which happened, people did these things – why did he have this feeling of recognition, of coming home? He remembered that during the only moment in the war when he had been in real danger, under fire, he had lusted uncontrollably for Shula, furiously determined that when the war ended, if he survived, he had to have her.

Once beyond the gorge, Menahem noticed that the displacement of the road eastwards had changed the familiar contours of the surrounding countryside. The little village where he always intended but never had time to stop and buy fruit and flowers had gone, hidden behind a ridge. The landmark of smoke rising from the chimney of the cement factory at Ramle, telling him how much time he still had to reach the office, had shifted from right to left of the highway. The airport – abroad, adventure – was now in full view.

Of course, it was deceptive, that accessibility. You couldn't just get on a plane; you needed permission from the army, arrangements with your secretary, making sure your partner didn't have reserve duty coming up. Reality meant that you stayed put. Shula and he were – how could he put it – a holiday abroad. She knew that too. They both had obligations.

Menahem looked after his women, his wife and daughters. Provocative as young women looked nowadays, absurdly provocative, putting it all out, he knew how vulnerable the girls were. Shula, somewhat younger than his wife, reminding him of his daughters, made him feel protective too. Shula was too earnest, too passionate in conversation. Men and women alike exchanged smiles behind her back. She was different from the other women, the other wives, who like Menuha dressed smartly, made up carefully, tinted their hair, trying to deny the years. Shula looked as if she hadn't noticed she was growing older, and there was no artifice in her appearance; she wore no make-up, and she dressed in the kind of tunics and trousers which had gone out of fashion years before. A schoolgirl's ribbon held back her long hair, which was thick but streaked with grey, and her slim arms and legs indicated a slight and boyish body under the loose clothes, while her hands (she had told him she was a physiotherapist), were well shaped but too strongly developed for beauty, like a dancer's feet. For some reason he could not understand – did he need to understand? – what attracted him was just that look of abandoned beauty, the lack of self-absorption, the vulnerability.

Menuha must never know, and it was fortunate that the two women lived in different towns. But while Jerusalem and Tel Aviv had once been worlds apart, too many people had recently started commuting up to Jerusalem, down to Tel Aviv. Menahem knew about one driver in ten on the road between the two cities at this time of the morning, and why they were there, and they knew him. Everyone knew Thursday was his Tel Aviv day, just as it was Jerusalem day for many of the lawyers, doctors and government officials he passed on the road. On a Thursday no one would notice having passed him going there or back, but on any other day it might arouse comment and enquiry. That was why he could only meet Shula in Tel Aviv on a Thursday.

Once out of the gorge and on the straight stretch of highway through the plain, all the drivers from Jerusalem accelerated, just as those going in the opposite direction were slowing down, readying for the climb through the hills. Menahem glanced briefly at the drivers coming from Tel Aviv. There was

Itsik, the industrialist, the pace-setter in his white Porsche (one of only three in the country, so he claimed) weaving in and out of the traffic. And as expected, there was a girl with him, laughing, showing her teeth, tossing her hair, head thrown back. Another few kilometres nearer the airport and there was Arieh in someone else's car, probably off the New York flight; the friend was driving, Arieh reading papers on his lap. Wealthy as he now was, he would always cadge a ride with people, often with Menahem himself. In the Volvo just behind was Moshe, a gift to the country's lawyers. You could make a living out of Moshe alone, as he was always fencing with the law. Probably going up to Jerusalem for a real estate deal, seeing what he could make out of the post-war boom in land prices.

Menahem glanced at the cars following the Volvo, to see if he could spot one of the scandal hunters from the press; one weekly had a man who followed Moshe like a private detective, camera and flashbulb on his back. A blaze of light and he'd be caught. Not that Moshe, or anyone else, cared. For Moshe, all legal problems could be solved by doling out cash. Menahem grimaced; he would have preferred not to have Moshe as a client, but the girls had to be put through college.

At the first set of traffic lights near Tel Aviv, Menahem took his left hand from the wheel to wave to Ron, whose curt nod reminded Menahem that they had not yet had that talk Ron wanted on malpractice suits, still rare in the country, but which Ron, with his large private clinic, was already encountering. Ron was a colleague of Amos, Shula's husband. He didn't give Menahem a second glance. Behind Ron came Mr Schulz the Jerusalem plumber, who until recently had gone down to Tel Aviv to get spare parts and returned with them in a plastic bundle in the sidecar of his ancient Vespa. Now he had acquired a new van. Menuha, who liked gossip, had told him that bandy, randy Schulz pinched the behind of every woman whose washing machine he came to mend. Perhaps the spare parts merchant had a wife, and had gone to Haifa to pick up supplies.

The new stretch of road came abruptly to an end in a seedy commercial district to the south of Tel Aviv. Menahem closed his window to keep out the fumes of the cars backed up in front of him, as they edged slowly into the crowded, narrow streets. Gross, slipshod women plodded in their dressing gowns to corner groceries; yards overflowed with garbage; derelict cars lay belly up in waste lots; smoke poured from the chimney of a small plastics factory in open defiance of the toothless anti-pollution law he had helped to draft. All this he usually passed without a glance. But today he took in the squalor and disorder, looking for something else.

There they were, the sleazy little hotels near the central bus station. Men and women he knew had tried to carry on their liaisons in such places, and been instantly discovered. The police knew they didn't belong there. There, or in Arab hotels. So many men were found out. Motti had taken his secretary to a hotel in Nablus and been accidentally pulled in by an army lieutenant conducting a house-to-house search for security suspects; Yossi was discovered in the Jerusalem Forest, in one of the abandoned summer houses, during a tree planting ceremony for American charitable women. Moshe's wife and Danny the pathologist were caught in an empty room in the medical school by the watchman. Every scurrilous story Menahem had ever heard returned to his mind. Only the young and single were allowed privacy.

Was he like Motti, Yossi and Danny, then? Even, perhaps, like Schulz? Surely not. He loved Shula. But who was to say that Yossi, Motti and Danny had not been in love, hiding for the sake of their families? What had been destroyed in the hotel, the summer house, the medical school at night? People even improved on stories; it was even said they had found Danny and the girl on the table in the dissecting room and that he had pulled his pants on and given the terrified watchman a tranquil-liser. Menahem didn't believe that story, but he had laughed too. Everyone laughed.

As she prepared breakfast for the family, Shula felt the foolish smile on her face; that, and her feverish eyes, would surely have given her away if anyone had troubled to look at her. No one did. Not at breakfast, anyway. Amos was always critical of her appearance when they went out together. If something was wrong, he would notice it. But at the beginning of a working day, Amos and the children were too busy with themselves to notice Shula. She had even been able to check, discreetly, on their timetables for the day. Amos would be at the hospital until seven that evening, the children would all be out playing football, or visiting friends. They would only miss her when they became hungry, towards eight o'clock.

'The family' – a joint, unwieldy obstacle to her meetings with Menahem. This was how she had begun to see them recently, and it appalled her. Now she looked at the children and at her husband in turn, willing herself to see them sepa-rately. Amos looked surlier than usual. That probably meant that a patient was dying, that he had lost a battle. He would come home in a temper, and if she was tense, too, they would quarrel. But she wouldn't be tense and angry that evening; she was unnaturally sweet, even now. The children snapped at one another, complained about their clothes or the snacks she was packing, but she didn't respond. Not one of them bothered to say goodbye. Amos was the last to leave; he didn't even close the door behind him.

So she was going to deceive Amos, to become an unfaithful wife. That was the way other people would see it, but it was all happening in a world so far away from her everyday life that it had nothing to do with Amos at all. She felt she had given

Amos fair warning; her meetings with Mènahem had been anything but secret. It was she who had asked Menahem, when the two couples met at a concert, if 'they' could consult him about a court case, a family battle over a small inheritance. She asked herself later whether it was a ruse – women were natural schemers – and wasn't sure. Amos, with no time to handle the inheritance matter, was gratified, not suspicious. Another man might have worried about the way she praised Menahem's skills, her enthusiasm at his handling of the case. Not Amos. He had even reacted irritably when she dutifully, hypocritically, reported the details of every consultation. Had she said that she was falling in love with Menahem, she was sure that Amos would have laughed at her. 'Be your age, *habibele*,' he would have said. Perhaps it was his very certainty that no man could challenge his possession of her, that she was too old and domesticated to arouse longings in any other man, that stopped her feeling guilt.

In Amos's book, only sexually unsatisfied or idle women had adulterous affairs. Shula was regularly attended to (that was the way Amos would have put it) and she had a full-time job. Had she confessed to Amos, even sought his help to free herself of her growing love for Menahem (which at one stage, panicking, she had thought of doing) he would not have taken her seriously. Amos her husband had always taken second place to Amos the doctor. Controlled and patient at the hospital – so everyone said – at home he was short tempered and dictatorial.

Menahem's life, as she understood it, followed quite a different pattern. People said he was an aggressive lawyer, dismissive and caustic to those who annoyed him, but to Shula he was gentle and sensitive. Was his behaviour in court and his office part of his professional manner, or did he – as Shula thought – actually dislike his work? There was a hesitance, a subtle insecurity, in Menahem's manner that had attracted Shula, signalling an unanswered need. So from the outset she had thought that – contrary to gossip – very little of Menahem went into his work, and she had set herself a perverse little exercise to prove it. At first, their talks had been quite impersonal: the inheritance, court procedures. Litigation in family affairs seemed to her degrading and unpleasant. The longer Menahem explained technicalities, the more impatient she became, until one day she exclaimed: 'This law is a specious business – all acting and pretence and manipulation. How can *you* possibly be a lawyer?'

That might have annoyed him, or made him laugh at her, if it hadn't struck at the heart of a private dissatisfaction. They had been at the seafront in Tel Aviv, near the rifle ranges and the cheap cafés, as private a place as they were likely to find, a place where he had taken her without explanation, inviting intimacy.

He answered her immediately. He had inherited the law, not chosen it, he said. His father had been a leading pre-state lawyer. His brother, a painter, had claimed the rebel's role, and Menahem, who had no fierce ambitions of his own, had gone into his father's office, trained for the succession. Shula was right, he said, and she could see that he was grateful for the insight. Middle age was changing perspectives. There was no question, he had said, hesitating a moment, glancing at her, of his changing in any drastic manner. It was rather a matter of facing truths.

From that moment onwards, they were in love. It wasn't what she remembered, the violent physical drive of adolescence which had entangled her with Amos. But wasn't love in the middle aged always a sharing of weaknesses and regrets?

She had not answered Menahem – no answer was necessary – and emboldened by her silence, he had put a hand on her shoulder. The first touch was an admission of mutual need and mutual desire; she had not moved away.

Menahem saw Shula coming when she was still on the other side of the crowded precinct – late as usual, probably breathless, but there was nothing he could do to stop her now, though Dudu and that junior from Haifa were sitting only two tables away. He should have remembered that Dudu took time off to sail the little boat he kept in the little marina below the square.

He rose and pulled out a chair, put out a hand to shake as if they were just acquaintances, but Shula didn't understand, or perhaps despised, the pretence. She flung her arms round him and kissed his cheek. He wondered what Dudu made of that. Then she took his hand and held it.

'Shula: There's someone I know just near us.'

'Should I care?' She wrenched her hand free in a gesture even more intimate than the embrace. Menahem liked the way her temper flickered, sensually. Menuha was slow to anger.

'Let's go,' she said.

'It would look better if we stayed.'

'All right.' She planted herself in the chair he'd prepared. 'Better?'

Dudu would have noticed the mockery in her face, if not the way she hid her strong hands in her lap, between her legs, a movement Menahem had come to recognise by now – shy, erotic.

'So what's new?' Dudu was standing over them, glancing at the closed file Menahem had placed on the table, and then, with frank, but puzzled, curiosity at Shula.

'Free advice for a friend,' said Menahem, weakly. 'My idea. Weather's too good to stay in the office.' Dudu's face showed him that he'd given himself away by explaining their meeting. Shula's embrace might well have been the high spirited, friendly hug of a family friend. Now he had made it suspect.

'I've been trying to make an appointment with this gentleman for weeks, but he's always too busy,' said Dudu. 'You're lucky, lady. How's Menuha?'

'Flourishing. Make it short, Dudu, I've got to get home, we have guests for dinner.'

'Gentle hint,' said Dudu, smiling at Shula and studying her carefully through the smile. 'I can never get Menahem to invite me out to a meal, you're lucky to get a coffee.'

'I don't eat in restaurants,' said Menahem shortly.

'Nor would I, with a wife who cooks like Menuha.' The grossness of the man. Was he warning Shula off? It was possible. Affairs conducted in public were everyone's business.

'Drop in early next Thursday,' said Menahem curtly.

'Sure thing,' said Dudu. 'I won't disturb you.' He walked off.

The worst of it was that they hadn't even made love yet. The holiday cottage he had told friends he wanted to inspect for relations from abroad was rented. The staff of all the big hotels knew him from meetings with clients, while the small, out of the way places were those where you were bound to meet someone taking a short, out-of-season holiday. There wasn't a hotel or kibbutz rest house where he had not been at some time with his family and where he didn't know someone on the staff.

'Shula.' He leaned forward and lowered his voice though Dudu had gone. 'Givat Ha Sharon. About three kilometres this side of Netanya, the old road. You could get there with your own car. No one goes there, no swimming pool, no beach.'

She looked amused. 'I have an uncle there.'

'Uncle? I didn't know.'

'How could you have known? He's too old for field work now, works at the guest house reception. And he's the family gossip.'

'Hell.'

'Anyway I haven't got the car. Amos took it to the garage, something's wrong with the clutch.'

'Why didn't you tell me?'

'You told me not to say things like that on the phone.'

'Don't you believe I want to find a place? I combed the whole Tel Aviv area before I thought of that resthouse.'

'You need a woman with a place of her own,' she said bitterly.

If we were younger, he thought, we could go up to the forests, or to the beach once it gets dark. It's warm enough already. But in his mind's eye he saw Shula with dry grass in her hair, sand in her clothes, her face flushed and weary, going home to Amos. He was a husband, and a father these twenty years. He couldn't just drop the habit of responsibility.

Shula said: 'My clinic closes at five. I have the keys.'

His heart leapt. 'Let's go.' She didn't move. 'Don't hide your hands.'

'They're ugly.'

'I love your ugly hands.'

'What about your friend?'

'He isn't a friend.' But Menahem was sobered. He had just thought what Dudu would say if he found out about 'Menahem's physiotherapist.'

Menahem had to stop to fill the petrol tank of his car. Waiting in the filling station, Shula was conscious of trespassing, for a man's car was an extension of his home. She pulled open the glove compartment facing her and found a spray can of car paint, a box of matches, a screwdriver, a soiled car map — familiar objects which travelled backwards and forwards every day with Menahem. She took the sleeve of his jacket, slung across the back of his seat, and put it to her face; there was a faint trace of sweat on the lining. She liked that. Amos always smelled of the hospital, of chemicals and disinfectants which he could never quite wash off his skin.

She watched Menahem joking with the petrol pump attendant. He searched in the pocket of his trousers for small change, good humoured, excited. It pleased her to think that she was the cause of that excitement. When he eased himself back into the car, she noticed that the skin at the back of his neck was dry and his belly sagged a little under his sweater; it was these signs of age which she loved and which reassured her. She would not have had him younger.

'What's the matter?' he asked, noticing the emotion in her face. He put his hand under her chin and turned her towards him for a kiss, his face tense and serious with desire. But she lowered her head and nuzzled against his hand. 'Nothing,' she murmured, 'nothing.' But his gesture had disturbed her, reminding her of Amos, who always turned her face to him when she complained of a headache or other ailment. It wasn't, in Amos, a prelude to lovemaking, but an impersonal, routine inspection of her eyes and colour. She didn't want to think of Amos now.

Shula directed Menahem to the clinic. Not a word was spoken between them until Shula had unlocked the door and they were in the darkened corridor, when Menahem said, his voice harsh with frustration: 'You said it was empty, but look, it's open, don't you see, there's someone there.'

There was a light at the end of the corridor, and the sound of voices. Shula said: 'I'm sorry. Maybe someone's broken in, we'd better go and see.'

The room with the light on was the largest treatment room. The leather couch (had she been thinking of that? it looked hard and uncomfortable) had been pushed to one side and a crowd of white clothed boys and girls were lunging at one another, arms outstretched, tumbling clumsily about, urged on by a perspiring young man whose glasses had fallen forward on his nose. He rounded on Shula and Menahem, complaining: 'You see! I can't do anything with them! Hopeless! They've no idea.' He turned to the boys and girls, who now were giggling and slapping one another, pleased at the interruption. 'Stop this straight away. Start again!'

'*Habibele*, what are you doing here?' Varda, one of her colleagues, was standing on the other side of the room. She too was in white, a sash across her chest, panting and smiling.

'And you?'

'Judo, can't you see? I told you we're starting classes. Wonderful for the figure, why don't you join? Hallo!' The greeting was for Menahem, and Varda patted her hair as she surveyed him frankly. Divorced and childless, Shula thought angrily, Varda would have no difficulty in providing an empty room.

'Varda – Menahem, my lawyer,' she said. It was safer to be straightforward, because Varda frequently saw Amos at the hospital.

'My hand's too sweaty to shake,' said Varda, coyly.

Menahem paid no attention to Varda. Shula's embarrassment was so plain that he had to prompt her. 'Didn't you want to collect something?'

'Oh, yes,' she said shakily. 'There was a document I left here in a book. The cupboard with the files,' she added.

'Well, go ahead,' said Varda. 'Don't let us bother you.' Her eyes were on Menahem. The judo pupils, who had fallen silent, were staring at them now, and so was the judo teacher. Shula rummaged in the cupboard, failed to find a book, apologised, said she had left it somewhere else, though she knew her clumsiness, her confusion were inviting curiosity. The chaotic noise and laughter resumed only when they were walking down the corridor again.

The streets outside were crowded with people coming home from their offices, children out of school. They were jostled by the crowd, people strolled in the road and cars were being parked on pavements. There were no vacant rooms, no isolated corners; a couple of schoolchildren were sitting on the bonnet of Menahem's car, sprawled out tracing patterns on the windshield; they only slithered off at the last moment when he turned on the ignition.

'Let's get out of town,' he said.

When Menahem stopped the car by the beach, he realised that he had made a mistake, that he should not have brought Shula here. It looked like the kind of place where a truck driver would rape a hitchhiker. He had remembered the beach as pleasant, but that had been on a weekend visit with the children, years earlier. The beach had been lonely then, well away from town. Now Tel Aviv was beginning to catch up with it. The road ended in a patch of greyish sand dotted with rough scrub. Sand covered steps led down from the road to a tar stained stretch of beach, separated from the road by a low wall. There was an acrid, foul smell from a garbage dump nearby. It looked like a place where builders and developers had begun work and run out of funds. The only building in sight had been abandoned at the second storey, its outer walls complete, the window frames blank eyes through which the cloudy spring evening sky was visible. There was no shelter, no cove in sight. The beach itself was narrow, and winter storms had thrown refuse up against the sea wall.

'Let's go,' said Menahem, turning the key in the ignition again. 'You'd better be getting back. It's terrible. I remembered it differently.'

Shula shook her head. She opened the door of the car and ran down on to the beach. He locked the car and followed her, looking at his watch. In about an hour he would have to start for home.

The sun glowed on the horizon, a warning beacon.

Shula was standing at the water's edge. The air was chill; she shivered. 'Do you want my jacket?' he offered, but she shook her head – angrily, it seemed to him. She was right, he thought. With his caution and his hesitations they had bungled the afternoon. They should have gone to a big hotel and damned the consequences. Shula's back was turned to him. Perhaps she regretted the whole idea and couldn't say so. When he had tried to kiss her, turning her face with his hand, she had drawn back. Despite the urging of his body, he couldn't reach out for her now, he needed a sign. He was accustomed to a woman who turned to him instinctively, even in her sleep.

In the car, on the beach – she didn't care where it was now. She'd lie down with him anywhere. But now he gave no sign of wanting her. His apologies about the beach were, she thought, apologies for himself, gentleness and consideration concealing the failure of desire. They were just a couple of middle-aged adolescents, after all, uncertain and absurd; the real adolescents had looked at them and giggled. Dudu and Varda would have managed things better.

They stood side by side at the edge of the sea. With great delicacy, a wave deposited at their feet a plastic bottle, a piece of wood shrouded in seaweed, and an old rag. As the wave receded, it sucked the sand from around a large and glittering seashell. Instantly, Shula and Menahem stooped to pick it up at the same moment, with the same instinct: to take it home for the children. For his children, though they were too old now for seashells, for hers – a reflex from years of parenting. But as both tried to pull the shell from the hard damp sand, their hands touched, and suddenly, angrily, she caught at him and pulled him away from the sea. The strength in her hands was amazing and Menahem did not resist, stumbling after her, his shoes sinking into the soft sand. Near the sea wall they fell to their knees, and now it was he who reached for her, toppling her beside the wall. The light was fading now.

There had been no sound – only a silent explosion of light, prolonged and intense, focused in a beam that passed across their locked, part naked bodies once, twice, and – when it paused on them a second time, accompanied by a giant burst of laughter, suppressed as the loudspeaker which relayed it was switched off. Now there were only small, remote voices talking; a crackling, dry snap of sound. The searchlight moved away, raking other corners of the beach. Then the engine whose hum they had not heard as it approached started up again, the bright light was extinguished, and the coastal patrol jeep reversed away from the ridge of the sea wall and moved off slowly down the road.

Neither Menahem nor Shula made any attempt to shift themselves from where they lay entangled. Menahem eased his arm and a tin can rolled against a stone; the knuckles of one hand, which still cupped Shula's head, rubbed against a bag full of garbage. One of his shoes had come off and when he moved his foot something viscous clung to it. Stones were biting into the small of Shula's back and there was sand and grit in her face which she could not brush away; one arm was twisted under her, and with the other she still pressed Menahem's head to her breast.

But neither of them moved, not wishing to hasten the moment when they would face one another in the light.

THE BATTLE FOR RAFI

I NEVER MET Rafi. So I never found out how it worked out, whether I was right or wrong. Perhaps that's why I keep thinking about that boy and his parents, going over the story in my mind again and again, wondering whether there was something else I might have done.

It was about three weeks after the end of the Yom Kippur war. The first shock was over, and the recriminations had begun in earnest. We knew who had gone and who had survived, by then. At least, I thought we knew, until I got the phone call. David, a teaching colleague in the army reserves, rang me to ask whether I was still available for voluntary work. After school hours, of course. Was there one morning a week I had free? Two, I said glumly, forcing myself to be truthful. Teachers are good stopgaps, and I'd served on those little committees which break the news to bereaved parents – on condition that they weren't parents of kids in my own school. Two mornings, I said, and perhaps an afternoon. I wanted that time for myself, but my own husband and sons were safe, and the war wasn't over for everyone. David said: 'They really need a trained psychologist, but there isn't anyone available; so just use your common sense.' Talk about a back-handed compliment.

He told me to report to a news agency near the army compound, and go down to the basement. Was it something to do with bereaved families again? I asked. Not quite, he said, not exactly. He wouldn't say more.

There were three men waiting in the basement: David, an army education officer, and a technician sitting in front of an ancient moviola. They explained that the film I was going to see was of Israeli prisoners of war in Syria. The film had been shot by television reporters from an European company; it was rough footage, I was to understand, and that was why it was so repetitive. What I saw was about fifty Israeli kids, their hands tied in front of them with Arab headcloths, and they were being pushed forward by soldiers, Syrians I supposed, into a field or open space. Then there was another sequence which showed them sitting there, their bound hands now behind bent heads, though some had raised their heads as far as they could and were glaring at the camera. Each time one raised his head a soldier came over and pushed it down again. 'They're not supposed to show their faces,' said David. 'That's the whole point.' I didn't understand.

All the kids were very young – boys just out of school, the new recruits who'd been at the front for the first time when the Arab offensive began – and they didn't look at all like the obstreperous, noisy, self-opinionated kids I'd known all my teaching life. They looked beaten, sullen, and afraid, just like those Arab prisoners shuffling along without their boots in the newsreels we'd seen after the other wars. Except that these were our boys, and they were shuffling not because they hadn't any boots, but because someone had removed the laces.

I must have groaned.

The officer said: 'The problem is that we can't identify them all. We have a rough idea, there are lists of the soldiers in each platoon, but the picture isn't complete. We were supposed to exchange lists of prisoners, but they won't hand over the list they have. Psychological warfare.'

'Can they do that?' I asked, stupidly.

'They can do whatever they want,' he said. 'The real trouble is that while the numbers are right we're not sure who they are.

There are two in hospital we know about, the Red Cross has visited them. But we've had a few unidentified bodies from that front. They grabbed a few boys and shot them at point-blank range, and their identification discs were taken. So since we're not sure who the dead boys are we're not sure exactly who these boys are either. And that's tough on the parents.'

'What have you told them?'

'Everything we know. Not much. A couple of American journalists in Syria talked to the boys who are prisoners and got a few names. We've used all the data banks and identikit stuff on the material we have, but we're at the end of the road now till we have an exchange of prisoners. It'll happen sooner or later, but the parents are going through hell meanwhile. We have two couples who've recognised the same boy – you can't see much of him, he's in the corner there – but he can't belong to both of them. And then there's another couple – the parents of a boy called Rafi. The father says he's sure that the one in the third row on the left, with his head raised, is Rafi. You can just see a corner of his cheek, and his hairline. The mother says it isn't him.'

'When do you think we'll get the names?'

'Probably not long before the actual exchange; we've got twice their number of prisoners so they're playing nasty. They held out against Red Cross visits for days. Now they've gone in but – we've still had no names. One of the kids shouted his name, but he was dragged out. You can see that they won't let them show their faces.' I asked how I could help.

'Just talk to the parents. That's all. Talk, pass the time with them. We've opened an office for the parents who want to come and talk, we're the half-way house to the kids. They haven't all turned up. The office is supposed to pass on information as we get it. In fact what we're doing is providing therapy.'

I asked to see the film again. The machine flickered as the

technician rewound the reel and the rows of ragged boys danced backwards out of the field. I wondered aloud where they were.

'The TV reporter said it was a fairground. They put the boys on as a kind of propaganda show, people came to look. They're in a prison now.' David jabbed at the screen with a pointer as the film was shown again. 'We know a lot about the boys who managed to show their faces, the one in the second row for instance with his head up. He's a kibbutznik, and the reporter said he was encouraging the others to raise their heads, but it wasn't easy, you can see the Syrians were standing over them with rifles. The one on the right with the curly hair is a religious kid who volunteered to help with front line services over the fast. The computers didn't even register him as being there, he was officially missing somewhere else, so that's lucky for the parents.'

The officer looked displeased at all this information getting out, and cut David short.

'What the parents need is support. We'll keep the office open for as long as they keep coming.'

Officially, the parents were confined to a shed near the perimeter of the huge army compound, but I noticed that quite often they managed to wander around and even get into other buildings in the hope of finding their sons' files, or someone responsible. I never saw them challenged, or even stopped; and soldiers hurrying from one building to another just dodged round them. I think everyone knew who they were, bereaved parents or potentially bereaved parents, and gave them a wide berth.

They were a kind of unfortunate by-product of all that was happening, of the war that had struck us with no warning, of the end of all the talk about being a great power in the region.

No one wanted to notice them though no one could really ignore them.

David had told me to think of myself as a parent-teacher committee, so I talked to the parents about their kids as if they'd not done very well that term, as if going up a class next term was dependent on their behaviour from now on, as if they were on probation.

Not all the parents turned up every day. Some came in the morning, some after work. But after a few days I was able to make a kind of personal roll-call (I had no access to army files, as I had no official status) and to form a picture of the kids in my mind. Most of them had been at school till a few months earlier, which made it easier; we could chat about studies and future prospects. Most of them also had steady girl friends, so I heard, but the girls weren't invited to the office; that was the parents' privilege.

In the first few weeks with a new class, I'd often made a mental picture of the parents from the kids, even before I got to meet them, but I'd never tried doing the reverse. It wasn't easy.

I wondered how the boys on the film were standing up to being kicked around and humiliated. That wasn't something they'd been taught to do, even − to judge from what my own boys said − in basic training, however tough they made it. All our kids are emotionally coddled − perhaps because at the back of our minds is the thought of the army, and somewhere in our minds, and in theirs, the thought that maybe they will never get to grow up. Together with that they're too innocent, or too callow, to understand real hostility. So I wondered how long they could endure imprisonment, these boys who'd been so praised and pampered, who'd raced their jeeps round corners laughing at old people who had to get out of the way.

I wasn't too worried about the rebellious boys, the ones who'd lifted up their heads and had them cuffed down again by the Syrians. The kibbutznik David had pointed out looked just like the kind of boy who gave you hell, that handsome impudent look that meant chaos in class. The boy I worried most about was Rafi, the boy who had been recognised by his father but not by his mother. For some reason I didn't like that disagreement. I wanted to meet his parents to find out more about him, and when I did meet them, I worried more than ever.

I met Rafi's mother, Lior, first. I thought she was the psychologist who was supposed to take my place after the first week, and never turned up. There were only three of us on duty in the draughty shed, an old Nissen hut raised on a concrete platform to keep it away from the damp field: an army chaplain, a young medical student with the key to the medicine cupboard and myself. The two men and I sat drinking tea, eating dry biscuits – I can still remember the taste, there was a vague odour of paraffin – and going endlessly over the same ground with the parents who wandered in. Sometimes we drafted petitions to be sent to international organisations, and every now and again we rang the Red Cross offices, or the news agencies, to see if there was anything new. There wasn't.

Rafi's mother was sitting there ready, on our side of the table, when I came in. The men hadn't arrived. She was a neat, prim looking woman, with her hair pinned up in a bun, blue eyes much magnified by her glasses, wearing an old-fashioned dress with a ruffle at the neck. She began by asking if there was any new information, and I told her that a Swiss journalist was arriving from Damascus that day, and we expected news from him though he hadn't been allowed to take photographs. Then I made the mistake of asking if she was taking over that day, as I was finding the job rather a strain. So it was awkward when she told me that she was Rafi's mother.

We both ignored what I'd said and began to talk about her

son. She said that she was pleased that she knew that he had definitely been taken prisoner, that he had definitely been serving with that unit. That was better than to wonder, as some parents did, where the boy had got to, whether he hadn't perhaps been sent somewhere else. Some of the boys in the unit had gone on leave over the New Year; some had been on their way back to the front. But Rafi's friends – those who had come back – had said they had seen him in the bunkers that were overrun. Those were the facts, she said. All the rest was guess-work. She looked squarely at me, as if daring me to disagree. Her training, she said, had taught her not to make guesses, except when they helped bridge the gap between two irreconcilable facts. What did I think?

I was taken aback. The other mothers had counted the days of their sons' captivity, packed gift parcels, and had tiny stratagems to keep them going, signs which convinced them that their boy was still alive: what he had said or done during his last days at home, or projections of the Syrians' probable behaviour. It was enough to listen, or sit silently with them, nodding. But here was Rafi's mother proposing a hypothesis on scientific grounds and asking me to agree or disagree with her. I said I agreed.

I asked what her profession was, and she said she was a research biologist. She asked me what I did and why they had chosen me to counsel the parents. I couldn't really answer that, but I tried, conscious of the fact that my explanations sounded hollow. Suddenly she asked me point blank: 'Do you think they're still alive?' She meant, she added, the boys in the film. Her 'you' was in the plural, asking me to speak for the army in general, which I couldn't do, but what frightened me was that she'd asked her question as if any answer, as long as it was accurate, truthful, would be accepted. Her blue eyes, grotesquely enlarged, it seemed to me now, by the glasses, showed no apprehension.

I started reciting what I hoped was a convincing summary of the facts. There was the evidence brought back by the journalists, I said, the fact that the kids were being kept together, had been filmed and could be counted, which suggested that no one would be hurt now, it would be too public. Of course we knew there had been murders, everyone knew that, but they had taken place immediately after the fighting ended, it was thought, not in prisons. The Syrians were using the families to create political pressure, perhaps hoping for concessions on our side. There would be no point in that if the kids weren't alive. And so on. I wouldn't have dared talk to the other parents like that, and I wished her husband were there too. All the time I was talking she kept those owl eyes on me, and when I'd finished, she gave a small involuntary sigh, as if she'd been holding her breath. Then she stood up, took down her coat and consulted her watch. She'd be back when the Swiss journalist arrived, she said. There was no point unless there was fresh information. I watched her go out of the door. From the back she looked even more like a girl.

As you often do, I formed a mental picture of her husband, who as far as I knew hadn't appeared in the office at all. Perhaps she was representing them both. He would be a man, I thought, who closeted himself with his worries. She had a German name, so I assumed he would be a fellow *yekke*, a fellow scientist or perhaps a government employee, a Herr Doktor, precise and controlled, the kind of man who wears socks under his sandals in summer and a scarf in winter. I could imagine mother, father, and son playing chess together, listening to chamber music, very rarely watching television. A bit inhibited, a bit secretive, even from one another, Lior and her husband; parents of an only child (I'd established that) who had always worn warm vests in the winter, did tiny precise drawings in one corner of his exercise books, made bookmarks and ashtrays for his parents in handiwork classes. So Rafi might

68

have great inner strength, like his mother, or he might be horribly vulnerable and shy.

A few days later a crowd of parents gathered in the shed to meet the Swiss journalist. I translated for the parents who didn't understand his English. They had brought photographs of their sons for him to identify, but he was bewildered, and afraid to make mistakes. Quite obviously, these snapshots from family albums and instant photo booths bore no resemblance to the boys he had seen in a quick tour of the prison compound. He said they were being held in a separate wing, and that he had tried to count them. The number seemed right. The parents bombarded him with questions. Had the boys received the parcels they had sent through the Red Cross? Had he spoken to them? He begged me to explain that he'd only been allowed to speak to the boys who were in hospital, and whom he understood were getting adequate medical treatment. The boys were being treated 'correctly' he thought.

At this, one of the fathers, a hulking fellow with unkempt hair, wearing an old army windcheater and smoking one of those thin cheap cigars, snorted audibly and pushed his way out of the room. I was relieved, because the reek of the cigar had made the steamy room unbearable; it was raining heavily outside and the windows were closed. The Swiss was asked increasingly difficult questions. Why hadn't he insisted on talking to the boys? Had he asked the Syrians the reason for the delays? 'I am neutral, my country is neutral,' he said. 'Now I must go and visit the Syrian prisoners here.' He smiled at me in an embarrassed way as if he expected help. I conveyed official thanks, though I wasn't an official; the officer in charge hadn't turned up.

The parents watched the journalist go, and then they gathered up their photograph albums and the parcels one or two had brought in case he was returning home through Damascus, which he wasn't. When the last of them had left I sat on in the office alone. The visit had depressed me, reminding me how petty our troubles looked to the outside world.

The hulking man with the stinking cigar pushed the door open and walked over to the tea urn, where he drew himself a plastic cupful of hot water, shovelled in a spoon of our instant coffee and threw himself into the chair opposite me, the cigar still clamped in the corner of his mouth. Suddenly he wrenched it out and threw it on to the table. 'So what are we doing about it?' he demanded, 'What are we doing to get them out?'

'What do you mean?' I asked nervously. I knew the man's name – Shlomo – and his surname, though I'd never talked to him. The medical student, who kept out of his way, said he thought he was potentially violent. He had led the parents in a demonstration one day, but now they too avoided him. That had been before I was called in, and I didn't know the reason.

'Aren't you from the Foreign Ministry?' I explained hastily that I wasn't.

'So what the hell are you doing here?' I tried to explain but he wasn't interested. 'We should go in and get them out,' he said. 'We know where they are, it's outside the town.' Now I remembered hearing that he'd urged the army to break the ceasefire and launch a rescue attack, and the rest of the parents had dissociated themselves. They didn't want other kids' lives endangered in a suicide mission, because that was what he was proposing.

I said that I'd heard people were working hard behind the scenes; that the Americans were doing their best. I assumed this was happening, though no one had told me so.

'Rubbish,' he said, 'no one's doing anything. The Americans don't give a shit.'

'Perhaps we shouldn't have given them the list of their boys till we had ours,' I said, hoping to look less feeble.

He laughed harshly. 'They don't care about their own

people. They don't give a shit whether they get them back or not.' I said I couldn't believe that.

'Oh can't you,' said Shlomo. 'Then you're like my wife.' It didn't sound like a compliment. 'We have to do something,' he insisted. 'We can't just let them rot. We know what their prisons are like.'

I had no answer.

'Mind you, my boy's all right,' he said, as if I'd asked a question. 'Tough kid. Got both his arms and legs. I saw that in the film. Kept his head up too. You can't see the face but you can see the shape of the head. Setting an example.' I asked who his son was, and he told me.

My first thought was that they must have been divorced, since their surnames were different. This man had one of those invented Hebrew names, not a straight translation from German or Russian. A self-named man, Shlomo. If they were divorced, perhaps it was the reason for the tension both of them projected, an extra tension. It was hard enough, I thought, to face this situation as a couple or a family. I couldn't imagine facing it alone. I'd wondered what I would have done if a son of mine had been missing, and I'd concluded that my husband and my other kids would have taken the stress with me, like stones in a wall. We'd all have had to forego something of our individual feelings. That didn't look like the case with Rafi's parents.

I wondered what had brought this pair together. Shlomo was difficult to place. I'd put him down as a lorry driver, or a mechanic, but now I settled for farmer; there was something about him that was ill at ease in the town. From a cooperative farm, perhaps. Certainly not a kibbutznik. He wasn't the husband I'd associated with Lior.

He brought his hand down on the table with a thump, indicating that the conversation was finished.

'I wish I could help more,' I said lamely. 'We can only wait.'

'Rubbish,' he said, but not to me. 'Have you seen the picture of my boy?' he asked abruptly. I asked whether he had the photograph.

'Couldn't find the album.' he said. 'She's hidden it some-where. I'll find it, though. Want to come round and see it?'

None of the other parents had tried to strike up a friendship. They associated me with their ordeal and didn't want to see me outside the compound. But I couldn't refuse, though I was afraid his ex-wife would resent my visiting him. He gave me the address. It was in town; so I was wrong again.

All that afternoon I couldn't get Rafi's parents out of my mind. It wasn't just the fact that they didn't seem like a couple. She rejected intimacy and he invited it. She looked like someone from a different country, a different era, and he was a caricature of the tough old sabra with his shabby windcheater and his abruptness. I couldn't imagine what sort of a boy this couple had produced together.

Their names were both beside the door, but on opposite sides. His was on a visiting card with 'Desert Tours' engraved under-neath, and hers (the surname alone) on a small elegant brass plate, very worn – probably a family heirloom. They occupied the ground floor of one of those curious houses, semi-oriental in style, with turrets and arched windows, which the first Jewish architects built in old Tel Aviv, reminders of a time when this was a town for dreamers. There was a garden with old palm trees and dusty cacti; but the house was surrounded by high-rise office buildings. I wondered immediately where Rafi would have gone to school, because there wouldn't have been anywhere he could go out and play with his friends; he would have been isolated with his parents.

Shlomo opened the door barefoot, wearing a singlet and trousers. He led me through a hall to the living room, which was dark, chilly, and full of heavy mahogany furniture, which

I guessed was also Lior's inheritance. He had found the photograph album, which was ready on the sofa. The album was the old-fashioned kind, too, with 'My Childhood' on the cover. None of my kids would have agreed to an album like that.

'You'll see,' said Shlomo, as he motioned me to sit and opened the album. 'It's the shape of his head. I knew from the head that it was Rafi. When they're babies you see the shape best, before they grow hair. I'd know his head blind.' He said this so savagely that I was alarmed again. I asked for some light, in order to see clearly and also because I didn't like sitting in the dark with him.

The first photograph showed his wife at the seashore. Lior had long hair then, covering her shoulders, and she had her feet in the waves, and was very pregnant. She looked beautiful and awkward, like a swan on land. I wondered which of them put that photograph in the album. I thought that if it was a family joke, a picture of Rafi before birth, it would make them a bit more normal. But it wasn't the joke I expected.

'Rafi in storage,' he said. 'Women are warehouses, aren't they?' He flipped over the pages rapidly. There were many snaps of a baby, then a few of a small boy with toys, carefully posed. By our standards it was a modest collection. Shlomo said, 'Rafi hates being photographed.' The photographs over which he now paused confirmed this. Some had been taken when the boy was unaware, perhaps, of the camera; he was constructing models, or working at a desk. But what he wanted to show me was the photograph of a boy standing awkwardly, unsmiling, in army uniform. Kids like clowning for the camera, and at first I thought he was acting up, heels together and giving a stiff salute. I looked more closely, to see his face, and then I saw that the smile was a forced grin. Perhaps he thought he made an odd soldier. It was a disturbing photograph.

'Handsome boy,' I said, because that was true.

ASHES

'A man,' said Shlomo. 'When he gets out of the army we'll make a team; he's coming in with me.'

I asked if he was in business, unsure what Desert Tours were. 'I'm a guide,' he said. 'One man show. One trip a week, four days, the hard way. Most of it on foot. Going over the old patrol routes. Mostly for our own people, plus a few tourists. It's too tough for most of them.'

I heard keys turn in the lock across the hall.

'Lior,' he shouted. 'See who we've got here.' So they were indeed a couple. I was pleased that Lior had arrived because I wanted a little formality.

She looked tired; strands of hair were escaping from the bun at the back of her head, and I discerned a faint, momentary resemblance to the girl on the beach. She asked Shlomo whether he had given me tea.

While she was in the kitchen Shlomo shouted again, impatiently: 'She's recognised him. I showed her the photos and she agrees about the shape of the head. Don't you?'

There was nothing I wanted to do except to go home. Lior didn't answer. I decided to say nothing and let them both interpret my silence as they wished.

Lior came in carrying a teatray. 'I'm sorry there's no cake.'

Before I could answer, Shlomo said, 'She didn't come to be fed, she came to check the photographs.'

Lior looked at neither of us. 'Where did you find them?' she asked.

'Where I told you. She identified him straight away.'

This was so outrageous that I started to say something but Lior, who was pouring the tea, said: 'There were a lot of boys with their heads down; he wouldn't have wanted them to take his picture.'

'He'd have kept his head up. He'd have wanted us to see him. He wasn't afraid.'

74

'What difference does it make?' said Lior wearily. 'It's all guesswork.'

'I know the shape of his head. You may not, but I do.'

'It's not fair to our visitor to argue in front of her,' said Lior. 'Forget it,' I said hastily.

As if explaining something which was not clear, she said, 'We would feel easier in our minds if we could have recognised him in the film.'

'We did.' Shlomo glared at her. 'How is it you can't recognise your own son?'

Lior asked me if I would like to see Rafi's room, and I gratefully agreed and followed her out.

'He is very tense,' she said. 'He cannot bear the uncertainty.'

I was looking at Rafi's room. There was a tank of fish, a collection of seashells, a tennis raquet and an antique revolver. It could have been one of my own boys' rooms, except for the tidiness. On a shelf over his bed I noticed a collection of small model cars, rather battered.

'My boys would be interested in those,' I said. 'They look very old.'

Lior nodded. 'Museum pieces now,' she said. 'German. My father brought them out with him in 1935. I played with them when I was small. I had no other toys.'

Shlomo had followed us into the room and he, too, was looking at the cars.

'I told you to put those away.' He brushed them off the shelf into a heap on the bed with one sweep of his hand. 'He's not a child any more.'

'He doesn't play with them,' said Lior to me, trying to explain away Shlomo's anger. 'It's a collection, a hobby. In the family. He likes them.'

'Only because you keep going on about them. To keep you quiet.'

Lior said nothing. Shlomo laughed and said to me, 'You see, I have two kids to look after.'

He went over to Lior and ruffled her hair. It was an affectionate gesture, but, in front of me, it was an affront to her dignity. 'I never had time for these hobbies she talks about,' he said, challenging me to disagree. 'We were too busy. I had to earn my own living when I was Rafi's age, and the rest of the time I was in the youth movement. We were all in the youth movement in those days – even Lior.' He squeezed her shoulder so hard that it must have hurt, but she did not move, looking straight at me, as if he hadn't touched her.

'Have you got kids?' he asked me.

'Four.'

'*That*'s a family,' he said, to Lior. 'All boys?'

'Two of each.'

'We wanted more,' said Shlomo, putting his arm round Lior, who stood like a statue. 'But she couldn't. Not her fault. But it's a problem having an only child if he isn't the sociable type. I was an only child too, so I know. You have to push them out into the world. I bet yours are off on their own most of the time, right?'

'A bit too often for my liking,' I said, my eyes on Lior.

'A boy can't be too independent,' said Shlomo. 'You listen.' He left Lior and came over to me, putting a heavy hand on my shoulder. I thought he was unable to talk without seeking physical contact, but he was threatening. 'You know how a boy survives an experience like this – being a prisoner? We know what they're like, we know the way those boys are being knocked about.'

I glanced at Lior, but she had turned away and was carefully replacing the model cars on the shelf, one by one. 'The kids have to help one another. Encourage one another. They're not alone. They don't want to be alone. It's no use thinking you're apart, thinking you're superior. Understand?'

I nodded. 'Good,' he said. 'I've been trying to explain to her' – he talked as if Lior had left the room – 'to reassure her, because she's worried, any mother would be worried, but she thinks he needs books. Books she's been sending him. Think he's in a rest house?' This was addressed to Lior's back. After a moment or two he shrugged his shoulders and went out of the room.

Lior finished with the cars and took down a recorder in a soft cloth sheath, hand embroidered with Rafi's name. 'He played this at the academy.'

'Does he study music?'

'He did for a while. Then his studies began to take up too much of his time. But he'll come back to it. It was the same with me. At some stage studies come first. When he leaves the army he'll study applied physics. He has exceptional talent. All my family were gifted in the sciences.'

'That's nice,' I said.

'I believe,' Lior said, 'that when people are in a difficult situation, they need their inner resources. I mean what they have learned and studied, whatever can make them forget their immediate surroundings. Then the past and future become more real than the present.'

'That must be very difficult at Rafi's age,' I said.

'Not if you are properly trained,' she said. 'I've done it myself.' Her eyes became luminous. 'Rafi has a wonderful memory,' she said. 'He has inner strength, and he will be able to abstract himself from everything around him. That will enable him to survive.'

I rang David that evening and said that I thought that with Rafi's parents I was out of my depth and that a psychologist was needed. He listened to what I told him and said that perhaps I should consult Rafi's regular class teacher who was also his counsellor. When I did so, I found that the teacher knew that Rafi was a prisoner and she wanted to hear all the latest information. I asked her whether the boy had made plans for his future, after the army. There was a short silence at the other end of the line, and she said that Rafi was a very gifted boy who for some reason had postponed all his plans for studying until after army service. His final grades had been so high that he could have served in the special unit enabling him to study and do his service at the same time. It was surprising that he hadn't done so. Beyond that, she couldn't or didn't want to tell me more. I know when another teacher is holding out on me, but I didn't press her.

After my visit to their home I had expected Lior and Shlomo to keep away from me. But Shlomo appeared the next day and said he wanted to speak to me alone. We took a walk along the gravel paths of the compound in the pouring rain. Shlomo ignored the rain, I put up my umbrella. He went on talking with the rain pouring through his hair and running down inside the collar of his windcheater.

He wanted me to understand, he said, that his wife was out of touch with the real world. Gifted, yes, exceptionally, and always had been. He was very proud of her, though not an academic type himself. She had been the youngest graduate awarded a lectureship in her subject, and for that reason had never spent much time with Rafi after he was weaned. It was Shlomo who'd changed the nappies, given the feeds. He wasn't saying that she wasn't a good mother – she was extraordinary. He himself could never have given Rafi a fraction of the education she gave him. She had guided Rafi through school, supervised his reading, helped him get good marks. But I'd agree, wouldn't I, that good marks weren't the only thing in life? His role had been to prepare Rafi for life.

Lior, good luck to her, had been over protected. He'd helped protect her. He had been her group instructor at camp, in the youth movement, he'd married her when she was only just eighteen, a little immigrant girl from Germany, because he had seen she would never survive army service. She in her turn had tried to protect Rafi as she had been protected. Music lessons – absurd, the boy was no musician – and so on. All this had gone on until Rafi's barmitzvah. At this point, Shlomo said, taking the lapel of my coat with his fingers, he had to intervene. He'd made Rafi into a man. He'd taken him all over the country, over the toughest terrain. Rafi knew how to ration himself water, drink just enough to stop himself drying out, no more. There was no gun the boy couldn't handle. He could use his fists, and he could drive long before he was allowed a licence. All this to ready him for the army. No one was going to knock *his* son about, or make fun of him.

There were a few things he hadn't been able to get into Rafi's head, just the same, he said, like how to get on with the gang. At school Rafi had kept to himself, acted superior. But where physical stress was concerned, said Shlomo, pulling together the edges of his collar, finally realising how wet he was, Rafi was fearless. That was where character told; the rest was nonsense. I said I was sure he had prepared Rafi very well for his ordeal. He nodded, grimly. 'I hope so,' he said.

The same day, just as I was leaving the shed, Lior appeared, and asked whether she could speak to me privately. I was longing to go home; one of my sons, Mickey, who was stationed in Sinai, was home for twenty four hours and I wanted to see as much of him as I could. But Lior's face reminded me that her war wasn't over. We walked out of the compound and went into a draughty little café in a nearby street. She was carrying a book wrapped in brown paper, and the first thing she asked was whether I could keep this parcel for her for a few weeks. She realised, she said, that this was an odd request, but it was important. She was sure I could be trusted.

We made conversation while we drank our sour, half-cold

coffee. I asked about her work and she said that while she was working she thought of nothing else. But Shlomo, she said, was out of work – all the tours had been suspended since the outbreak of war and not enough men were demobbed yet to make it worthwhile – and that made things hard for him. I must have realised, she said, that the army had not called him up this time. He wasn't the only old soldier left at home, but he resented it terribly. She suspected that he also didn't want to go back to travelling, in case news came about Rafi.

I asked whether Shlomo had always been a guide.

'He's done everything,' said Lior. 'In the old days there were plenty of jobs for a man without much education – you'll have guessed he didn't study much – but who wanted to do the really rough work, in the difficult parts of the country. When things became more organised here he went to Africa for a while, teaching trade union work. But he missed us. We had to compromise, he and I. He wanted to live in the south, some-where in the desert, but I had to stay near my lab. He under-stood that. What he didn't realise was that the country had changed. Challenges are different now. People want skills today, not pioneers. The country's too small now for adven-turers. Shlomo's an intelligent man, he should have gone back to school. But he didn't want to risk failure.'

I said that not everyone was cut out for studying.

'Rafi is,' she said.

There was something I wanted to say to this woman, though I had no business to say anything at all. I got ready to phrase it. I wanted to say that parents always found resemblances between themselves and their children; it began when you looked at a baby and said that this was the father's head, the mother's eyes. It was hard not to do this, and yet when we do it we're taking something of the child for ourselves – not always to the child's advantage. Anyway, I'd tried not to stake too many claims myself . . .

She said suddenly: 'Rafi was afraid.'

My little homily was as stale in my mouth as the coffee.

'Everyone's afraid, that's natural, my boys . . .'

'No, no,' she said, as if Rafi was unique. 'He was afraid all the time. He was sure he was going to get killed. He knew there would be a war. He wrote it all down there' – she gestured at the package – 'in his diary. That's why I don't want Shlomo to see it. He thought he'd made Rafi strong.'

I took the package and shook hands politely, because she offered me her hand in that formal, Germanic way of hers. I suddenly wondered – it was an insane thought but there it was – whether that was how she had said goodbye to Rafi.

The diary ticked away in my mind, and day by day I worried more about Rafi's premonitions. It was very likely that, as Lior had said, a sensitive kid like Rafi would fear death, and I felt it was good that he had written it down. But it was hard to contemplate that boy, with his mocking salute, tied up and knocked down, if not worse. By now I wanted desperately to know more about Rafi. But I couldn't open the package and read the diary, something which would have helped me come closer to him.

About a week later one of the girl soldiers rang me at school. Could I come to the compound when I finished teaching? There was some news, and Rafi's mother wanted to see me. I was scared, and sounded it. Nothing important, said the girl. It was just that they'd received an extra sequence of the television film, and Rafi's father had lost his self-control.

When I got there, a group of parents was standing outside the shack, chatting in low voices like people at the scene of an accident. Inside Lior was helping the girl to put things right. The filing cabinets had been flung to the floor, the urn was lying on its side in a corner, and there was coffee everywhere the colour of dried blood. I didn't need to ask who had done the damage, so I asked what was on the film. The extra footage showed that the boy who had raised his head for a few seconds, whose cheek was visible, wasn't Rafi at all but another kid. The parents had identified him, and everyone was pleased that one more name was on the list. But Shlomo had gone berserk. Lior had come to apologise.

I wondered what she wanted of me. She took me aside and said: 'He blames himself.'

'For what?'

'Rafi could have been in the academic corps. He wouldn't have been in the front line. He wanted to please Shlomo.'

I said nothing.

'Now he thinks Rafi probably resisted capture and was shot. He blames himself. He thinks Rafi's dead.'

'That's ridiculous,' I said, though privately I thought it wasn't.

'I can't help him,' said Lior desperately. 'I haven't given up just because the boy in the film wasn't Rafi, I knew it wasn't him. I know he's alive. Thank you.' She went, having said what she had to say. The girl soldier and I picked up the remaining fragments of the mugs and cleaned the floor. We didn't talk.

'Hey! They're coming back! The plane's arriving before the list.' My son Mickey, home now, and keeping his radio on all the time, was shouting at me from the bathroom where he was shaving. 'Put the telly on, the cameras are at the airport!'

We all sat round the set and my kids tried to keep me calm. My small daughters sat jammed up against the screen as if they'd see better that way and Mickey kept his arm round me; they all knew about Rafi and the others. As the commentators droned on about American intervention, stretcher cases and the mood of the crowd at the airport in that infuriating way they have, I kept trying to get David on the phone to find out what he knew. But there was no answer either from his home or from Shlomo and Lior's. They'd all gone to the airport, obviously. I hadn't been told. But of course I had no one to meet. So I had to watch everything on television.

I couldn't see Lior in the crowd, because she was too small, but I spotted Shlomo towering over the other parents in that old windcheater. The reporter interviewed a few parents, but not Lior or Shlomo. I saw one of the other parents pat him on the back, but he didn't smile. I watched the plane touch down and the crowd press forward to the barriers on the tarmac, and Mickey remarked sarcastically about the politicians who were there, getting in on the act.

The door of the plane opened and the boys started coming down the gangway. I recognised a few faces straight away. I kept calling out names, and tears were rolling down my cheeks, and Mickey held my arm tightly. The boys didn't look too bad, at this distance, but their faces were grim. When I remarked on this Mickey said sharply 'It's not a football team coming home, Mum,' and automatically I looked at their boots. They were all wearing brand new shoes with laces, and I wondered who had given them the shoes.

'Well, is he there?' asked Mickey, but I couldn't see him. There was a moment when no more boys seemed to be coming through the door, and I thought: that's it, his premonitions were right, Shlomo was right, he's dead.

Then I saw him. It wasn't more than a brief glance, because the cameras were cutting back and forth between the kids and the crowd, and the moment the boys were off the plane they were gathered up by their families, who'd been allowed on to the tarmac, and carried away.

I recognised him immediately from the photograph in the album. His face was very drawn, and he was slighter in build than I'd imagined, not much taller than his mother. He came through the door and down the gangway at a trot, and disappeared into the crowd like the rest. I wanted to get through the screen into the picture, to get closer, but he'd gone. Then they brought another camera into play, perhaps up on a boom, and I saw him again, and this time, I could see Shlomo and Lior together waiting for him. I couldn't see their faces clearly but there they were, waiting.

Rafi walked right past them.

I'm quite sure of that, because I saw it happen, and they moved forward, but he was too fast and they must have been too astonished to intercept him. I think he went towards a girl, but I can't be sure of that. But one thing I am sure of, and that is that he saw his parents waiting for him. The camera was on him for several seconds as he got near them, and he was looking at them, in their direction, but quite without expression. He just went past them.

There could be many explanations, of course. Perhaps he was in shock, and just didn't recognise them. That could have happened. Maybe they were all reunited later. They must have run after him. I spoke to David about it, and he told me that I shouldn't interfere, that it was none of my business now; I'd done my job.

No one has claimed the diary.

The trouble about watching things on television, from a distance, is that you can't call the shots. People, strangers, disappear out of your line of vision. The moments of crisis pass, the moments of truth. Perhaps it's just as well.

DOLLS

THE NEWS THAT Shmulik Weiss was in trouble again ran round the Tel Aviv café circuit like flame along a fuse, with a heartwarming charge of gossip at the end. Shmulik's troubles were part of the non-stop entertainment he provided. They were not the kind of trouble that lands a man in jail – at least, not for more than a few days until a much publicised exit – or destroys his vigour and good health. Shmulik was always on the point of bankruptcy; his property was always in danger, his yacht spent more time in the tax warehouse than in the harbour, and as it was towed across town once more, people cried, 'There goes Shmulik's yacht again,' and the policemen grinned. He was always saved at the last moment. He would bring over a French-Moroccan pop star, an American rock group, an African musical, and make a fortune all over again. In a matter of months the fortune would be gone, but Shmulik himself was always the best show in town.

What made him so popular was that he spent his profits on mounting local entertainments – a festival on the northern border, and the hell with the Katyushas; a Bedouin musical called 'Nomad' with hundreds of tribal extras; a Purim celebration in which he dropped parachutists in biblical costumes carrying sacks of sweets over sad little 'development' towns in the Negev. He organised free shows for the army in wartime, and staged peace demos between the wars. He had been one of the first to get together with the Palestinians in exile, when there was a law which made that illegal. His prosecution was great publicity for the idea, so the case was dropped. Anyway Shmulik had no politics. A leading newspaper deplored the way he threw his money around, calling him a clown, and the next day he rode down Dizengoff on a huge float in a clown's costume, showering the crowds with leaflets on the latest cause he had taken up that week: pollution. A team of specially hired sweepers followed to collect the leaflets. One day he would ride around in a scarlet Cadillac, a real gas guzzler, and the next day he took it to pieces and let his favourite sculptor make an installation out of the remains, bought a motorcycle instead and parked it on the pavement of his favourite café.

Two things endeared Shmulik to his public: his carefree way with money and his equally carefree way with women. When most people were in overdraft by the second week in the month, and hurried from one bank to another in search of loans on easier terms, it was good to watch someone juggling with millions without a thought for his bank balance. When most men found it hard to arrange a weekend in Paris or Istanbul without endangering domestic comfort and the hard-earned share in the family apartment bought by their in-laws, Shmulik's girls – dancers, singers, models, so openly paraded, so easily changed – fed their fantasies without ill feeling. For no one would really be in Shmulik Weiss's place, because of Annetta.

Shmulik had been married for twenty years, and for the last fifteen, Annetta had been in a wheelchair, paralysed from the waist down, the result of a car accident on the Eilat road when, so the story went, she had been sharing the driving with Shmulik, with Annetta on the accelerator and Shmulik, arms around her, at the steering wheel. No blame, therefore, attached to anyone, and Shmulik had done everything possible to compensate his wife. Occasionally he even took her abroad, Annetta wearing dark glasses and a picture hat, with Shmulik pushing her wheelchair himself. She had a separate settlement so that if Shmulik lost all his money, so they said, creditors couldn't touch her. When he was in the country he never spent a night away from her. The weekly journal which chronicled Shmulik's adventures ran endorsements by Annetta of Shmulik's love affairs. 'Annetta: let Shmulik live!' was a typical headline. She told reporters that a man like Shmulik couldn't be expected to live without women. On the other hand, girls were to understand that his only real commitment was to his wife, world without end, amen. There were to be no financial or emotional demands. It was a privilege to have been to bed with Shmulik, a quality control seal. All Shmulik's girls had gone far. And Shmulik only liked young girls; married women were ruled out, in line with his warm hearted, absolute candour. Everything was above board, from Shmulik's tax debts ('Shmulik: I owe the Income Tax Two Million') to his last girl's newest lover, for these girls would remain in the public eye for several years, part of the still glowing galaxy.

Only Annetta enjoyed total privacy, without being forgotten – a conjuring trick with memory. Shmulik had put her in a penthouse on top of one of the highest apartment buildings in the town, where she had a roof garden tended by an Arab gardener, a telescope and two Thai maids. Select guests were brought up to visit her and reported that she looked as young, beautiful and slim as she had fifteen years earlier. She read horoscopes, did tapestry work, and when Shmulik brought her down in her wheel chair in the king-sized elevator, to a premiere or a New Year's Eve party, smiling and waving a pale hand, tears stood in people's eyes and they said what a fine man Shmulik was, what an enormous sacrifice, what a mitzva he had done looking after Annetta all these years, even giving up parenthood for her sake.

To speak ill of Shmulik was to show yourself mean minded, puritanical, grudging. Even those who, just to be different, said that they disliked the whole Shmulik circus – Annetta, Chubchick Laufer, Masha and the rest – couldn't keep it up when they met Shmulik himself, felt the frank pressure of his hand, responded to his energy and goodwill, accepted his favours. Even a man as generous as Shmulik had his rivals, however, and it was they who had spread the vicious rumours. There was the story of the Bedouin extras in Nomad who had never been paid and were threatened when they complained; the story of the Mercedes Shmulik had given a slum family in his pre-environmental days, which had been mysteriously stolen and replaced the following week by a small second-hand car; there was the story of a boyfriend of one of Shmulik's conquests, who had been forced to eat, with mustard, an insulting and threatening letter he had sent Shmulik, and another – a fiancé – who had been paid to disappear. There were even rumours that Shmulik was gradually smuggling a fortune abroad on those talent-spotting excursions of his, and was soon going to leave for good, without Annetta; and that the separate settlement, since the basic capital was Annetta's, left her by her tycoon father, was no more than a canny arrangement with a captive treasurer. But these rumours, too, were public property, and the papers published them in order to squash them in one of those features authorised by the penthouse: ('Annetta: The Lies about My Husband').

Shmulik's most recent trouble remained in the café circuit and did not get into the newspapers. To be honest, the café circuit itself was not what it had been. Times change, old friends who survived the wars and the traffic accidents died off, a new generation grew up which scarcely recognised his name, the journal which had retailed Shmulik's adventures went bankrupt, cable television arrived and with it a host of instant celebrities more familiar to young people than Tel Aviv's once legendary figures, and the numbers of those who had heard about

Shmulik Weiss's new trouble were now somewhat depleted – a handful of journalists and actors fallen on hard times, now that most of the papers had closed down and the theatre wasn't what it had been. They needed Shmulik to prove that things hadn't really changed, that show business would revive again as it always did; there were rumours that he was launching a pirate TV station offshore to outdo all the others.

The latest trouble was a girl called Buba, 'doll'. All women were dolls in Shmulik's circle, but in Buba's case that was the only name she went by. Buba was a girl from nowhere, not a budding singer or model like those Shmulik had picked out in the past, but a waitress in the new restaurant called Shmulik's which he had opened in the port area, and which had been recently fashionable. She had caught his eye one Saturday night when he was making the rounds of the tables set out on the pavement and chatting to those who were old friends and – that was the way things are these days – even to those who weren't. Even American tourists chatted back to this pleasant faced guy with the grey hair and the sandy sideburns. He had sent Chubchick Laufer to proposition her, which was the way things had always been, with a phrase famous in that circle, 'It isn't for me, doll, it's for Shmulik.' Those in the know roared with laughter, but the girl herself didn't even smile, shrugged her shoulders angrily and walked off to the kitchen.

Chubchick Laufer reported back to Shmulik, who just frowned a moment and went on chatting to Chaimke, the fat sculptor who was preparing an exhibition called The Metamorphoses of Shmulik, an installation piece of acrylic dummies and computers which stuttered out stories of different phases of Shmulik's career – war, women, show business and all. Later he went into the kitchen to taste some of the dishes the chef was preparing, and Laufer thought nothing of it at the time, but one of the cooks told him later that Shmulik had spent a long time talking to Buba, whom he had backed into a corner near the salads and was feeding with spoonfuls of a new dip. At one stage, the cook said, he popped a hot pepper into her mouth, and when her eyes ran with tears, had carefully scooped it out of her mouth and poured in a glass of a freshly opened best Cabernet Sauvignon, Golan Heights variety, drop by drop, swallow by swallow. All this the cook told Laufer three months later, because although Buba was in a sense the cook's copyright, it was the end of the month and Laufer was a well-known journalist offering good money. Buba, he said, was just a very simple girl from Afula, the back of beyond. The cook thought her family was Rumanian, one of those who never made good and got stuck there with the Moroccans, but the others maintained that she was a Moroccan herself. She spoke so little that it was difficult to tell.

Chubchick Laufer told the eager inner circle that he really hadn't given Buba another thought until he heard what the cook had said. She was just shy, fat, rather stupid, with a pretty face, admittedly, but with the kind of looks you saw in old photographs of the first immigrants to Palestine: heavy eyebrows, thick plaits, big boobs and thighs, like Stakhanovite peasant girls.

'Certainly doesn't sound like Shmulik's type,' said Masha, who might herself have looked like that thirty-five years previously but now had short, ash blonde hair, a peaked, surgically altered face, skinny flanks under her jeans and a dancer husband some fifteen years younger than herself. She still chain smoked, contemptuous of the risks, though her laughs turned into coughs and her perfume was salted with tobacco.

'Perhaps she reminded Shmulik of his mother,' mused Chaimke.

'Never knew his parents,' said Laufer authoritatively. 'They left him in a convent for safety during the Holocaust.' Laufer was writing a biography of Shmulik and hoping desperately that people would still know his name when it came out.

'Do finish, Chubchick,' said Masha. 'Did he take her into the yard there where the dustbins are, I really think he might put in a proper lavatory, not that shed—'

'Nothing happened at all,' said Laufer as if retailing the most lascivious detail. 'Nothing. She ran away, never turned up in the restaurant again. But apparently – you won't believe this – Shmulik found out where she lived and took her down to that village on the Red Sea, where the Egyptians have opened a hotel, you know, got her a job as a chambermaid, and he's been keeping her there ever since, feeding her on fish like a pelican.'

'In *Egypt?*'

'In Egypt. He has a share in that hotel, you know.'

'You mean in secret?' said Masha, astonished and resentful. 'Without anyone knowing – except you, of course.'

'And it stays that way,' said Laufer determinedly. 'It's not even in the book.'

'But he's here all the time,' Chaimke objected. 'When does he have a chance to go down there?'

'If you hadn't noticed,' said Laufer smugly, 'he's become very friendly with Yaakov in Southern Command. The one who handles liaison with the Egyptians. I worked out that he goes up and down by helicopter three or four times a week, but he's only taken me with him once.'

'But why bother?' Chaimke enquired. 'Can't he screw her in Tel Aviv?'

Laufer pushed his chair back and stood up; dramatically, he scooped air out of a shape in front of him, the shape of a woman's pregnant belly.

'No . . .' the friends drew out the syllable in horror.

'Yes,' said Laufer. 'It doesn't show yet,' he added. 'But it's there all right. I saw her puking into the kitchen sink, and anyway he told me. He's very proud of it.'

It was clear to everyone why this choice piece of information had not got into the papers. The faces which had lit up when

Laufer's bombshell exploded darkened immediately. Chaimke thought of his exhibition, Dudu of a forthcoming court case, old Shimon the actor of the chance he had of appearing in a television 'This is Your Life' starring Shmulik – he'd known Shmulik longer than anyone, right back to the days of the immigrant youth camps. Nobody gave parts these days to actors with heavy Russian accents, the new Russians had professional coaching and spoke Hebrew like *sabras*. They were all silent, until Masha, speaking to no one in particular, voiced what they were all thinking.

'He'll put everything away in the child's name. Men that age go mad when they're fathers for the first time. He might even leave Annetta.'

Laufer laughed. 'Not unless he wants to end up on the beach, he won't.' He turned to Masha. 'Any ideas?'

'It's suicidal,' she said. 'Annetta's bound to hear of it. Her doctors know everything that goes on in town. I don't suppose Shmulik will risk Buba having his child anywhere but Tel Aviv or Jerusalem.' She blew a smoke ring and watched it drift away. All those round the table suddenly remembered that years ago, there had been a rumour that Masha, a long term rival of Annetta's but less complaisant of Shmulik's other affairs, had aborted a little Shmulik herself on a trip abroad. Shmulik treated Masha these days with elaborate courtesy but rumour had it that she was the only woman he had ever feared.

'So what do you suggest?' asked Chaimke.

'It's no use trying to change Shmulik's mind,' said Masha. 'We have to concentrate on Buba. Are you sure she really wants the baby?' she asked Laufer.

Laufer pantomimed surprise. How should he know what a half-witted *Schwartzer* from Afula wanted, he asked. This one time in his life, he said, Shmulik hadn't known what he was getting into. He'd thought he could keep her somewhere out of sight, and it hadn't worked, but as for the girl, his impression was that no one gave a damn about her and she was one of those girls who had a baby to be sure that they'd get a free smile now and then.

'Find out when she comes up for medical checks,' Masha instructed Laufer. 'I'll adopt her.'

A day-long watch was kept on all the entrances to the best private clinics in Tel Aviv, and sure enough Buba was spotted: Shmulik had not risked accompanying the girl, who was brought by his Nigerian driver. Masha, alerted by mobile phone, made a totally unscheduled visit to the same doctor half an hour later, and later left the clinic by a side door with Buba, having struck up a friendship in an environment where even a girl more intelligent than Buba, preoccupied with other matters, would not have been suspicious.

A few hours later, while Shmulik's driver was coasting helplessly round the block, wondering whether he dared tell the boss he had lost his girlfriend, Buba was sitting in Masha's flat with her feet up, with Chaimke doing a portrait of her using Masha's make-up, old Shimon telling her she looked exactly like Rovina in the Dybbuk (and who Rovina and the Dybbuk were) and Chubchik Laufer taking down the story of the romance for – he assured her – a chapter in the biography.

'We all love Shmulik,' said Shimon, 'but it's a crime to keep talent like yours to himself.'

'Spielberg's making a modern version of Samson and Delila and he hasn't cast the woman yet,' said Masha. 'We've been talent spotting for him and I thought we'd found just the girl, but when I saw you in the clinic, I rang her on my mobile and told her to go for the Scorsese job instead.'

'Now, let's see if I've got this right,' said Chubchik Laufer, strumming away on his laptop. 'You came to Tel Aviv to go into modelling, found your measurements weren't right'—

'Too voluptuous,' said Shimon, 'It's a pleasure to see a girl who isn't anorexic'—

'Went to work in Shmulik's restaurant because it's where you heard all the American producers go to eat'—

'And ended up on the beach in Egypt,' said Masha sadly.

'Never mind,' said Chubchik, 'this time it'll all come right. We were all looking for a new face to promote, and it was lucky for us you came along.'

Buba's huge brown eyes filled with tears. 'But . . . I'm pregnant,' she stammered.

'That,' said Masha briskly, 'can be seen to.'

But it wasn't so simple. There was no question of going back to the same gynaecologist, who knew perfectly well whose girl Buba was and would not risk his private practice, his elegant surgery with the Chagall prints and the five-channel stereo system linked to twenty sets of earphones to while away waiting time for the ladies, even for twice the usual fee. And this consultant had warned off almost every other reputable practitioner in the Tel Aviv area. Masha, who was playing the role – not wholly convincingly – of motherly older woman helping careless young friend, discovered that the same was the case in Jerusalem and Haifa. Queues unexpectedly lengthened, urgent operations intervened, and one doctor was summoned away at the last moment, when Buba was in the chair and about to be anaesthetised. There was no gynaecologist of repute (for they were a worldly set of men and women) who had not heard of Shmulik Weiss and Annetta and who was not alerted in time and informed of the real situation. There was also the risk that Buba, naive and dumb as she was, would somehow be impelled to confess the truth to Shmulik, naming names and getting them all into trouble.

Eventually, however, they found the right woman: a sturdy Russian doctor whose clientele had diminished as her sister immigrants discovered the pill, and to whom the name of

Shmulik meant nothing at all. Time was running short, Buba had stopped vomiting and grown rosy faced, and Shmulik was providentially away in New York. Masha escorted Buba to the Russian's surgery, assuring her that she was in good hands, and breathed a sigh of relief when the door closed behind her. But when the time came to take Buba home, or rather to take her to Masha's, where chicken soup and blintzes had been promised, they found the girl in tears. The Russian doctor assured them airily that this was common, the result of the anaesthetic, that hormonal difficulties were to be expected for a few days, and that everything would pass; but it did not. Buba lay and wept, and wept. Shmulik would never forgive her, she said over and over again, and Chubchik, Shimon and Chaimke, called in by Masha, conferred in Masha's tiny kitchen. Something had to be done to cheer the girl up before Shmulik returned from the States to be confronted by the story of a sudden miscarriage – the story in which they had rehearsed Buba for days. In her present mood, she was more likely to tell him the truth and sink them all. None of their promises of talent scouts and meetings with producers – local ones, it had to be said, not Americans as they had promised – who were in on the story and who had been bribed to give Buba a walk-on role in their latest film, could wean Buba from her post-natal depression, as Masha called it. Buba lay on Masha's *chaise longue* on the balcony overlooking the sea, refused to eat, tossed and turned, day and night, for the mandatory three day rest, and then showed no signs of being able to get up and go, whether to Eilat or anywhere else. Her worry over Shmulik, it emerged, was inspired less by love than fear; she was afraid of what he would to do to her. Buba already looked a haunted girl, with dark shadows under her dark eyes, and what were discovered to be fine bones showing under her formerly plump cheeks.

At this stage Chubchik had what he thought was a very good idea indeed. He went into a toyshop in Dizengoff and bought

Buba a present, something which he thought, so he told the others later, would restore her to her habitual placidity. He turned up at Masha's flat that evening carrying a large coffin-shaped box from which he extracted the most magnificent Italian baby doll any of them had ever seen, made not of the usual plastic but a material resembling that of the old-fashioned china dolls in museums. It was dressed in pink satin, had pink buttoned shoes, and Chubchik handed it reverentially to Buba, who was lying on the *chaise longue* on the balcony in the warm Tel Aviv sunset, with her uneaten blinzes on the tray beside her.

'Look, Buba', he said. 'A present from Shmulik.' As she stared at it, Chubchik laid the doll flat beside her, to show her how its eyes closed with the faintest of clicks, no louder than the tap of a spoon on an eggshell. Then he held it upright. The doll's eyes opened, with another faint click, and from somewhere under the pink satin a voice said: 'Ma-ma.'

Buba left Masha's flat that evening, and she did not go back to Egypt, or — as far as anyone knew — to Afula. All Shmulik's frantic searches for her, when he returned from New York, failed to locate so much as the toenail of his pregnant girl friend, as Chubchik dramatically put it. It was not until about a year later, that Masha and Chubchik, strolling down Dizengoff one afternoon, paused in front of a shop window where an American soap opera was playing on ten television screens, and where from every angle they were confronted by Buba — a different Buba, much thinner, darker, tragic and angry, in a dramatic confrontation with the hero of the series, and speaking very fractured English, but Buba none the less. She was playing the role of a Mexican immigrant. How Buba had made the transition to Los Angeles no one really knew. There were stories of her having been picked up by a talent scout at a café table in Tel Aviv (those cheekbones, that body once hidden underneath the puppy fat), others of her simply having got on a plane to the States and gone straight to Hollywood, but if Shmulik knew he had been duped, he was not telling anyone. When her name was mentioned – an invented name, an assumed name under which, in the soap world, she became briefly famous – he would just shrug his shoulders. And Chubchik Laufer, once life had settled into its familiar course again on the café circuit, took all the credit for himself.

TEMIMA

I THINK WE should still have been married if it hadn't been
for the difference in the hours we slept. He was always awake
when I wanted to sleep, and when I woke up he was always
sleeping. Until I met Matt, I thought people slept when they
were tired and woke up when they'd had enough sleep or they
had to go to work, but with Matt even sleep was a complicated
business. He said that there were peak times for every activity,
and other times when you were working against your 'metabolic
rate', when nothing you did would be any good. If you changed
your sleeping habits, he said, you'd just be fighting yourself.

Matt was very interested in how he functioned. He said that
metabolism – which I'd never heard of before – was decided
partly by inheritance and your body, and partly by the climate
of the country you were born in. Perhaps he was right. Until I
met Matt, I never knew anyone who didn't get up at dawn.

When people tried to comfort me afterwards, they said that
the marriage hadn't worked because of our different back-
grounds, because he was American, and Ashkenazi, and white,
and I was Yemenite, and Sefardi, and black. Or because he was
so well educated, and I'd only had eight years at school. That's
all nonsense. I know quite a few Yemenite girls who are
married to Ashkenazi boys, and it works out well, though some
of the boys say it's easier to marry an American tourist than to
court an Ashkenazi girl from round the corner.

Matt and his friends were very excited about my coming

from a Yemenite family. They thought all Yemenites were dancers or jewellers, and they were always talking about our marvellous talents and wonderful looks. As if I hadn't always wanted to be blonde, like those sabra Ashkenazi girls with their long pink legs sticking out of their shorts, all called Tami, not Temima, like me. Temima means innocent in Hebrew. But innocent means stupid too, so I called myself Tami short for Tamar, which is a good sabra name.

Anyway, Matt loved the dark colour of my skin, and when I met his mother she said everyone back home was thrilled he was marrying a Yemenite. I didn't like that. I didn't love Matt because he was American.

And it wasn't education that was the problem. If I'd been more educated, Matt wouldn't have been able to teach me so much. He loved being my teacher. He wanted me to learn everything at once, like metabolism and chiaroscuro and the New Testament and the *Mahabharata*. Chiaroscuro was the way painters play with light and dark. The way the light shows up the dark and the dark the light. Matt said that there was a whole world beyond Israel and Jews that I ought to learn about. If you lived in Israel you had to understand the countries outside, because it was such a small place in a little corner of the world.

He explained all this to me with pictures and stories, teaching me from the pictures in his big art books. He hadn't any socks or saucepans but he had all these books, not like my father's sacred books but with pictures. He taught me about Jesus from all the paintings of those ugly babies with grown-up faces, and the ones of the man on the cross, and Krishna and Buddha from the photographs of statues.

My father was very angry when I told him that as far as Matt was concerned I had no education at all. I was considered the cleverest in the family, and I'm very good at figures. If it hadn't been for the fact that they wanted me near home, I would have gone to night school straight away and then to a bank, I would never have worked in the post office and never have met Matt. I was much better at figures than he was, and that's why I knew how to manage money and he didn't. I couldn't even send him out to buy a kilo of tomatoes; they gave him the wrong change and he never noticed.

I worked at the post office because after what had happened with my sister, the family wanted to keep an eye on me – so I went on living at home. My sister was better looking than me and she served in the army. A colonel seduced her. He ran a liaison office with the UN people, and when he wasn't interested any more she went off to Sweden with one of the UN officers. She works in a bar now and she's thinking of going to Canada. She writes to me but my parents don't write to her. After these things happened my father wouldn't hear of my going into the army. He said that my sister's disgrace was his reward for being a good citizen and not claiming exemption for her on grounds of religion. He spends half his time in the synagogue, but the rest of us do as we like. He made me go and swear that I was an observant girl, dressed me up in long sleeves and stockings like the religious Ashkenazi girls wear, and told me to look at the ground all the time and not look any man in the recruitment office in the eye. He said that would show that I was modest, but I think it suggested to them that I was lying. They let me off anyway.

My father never really trusted Matt. He wouldn't trust any Ashkenazi after what happened to my sister, he said they were worse than the Arabs. My mother liked Matt because he was very polite to her, and wrote down all she told him about her herbs in a special notebook. But though Matt tried to talk to my father about life in the Yemen, my father wouldn't answer. He would sit in a corner and barely nod to Matt whenever he came to visit. He never got over the fact that I'd met Matt in the post office, and not in the accepted way, at a meeting between members of respected families.

This is how it happened. Matt came into the post office one noon near closing time to collect a registered letter. He looked so funny that I couldn't help glancing at him as he fidgeted at the end of the queue. It was clear that he'd just got out of bed. His hair was all over the place and his eyes were sticky, and he had his shirt on inside out, and he kept waving the collection slip at me as if he thought I'd close the position and go away. I was glad that he was the last, because I didn't have to hurry him. We were left almost alone, because at twelve thirty on a summer day everyone left on the dot, and only one man was there heaving the mail bags to the back door for the van to take away. Matt was so excited about the collection slip that I was sure he must be expecting money. All the young Americans who lived in our district – there were quite a few because it was what they called picturesque, and cheap because it was neglected, people like us left the old stone houses and moved into government housing when they could – got money from home in registered envelopes, and it was funny watching the look on their faces when they opened the envelopes and saw how much was there.

It was only after he'd torn the envelope open that he went to the front door, which was already locked, and turned to ask how he was to get out, and then looked at me and liked what he saw. And I liked what I saw too. He had a beautiful pointed face, rather girlish compared with the men I knew, with gentle eyes and a very full-lipped, soft mouth. I liked the way he smiled and tried to pretend that he was really not in a hurry, that he'd leave when I was ready. But I couldn't risk leaving with him because my mother might have been waiting outside, as she sometimes did, and so I said I still had work to do and let him out the back way.

But I remembered his name, Matthew Levine, and every morning I would look through the registered letters and the parcels and see if there was anything for him. After about a

week he came in one afternoon to buy airletters, and I could see
that he was getting ready to ask me something, and in the end it
was whether I was Indian, and I laughed and said no, Yemenite.
He said oh, he thought Indian because he had been to India,
and I said that must have been interesting but I was from a
Yemenite family. There was someone in the queue behind him
in a hurry who started complaining about girls who talked to
young men instead of serving the public; so Matt apologised all
round and left.

It wasn't long before he came back again, with friends. I
didn't like that, because they all stared at me and whispered
together. I had the feeling that he'd brought them to look me
over. One of his men friends, who had a very bold look, asked
me if I'd come to a party they were giving, and I refused. But
then I looked at Matt, who was pale and saw he'd done the
wrong thing, and I felt sorry for him. When the others had
gone – he almost threw them out – he apologised and said that
he'd wanted to ask me out himself, but didn't know how. I said
that another time he might speak for himself.

In the end I did go to that party. I managed to get another
girl in the block to go with me, which was the only way my
parents would agree to my going, and I was trying to keep them
happy because of my sister. I was embarrassed to explain all this
to Matt. When I finally did explain, he said that he thought all
Israeli girls did as they liked, and I said that because my parents
had suffered over my sister they were extra difficult. He wanted
to know about it, so I told him, though it wasn't something I
ever talked about. But he was so gentle and sympathetic that I
couldn't help it. Of course that drew us together, straight away.

Yet all the time I was telling him, I felt that I was cheating,
lying to my parents and to Matt. Because while I made out that
my sister's affairs had been such a terrible blow to the family, I
wasn't even a virgin myself. Something had happened a few
months earlier with the son of one of those respected families,

and it had practically been rape. It was just one Saturday evening, when a crowd of us had been fooling around near my home, and somehow we found ourselves left alone, near one of the darker hallways in the estate. The boy kept threatening me that if I didn't go out with him after that, he would tell my parents. But although I was afraid, I managed to keep away from him. All I thought when that boy forced me was that I was glad that the first time, when you were hurt and felt no pleasure, it wasn't with someone I really cared about. I knew something about it, you see, already, even if it was only hearsay.

Everything I knew about physical love I'd learned from my sister. She told me exactly what a woman felt when she wanted a man, and many other things, and when she told me, her eyes grew bright and she breathed faster so that her talking was breathless, and I could feel her physical excitement, though I couldn't share it. I was sorry for her, too, because the men she needed so strongly didn't care for her at all, and I thought that they must laugh at her behind her back.

I suppose it was partly curiosity about what I might feel that made me go to Matt's place, a room not far away, even before he had asked me to. That, and the fact that I felt so safe with him. What worried me was whether he would think badly of me when he found out that I wasn't a virgin. I'd heard so many stories from my mother about husbands who'd sent their new wives home again, and from friends who tried every trick to pretend they were still virgins on their wedding night. I couldn't quite believe that Matt wouldn't be angry. But in fact he never said a thing. It didn't occur to him. What he kept asking was whether I was ready yet, and was it good, and no one had ever suggested to me that men would ask you those questions, not even my sister. I was so surprised, and grateful, and in love with Matt that I cried all over him, with relief.

But I didn't want to meet his friends yet. I wanted us to be quiet and secret. He thought this was because I was afraid of my parents, and I let him think that. But the truth was that I didn't want to be shown off as Matt's Yemenite girl. In the end, he insisted, and we went to see his closest friends, a married couple. He said they were spending a couple of years in Israel to see how they liked it. Until he said that, I hadn't thought that perhaps Matt, too, was seeing how he liked it, and that in the end he might go away. He had a job working evenings in the office of the English language newspaper. He translated Hebrew novels, too, and he had those cheques from his mother. But it was never enough for him. He was very wasteful with money. Because he couldn't cook, he bought expensive foreign food and drink for us, until I started doing the shopping and he was surprised at how little money I spent.

The couple he introduced me to were not as bad as those other friends who had come with him to the post office. I liked the husband better, because he didn't make a fuss of me and didn't ignore me either. I could see that the wife was teasing Matt about me all the time. There are women who like to have an unmarried man around as well as their husband, and don't like it when the man gets a girl of his own, and she was one of those. What troubled me most, though, was the thought that these people came and went. My family, my people, stay in one place because there's nowhere else for us to go, and we wouldn't want to go there anyway.

When we'd paid our visit to the couple, and left, Matt saw that something was wrong. He was very sensitive. When I told him what I was thinking, he asked me whether I thought he was like my sister's colonel, someone who exploited women. I didn't dare say that my family would see him in that way, though I didn't, so I said no. Then he stopped in the middle of the road and asked me whether I would marry him if he asked.

That was a strange way to propose, of course, asking and not asking. I knew it was too early. I'd pushed him into it and he was trying to prove to me that he was honest. So I said that there wasn't any hurry, and he was relieved.

But I didn't like the way we were living. My parents knew nothing about Matt, but of course they knew that something was going on. I was afraid that there would be terrible scenes when they found out, and that Matt would be horrified by the way they would behave. I don't know what worried me more, his reaction or my parents.

There were other difficulties. His other friends, the ones who weren't married and were all very clever, made jokes about me, I knew. Behind my back I heard them call me 'the mail girl' and they used to ask me all kinds of questions about postage rates and delays. I used to answer them quite seriously, though I knew they weren't interested in the answers, and Matt got furious with them. But in the end he saw that my way was the best, and when they saw we were laughing at them, they left me alone.

All this time there was no problem at all with our metabolism. We always made love in the afternoon, during my lunch break from the post office and before Matt went to work. At that time of day, my mother was still at work – she was a cleaner – and didn't miss me, and my father fell asleep once I'd given him lunch. I'm afraid I pushed him through it to get out as quickly as possible and be with Matt. Matt was always fresh in the early afternoon because, though I didn't know it then, he'd slept half the morning. He had never got up early to go to work. Sometimes I was a little sleepy myself, especially as those were the hottest summer months, but Matt didn't mind that, nor did I. It was like being a little drunk, in his cool room with the blinds down, the heat outside and the different heat inside us. Afterwards I fell asleep and Matt woke me when it was time to go back to work. The clerks who'd tried to flirt with me for months guessed where I'd been, my face looked different, and made coarse remarks.

I suppose they, like Matt's friends, thought that all there was between us was what happened in bed. But that wasn't true. I loved Matt for his gentleness and consideration towards me, and he loved me – well, I don't really know why. Maybe it was because I was different to the other girls he'd known before, maybe for other reasons.

There was only one time that Matt hurt me before we were married, and it wasn't on purpose. We were discussing the wedding. He'd suggested that I wear a Yemenite costume, because his mother had written that it would make such a wonderful photograph. I was worried. We'd made all the plans, and his mother had bought the colour film, and I still hadn't dared tell my parents that I was getting married. I'd introduced them to Matt only the week before. He had come with friends, as if he were a prince with his court, I thought, but I hadn't actually told them how things were between us. Meanwhile Matt was wondering how I'd get on with *his* mother. He was on the bed, and he rolled over and looked at me and said, 'Anyway I think she's relieved. If I'd stayed in the States I might have married a black girl.'

I got up and dressed, with that pain under my heart all the time, and I was almost at the door when Matt suddenly realised that something was wrong. So he asked me what it was. I couldn't answer and I couldn't explain. It was much too complicated. He got up and took hold of my shoulders and stood there, near the door, looking at me in a puzzled way. I think that if he'd been dressed that would have been the end between us. But standing there stark naked, with his hair in his eyes, he looked so ridiculous that I laughed, I couldn't help it. I mumbled something about having to buy vegetables for my mother, and I went out, and nothing was said. I suppose that once you really love someone there comes a time when it's too late to find out something you don't like, because it doesn't make any difference.

In the end I didn't wear the Yemenite costume, because my

parents insisted that I wear a white wedding dress, with a veil, to be modern. Matt's mother was there with a little camera like a cigarette lighter. I kept thinking that she was going to light the cigarette in her mouth with it, she dashed about with it unlit, and it was very odd. She took pictures of everybody from strange angles, getting down on the ground and climbing on tables. My family stared at her and sniggered.

I still have all the photographs, though I don't like looking at them.

Almost from the moment we were married we had trouble with our metabolism. After the honeymoon, I mean. We went to Greece, and Matt told me hundreds of wonderful stories about the places we visited. The places themselves didn't look interesting to me, the landscape was like Israel, but Matt saw more in them than I did, because he had all those stories in his head. We were very happy. I think the best part was waking up next to Matt, though I always woke hours before he did.

It was when we were back in Tel Aviv that things began to go wrong. We'd decided that we were both going to go on working, exactly as before. Matt's mother couldn't send much money, and because he had to wait for most of his pay to arrive by post it was important for me to get paid on the first of every month. So I stayed in my old job at the post office.

We never kept the same hours, though we were living together. Matt was always asleep when I left. Once or twice I called him from work, and by eleven he still wasn't up. Or else he was lying in bed listening to music. Although I tried not to be annoyed, I was. For one thing, I wanted to air the sheets in the morning. Matt never remembered, and I liked to put the bedding out on the balcony the whole morning, so that it would soak up the sun and smell sweet. Of course he'd told me that where he came from, you couldn't put the bedding out of doors, he said it would be black when you took it in, but this was Israel, and I wanted to air the sheets.

When I got home at lunch, Matt wasn't there. Sometimes he went to give English lessons after his translation work, or went to the sea for a swim. I was very hungry, but I'd wait for him to eat, and he'd come in and say he'd already had a hamburger outside. That was a waste of money, and I'd taken trouble to prepare the dishes he said he liked. But soon I realised that he didn't notice what he ate. In my family the men were very demanding over food. If the rice was soggy, or the spices were wrong, they'd fly into a rage. I know it was considerate of Matt never to complain, but sometimes I wished he would.

In the evenings we'd go to see his friends, or see a movie. We never went to see my friends, I knew they didn't interest him. We didn't like the same kind of movie. The sort he liked had no story, and I'd begin to yawn. Then I swallowed my yawns because he said I shouldn't go to movies I didn't enjoy, and that he'd go with a friend. I said I always wanted to go where he went, and he said that just because we were married didn't mean we were Siamese twins. Well, that hurt, and he saw it, and was sorry.

Then something happened which I see now was very bad, though it didn't seem so bad then. It was in winter, and the afternoons were mild, and neither of us was as tired as we'd been after work in summer. We used to go down to the seashore at night and walk at the edge of the waves. At night you couldn't see all the tar and the filth on the beach, and the sea didn't look dirty and dangerous as it sometimes did in the day, but quiet like a big sleeping animal. Even on the shore we seemed to be riding on its back.

At about that time I bought Matt a book. It was about Greece, with pictures of some of the places we'd been to, and I thought it was beautiful. It cost a lot of money and had gold letters on the cover, and the paper was very silky and smooth. When he opened the wrapping paper and saw the book, he suddenly looked sad and turned the pages very slowly, though he wasn't reading. I knew that he didn't like it, though I didn't know why. But he said nothing, just closed the book and stroked the cover a little, kissed me and put it away. I don't think he ever opened it again.

That wasn't what went wrong; it was this. One night we'd just made love and Matt asked me what I did to avoid getting pregnant. He'd never asked me that before. I don't like to talk about love, and I was embarrassed when Matt and his friends talked in a casual cold way about what men and women do together. It made more sense to me the way my sister had talked. Of course alone with Matt I wasn't embarrassed; I laughed and said how funny it was he'd never asked, he'd taken it for granted that I knew what to do. And he nodded. I realised then that if he'd never mentioned that I wasn't a virgin, perhaps it was because he thought I was far more experienced than I was. So I told him what my sister had told me, that if at the end a woman moves in a certain way, the seed flows out again and can't settle. And he sat up and stared at me and said I couldn't be serious. Hadn't I been to a doctor and had myself fitted up, or given the pill? I said no, I was afraid of that kind of doctor and I wouldn't go to one until I got pregnant.

Matt lay down again and stared at the ceiling. He began to ask something and stopped. I think he'd taken those movements for part of the pleasure and nothing else. He was offended. Then he said that my sister was ignorant and ridiculous, and that if I hadn't got pregnant till then it was just luck, or perhaps I wasn't fertile. I said all the women in my family had children, my mother began when she was twelve, so that when she came to Israel they took her first two children away in the hospital, pretended they'd died and had them adopted, it happened to a lot of our women. Matt didn't believe that either.

I didn't want to argue with him, but I was angry. I said all right, just once I wouldn't make those movements and he'd see, I'd get pregnant straight away. He laughed and laughed, and said that he was glad to see that for once I could get really angry, and it ended with our making love again. At the end I lay quite still, and I got pregnant.

I'm very happy that I have Shammai. Some of my friends think he is a burden, and say that young men don't want a woman with a child. But I don't care about that. I don't think I shall want another man for a very long time, and it was Shammai who gave me the strength to bear everything that happened.

Shammai was the beginning of real trouble in our marriage. It was too early for us to have a child, but Matt didn't dare suggest an abortion, he knew I wouldn't agree. I was very pleased to be pregnant. Matt wasn't so pleased. When I wanted him to feel how the child kicked he put his hand there for a moment and then snatched it away as if he'd been burned. Yet he wanted to see the birth, because I suppose his friends did things like that. I wouldn't hear of it.

My family took over completely when Shammai was born. They made things worse between Matt and myself, because they behaved as if Shammai belonged to them, and not to Matt, and I didn't have the strength to argue. Matt refused to go to the synagogue for the consecration of the first born son. He said it wasn't something he'd ever heard of, and it discriminated against girls. That led to a complete breach between him and my family; they said it looked as if he didn't think he was the father.

Strangely enough, Shammai looked exactly like me, or rather, like my father. That added to Matt's feeling that Shammai belonged to me and my family, and not to him. He didn't have any special feeling about his first child being a son, and I think he might have loved a daughter more. The main thing was that he wasn't ready to be a father. He tried very hard. He gave Shammai his night feeds when I was too tired to get up, and it was because of him that I went on suckling Shammai for six months, and didn't go back to work. Those months were very happy, as I enjoyed being at home with Shammai, doing what I liked best, cooking and cleaning without having to watch the clock. All this was possible because Matt had got himself an office job. But it was torture for him to have to get out of bed at seven every morning, really against his metabolism. He cut himself so badly shaving that he gave up and started to shave in the evening instead. And in the morning I'd get everything ready for him, even half dress him, both of us laughing, and Shammai laughed too, seeing me pull Matt's shirt over his head.

It was during this period that I thought we could go back to making love in the afternoon. But Matt came home at two thirty, when his work ended, completely spent, fell into bed, and slept until evening or at any rate until Shammai woke him. Babies often cry when it begins to get dark, and Matt didn't like being woken. So there was no love in the afternoons at all.

Then Matt insisted that the doctor put me on the pill, though I said feeding the baby would stop me getting pregnant, everyone knew that, but he said he didn't want a whole tribe of children before he was twenty-five. Whenever my mother came to visit me he went out; he couldn't stand the way she always brought dummies, which he threw out the moment she left. Matt thought Shammai needed stimulus. He bought him a complicated toy we fixed to his cot with eight or nine different things to do, wanting him to play with the knobs and buttons, but none of them seemed to interest Shammai; I think he was too young. All he needed was to be cuddled or sung to, but all Matt wanted was to educate him, perhaps like he educated me.

One day, Shammai ran a high temperature and the doctor told me to take him to hospital for tests. When I got there I rang Matt who was still at work. They told me he'd left the job some days earlier. I sent a message home through a neighbour, as we had no telephone, but Matt only turned up at five, and by that time Shammai was better. They told me they'd keep him there under observation until the morning, and I stayed there all night with him. After an hour or so Matt said he was going home to sleep, so I never asked him where he worked now, and where he went when he left home in the morning. As I sat watching Shammai, I think I knew already that the two of us were soon going to be alone together for good.

As soon as Shammai was better, I took him to my parents and went to visit that married couple who were Matt's closest friends. I had the idea that they might know best what Matt was doing with his time. Matt was there, in the middle of what looked like an important conversation. He was amazed to see me, and annoyed. Everyone was polite, but I knew that I had done something wrong. When we left, together, he asked me why I was following him about. I'd been hoping that he would explain everything, that he was preparing to surprise me with good news about some interesting work he'd found, but he told me nothing, and he wouldn't look at me. We walked home together without exchanging a word, and I fed Shammai − he was on a bottle by this time − and when I looked at Matt I saw that he had tears in his eyes.

One day a friend of mine came to tell me that she'd seen Matt with a girl, in a seafront café. What sort of a girl, I asked. Quite pretty, she said, serious looking, with big spectacles and a camera, she looked like a tourist, maybe a relation, nothing to worry about. Of course, I said, his cousin, she's on a visit.

I kept telling myself that Matt couldn't possibly be making love to another girl, because his metabolism was terrible at the moment, he was sleeping at all hours of the day and working at home at night, he hardly ever went out from the time he lost his job. Whenever he did go out, I took Shammai out of his cot and held him close to me.

One afternoon, Matt went out for a walk and came back with the married couple, and they asked me whether I would like to bring Shammai and stay with them for a while, because

Matt had to go back to the States, he had to go home, they said, though I thought his home was with me. His family needed him, they said, though I thought Shammai and I were his family. His friends said they'd look after me until he got back.

Suddenly I remembered that time when he had come to the post office with all his friends, when he was courting me, because he was afraid to ask me out on his own. Now he was going to leave me, it was clear, but he hadn't dared say so himself, he had brought his friends to help him break the news.

I wanted to ask: what about the girl with spectacles, is she going too? But I knew deep down that she wasn't the reason, and I didn't want to embarrass him, he looked bad enough as it was. So I just said no, I'd stay with my parents. At the back of my mind I thought that if anything would stop Matt going, it would be the thought of Shammai with a dummy in his mouth. But they all looked relieved, and I knew then that there was nothing I could do.

Matt never really said goodbye to me. He wrote from the States that it wasn't working and that we both knew it. He offered me a great deal of money if I would agree to a divorce.

I accepted the divorce, and refused the alimony, despite the rabbis and despite my parents, because I'd begun working at the bank where I am now, and I earn a very good salary. I settled with Matt, instead, that he'd help with Shammai's education. I know I can rely on him for that, because he keeps in touch, and I know he feels responsible. I like the work at the bank, I'm good at foreign currency and quick with calculations, and I'm taking an evening course in economics.

I still have the wedding photographs, and the book about Greece which I gave Matt which he didn't like, and didn't take with him. These are the only things which remind me that I was married once, apart from my little boy. But Shammai looks like me, or rather, like my father, and he doesn't like to sleep very much, and the two of us manage very well.

IN TRANSIT

SHE CAME IN on an early flight from Brazil, on a brilliant spring morning. The other passengers belonged to an organised tour, carried cameras, and were presented with orange sunhats. She had no camera and no one was foolhardy enough to offer her a sunhat.

She collected her suitcase from the carousel only on its fifth journey around. Until then there were too many people jostling for position, and she stood aside until the field was clear. Although the suitcase was evidently heavy, no one tried to help her. She did not look as if she would welcome help.

She put the suitcase on a trolley and stood watching the scene taking place behind the glass wall which divided the waiting area from the arrivals hall. Beyond the glass, a crowd was inspecting the arriving passengers. People waved, fidgeted, knocked on the glass, a pantomime which she observed from the side, recognising no one, recognised by no one. The crowds on either side of the glass wall diminished, the carousel stopped. She was left alone apart from uniformed men: customs officials, armed policemen. She made no further move.

After half an hour had passed, a man without uniform but with an official manner came over to her. At first he spoke in Hebrew, which she did not understand; then in English.

'May I look at your suitcase and your papers? Keys, please.'

As he examined them he glanced at her: no sign of nervousness there, but hostility, yes, she was one of those people who hated having her belongings touched by strangers.

'Thank you.' He straightened up and frowned. 'If you're waiting for someone, this isn't the place.' He took her suitcase, and they went out through glass doors which parted automatically, and into the arrivals hall. The man put her suitcase on one of the red and green plastic chairs and went away. She sat down beside it.

Haim, a clerk newly recruited to airport administration, was reading *Time* magazine in his second-floor office when the buzzer went. It was only five minutes to the end of his working day, which had been spent checking cost-of-living allowances paid to airport staff, and incidentally acquiring useful information from the files about the girls who worked on the ground floor. The men who shared his office had gone home already.

'What?' said a girl's voice over the buzzer.

'*You* called *me*,' said Haim.

'There's a woman here, an arriving passenger, who's been sitting in the arrivals hall all day and hasn't moved. Will you handle it?'

'Isn't that Security?' asked Haim.

'She's been checked three times,' said the girl. 'She doesn't belong to Absorption either. They're always losing people, so we checked. Come and do something about her, they said.'

Haim decided not to argue. He liked to think of himself as a troubleshooter, an English word for which there was no equivalent in Hebrew. So far, his initiative had been cramped in airport service. He had written letters to the management suggesting methods for speeding up queues at immigration, cutting down on outgoing checks, and changing the seating in the departure hall. After a month he had been called into someone's office, and told: 'We read your letter, don't sit down, if you push them through immigration too quickly they'll jam the exit; if you hurry customs, they'll put pressure on Security, and those chairs are meant just for short waits. Keep official paper for your work.'

'Where are you?' he asked the girl.

'Dina, at Information, in Arrivals.'

Haim put *Time* in his jacket pocket and went downstairs. Dina was checking flight schedules at her desk in an almost empty hall, where the dust on the floor was visible in the shafts of late afternoon light coming from the glass façade. Dina was a pretty blonde girl with a glum expression which did not change when she looked up at him. Haim saw himself considered, challenged.

He put his elbows on the desk. 'Why do the pretty girls always look angry and the plain ones smile?' he asked.

'What do you want of me,' the girl said, in what was not a question, totally without expression. 'That's the woman over there.' She motioned with her head without looking in the direction of a woman in black, sitting alone.

'Why did you call *me*?'

'They told me to get someone from the second floor and you were the only one who answered.'

'What do they want me to do with her?'

'Find out where she's going, and get her there.'

'And if she's waiting for someone?'

'So go and find out.'

'Will you be here when I get back?'

'Doesn't suit you,' said the girl, again without expression.

Haim put up his hands in mock surrender. It was difficult to start without data. It would be so much simpler if the department were to run all the girls' relevant statistics through their computer: together with 'married' or 'single' there would be 'available', 'temporarily unavailable', 'pregnant', 'waiting for a termination', 'willing', 'preference for pilots', 'tourists', 'fellow employees' and so on. It would save time.

He walked over to the strange woman, wondering which

approach to try. Should he behave like a policeman? Or perhaps like a doctor?

'Good afternoon,' he said. 'I'm from airport administration.'

She looked startled.

'Can I help you get a taxi? Where are you going?'

The woman appeared to be thinking over his questions. 'I don't know yet,' she said finally.

Haim had a brief sense of disappointment. The woman was just a nut case; it was too simple. Someone had told him they coped with several a day.

He went back to Dina, who was doing her nails. They were long and curved, two rows of small daggers. Haim approved; he didn't like girls to have short, stubby fingers. He could feel these in the small of his back.

'Finished already?' she asked.

'She's crazy. Do we have a doctor available?'

Dina looked in the woman's direction. 'Doesn't look crazy to me. How do you know?'

'She told me she doesn't know where she's going. Quietly, just like that.'

'All right, I'll try and get a doctor. You stay with her.'

Haim went back to the woman. 'We'll have things fixed up for you soon,' he said, nodding reassuringly as if she had asked a question. The woman paid no attention to him. Haim offered her a cigarette.

'I don't smoke,' she said.

'Are you here for a holiday?' asked Haim, crossing his legs and hooking one arm over the back of his slippery plastic chair. It was the only way to stop his buttocks slithering sideways. He could scarcely believe that the woman had sat here all day.

She looked away, not at him, and said severely: 'I've already explained to you that I'm not sure yet. I came here on an impulse, and I may have made a mistake. The person I expected to meet me did not come, so I may decide to go to London. I really cannot understand why you should want to interfere.'

Her tone was authority personified, reminding Haim unpleasantly of the official who had rejected his letter. She was dismissing him. At first he was taken aback, wondering whether he had not made a fool of himself in sending for the doctor. The woman had spoken slowly and precisely, and her voice had a slight quaver, as if talking was tiring for her, but not a signal of distress.

Dina was on the telephone now. Haim mimed query by raising his right arm and wiggling his hand at the wrist. The girl shook her head as she put the telephone down.

Haim puffed a salvo of cigarette smoke in the woman's direction, and examined her carefully through the haze. He had been reading about body language, movements that gave things away; he might follow up with negotiation psychology, conversational strategy. If he was unappreciated in the Personnel department, he might consider a move to Security.

The woman opened her handbag, took out a handkerchief and blew her nose. He noticed that her hand shook slightly, like her voice. But her eyes were dry, her expression self-possessed and annoyed. He wondered whether he could ask to see her documents, and then decided to make his assessments first, check later. He put her at somewhere between fifty and sixty years old, widowed or divorced, wealthy. She had probably been very good-looking, years ago; he was not in the habit of looking carefully at women of this age, and he was surprised at the elegance of her clothes. What could be the point of dressing so carefully when she had nothing to offer?

He muttered, 'Back in a minute,' and strolled over to Dina's desk. There he turned, one elbow on the desk, poised to keep the woman in view.

'Well?' the girl asked. For the first time there was interest in her voice.

'Difficult to say,' said Haim. 'She has very expensive

jewellery, her handbag's real lizard, but she might be down to her last cent. Maybe she hasn't even the money for a taxi fare.'

'Detective, are you?' Dina looked sceptical.

'Wait,' he said cryptically, inhaling smoke.

'You'd be amazed how many mental cases we have in this place every day,' said Dina, suddenly voluble. 'Black Hebrews, hippies, junkies. And over at immigration they've got at least one stretcher case a week. When my aunt needed a gall-bladder operation it took three weeks to get her a bed.'

'Did you get through to the doctor?' asked Haim.

'He has someone in diabetic shock, he can't come straight away, I told you there's always trouble.' Haim did not want to listen to Dina's patter, sensing that it was not offered in confidence, but part of a stock-in-trade.

'She's in shock too, I'd say.'

'What was she talking about then?'

'She's not making sense.' He tapped on the counter. 'Needs care. They'll make her relax, then she'll talk.'

'You mean drugs?' asked Dina, nodding knowledgeably. She looked back at the woman. 'But she'd have to agree. I mean – she looks as if she wouldn't.'

'That's just on the surface,' said Haim. 'In fact, I think she might crack up any minute.' The confidence with which he said this, though he had not intended to go so far, impressed Dina. She looked apprehensively in the woman's direction. 'Four flights due in a few minutes,' she said.

'Don't worry,' said Haim. 'I can handle it.' He strode away from the desk, sensing that Dina was looking at him.

The woman had taken a leather notebook and a small gold pencil from her handbag and was making calculations. As Haim approached, she put it away.

He stood over her. He was not tall, but burly, blocking her light, and he knew that he was too near for her comfort.

'Look,' he said. 'If you'll tell me what the problem is, I can help you. If you want to go to a hotel, I'll fix it up. You want to make a call to the person who should have met you? I'll do that. Maybe we can get him here.'

She shook her head. 'No,' she said. 'I think perhaps he is not alive any more. I have to stay on my own, or go to London, to my son.'

Now it's all coming out, thought Haim, with a sense of elation.

'Well then, I'll cable your son,' he said briskly. 'Just give me the name and the number, it's on the house.'

'Certainly not,' said the woman. 'I know you want to help, but it is none of your business. I just need a little time to make the decision, and I would be grateful if you would just let me sit here quietly to think. I am not disturbing anyone.'

'You can't just sit around here, you know, this is a place for passengers. There are four flights arriving soon, and that means a lot of pressure. Noise too, this isn't the place to think. Just tell me what the problem is. Look, you don't know me, so that ought to make it easier. Right?'

The woman looked at him now for the first time. She had large, dark eyes, a white, powdered face. A ruin, thought Haim, almost with resentment. A woman this age ought either to be a comfortable grandmother or in some useful job. This woman wasn't self supporting – of that he was sure – but certainly used to giving orders. Supported all her life by some rich man. A man's woman, when the man was gone; that was his assessment.

She stood up; the high heels meant that she was slightly taller than Haim. 'Then I shall go to the restaurant,' she said. 'Surely one is allowed to buy a meal here.'

'Restaurant's closed for repairs,' Haim announced, 'There's a snack bar, not too comfortable I'm afraid. Can we buy you a coffee?'

'No, thank you. Please take my suitcase to the left luggage.'

As if she were talking to a servant, he thought angrily. He

watched her tap away out of the arrivals hall and in the direction of the bar. With bad grace, he lifted the heavy suitcase, took it over to the information desk and pushed it on to the counter. Dina was talking to a passenger, smiling, playing with the gold chain around her neck. Haim waited impatiently; then he lowered the suitcase over her side of the counter, letting it drop the few extra inches to the floor.

'What's going on?' Dina looked at the suitcase.

'Hang on to it. I have to keep track of her, follow her round the airport. Now she won't keep still. Keep trying for the doctor.'

'Why, what's happened?'

'I can handle it, but see if you can get some sedatives from him, send someone over to get them if he can't come himself.'

'Haim, if you need any help, I'm here.' She actually smiled at him, a friendly, schoolgirl's smile, not the kind of smile he wanted but a smile none the less. Progress, he thought, we are making progress, and set off for the snack bar, elbowing his way past the passengers who had suddenly crowded the airport.

The woman was sitting on a stool beside the snack bar. There was no cup in front of her and she was trying to catch the waitress's eye with a small, delicate movement of her gloved finger. Haim stood behind her. 'You have to get a ticket at the cash till,' he said loudly, 'I'll do it.' Before she could move he jumped the queue, snatched a ticket from the woman at the till, whom he knew, and was back, waving the ticket in the waitress's face. 'Coffee,' he said, 'black or white?'

The woman watched him stonily. 'I should have preferred tea,' she said, and he noticed that the quaver in her voice was more pronounced. 'Very well – black.'

He took the stool next to her. 'Now, we have to decide quickly, because there are only two more European flights we can get you on to, and one only,' he held up a finger as if talking to a child, 'one only to London. You don't want to sit here all night, do you?'

The woman was silent.

'Or why not stay on, tour the country? The Sinai coast is great this time of year. No, perhaps for a lady like you that would be too rough, simple accommodation, but there are very luxurious hotels in Eilat. Tel Aviv overnight, then Eilat. I guess you don't water-ski, no skin diving, right? But the rest would do you good. Then Jerusalem. If you like shopping for souvenirs, Jerusalem is the best place. Absolutely. Things that would cost you twice as much in Tel Aviv, coffee pots, necklaces – half the price in Jerusalem. You look like a lady who would enjoy the ruins. Here's your coffee.'

He tipped milk from a jug on the counter into her cup and pushed it towards her. Some of the coffee slopped into the saucer. 'Sorry.'

The woman was drawing off her gloves. She had bony white hands, lined by the seams of her gloves. Haim watched her with some of the distaste he felt for old women in bathing costumes at the sea. Her hands were naked but for one gold ring. She stirred the coffee and put the spoon gently back in the saucer.

'Hey, waitress,' said Haim. 'I said black coffee. The lady can't drink this.'

'It doesn't matter,' said the woman faintly.

'You asked for black, you'll get it,' said Haim determinedly, pulling her coffee cup over to himself. He drank, and the skin from the warm milk adhered to his moustache. 'I could see right away that you were a well brought-up person, not used to looking after yourself. You have to learn to push a bit, otherwise you get pushed. If you ask for black coffee you have to insist, right?'

'You are extremely impertinent,' said the woman, tracing an invisible pattern on the counter with her fingertip.

'You aren't letting me help you,' said Haim. He took a cup of black coffee from the waitress and put it on the counter. His left hand and arm were planted between the woman and the cup.

He saw her look at the coffee, but she clearly did not want to reach across and risk touching his arm. She was very pale; he reflected that she had probably eaten nothing since the morning.

'You aren't fair to me,' he said, leaning towards her. 'I'm doing everything I can to help you. In other countries people have to look out for themselves; here we care for one another, you know. In London airport you could sit for weeks and no one would bother with you, you could drop dead.'

Her eyes were still fixed on the coffee cup, and slowly, Haim withdrew his arm. As she reached for the cup he took an envelope of sugar from the saucer, tore it and shook the sugar into the coffee.

'I think you need energy,' he said. 'Drink up.'

The woman took one sip and put the cup back into the saucer, where it rattled till she let go of the handle. 'I don't take sugar,' she said. 'I should like to leave on the London plane.'

'Right,' said Haim with alacrity. 'I'll fix it.'

'Well?' asked Dina. She had been combing her hair, and now shook it back over her shoulder in a pretty gesture. 'You have milk all over your moustache.'

Haim sucked at the hair, looking at Dina. 'That doesn't make you feel bad?' he asked. She shook her head. 'Some people can't stand the sight of skin on the milk,' he said. 'Fussy people.'

'How's the lady?'

'She wants to leave on the London plane,' said Haim and Dina looked at him admiringly. 'I'll check,' she said, looking at her watch. 'Mind you, Chava was supposed to replace me at three thirty, she's late, it isn't really my shift any more.'

'Wait a second,' said Haim. 'I don't think that woman ought to leave. She ought to be in hospital. She isn't fit to travel, and what happens if she breaks down on the plane? They'll blame us for passing her through.'

'You keep saying she's going to break down,' said Dina, 'but it hasn't happened. You said herself she's made a decision. She wants to get out of here, so let her go.'

'If that's what you think,' said Haim, conceding the point. 'Book her on the flight to London if you can. I'll get her details.'

The woman had left the snack bar and was walking towards him, it seemed to him unsteadily. Was it his imagination or did she look suddenly distraught?

'Is there room on the plane?' she asked.

'I don't know yet,' said Haim. 'Come and sit down, you look bad.' He guided her, his hand under her arm as she almost collapsed on to the chair.

'Flights are heavily booked this week, you know, holiday time,' said Haim rapidly. 'Even for people like us who work at the airport it's hard to get a seat. Of course, we'll do our best to get you on if it's in our power. You've made it very difficult for us, sitting around here, if you'd made up your mind this morning there might have been a chance, they put on an extra flight to London at midday, but you missed that one. Wait a minute, though, I can see one possibility. If it's really a hard case, somebody died or something, I know some one who could get you on the plane, but you'll have to tell me the whole story. All the details, all the names, once I've got that straight I might even be able to get you upgraded, a first-class seat, they're sometimes empty. If you'd just start talking.'

She had one hand in front of her eyes now and had turned away from him. Haim looked her over carefully. She wasn't carrying the handbag; must have left it at the bar, he thought. Leaving her, he ran to get it, and returned to Dina.

'That's it, she went to pieces,' he said briskly. 'How about the doctor?'

As Dina spoke to the doctor on the telephone, Haim watched the woman. He felt like a trainer with an athlete he had put through his paces. She was weeping freely now, her head bent low on her hands. Passengers were streaming into the arrivals hall, pulling trolleys, nudging forward children festooned with spare coats and parcels. No one paid the woman any attention.

'He's coming now, says he'll take over,' said Dina. She looked towards the woman and made a face. 'Maybe we ought to go over to her?'

'No, leave her alone,' he said. 'She doesn't like people talking to her.' He tucked the lizard handbag under one arm while he lit a fresh cigarette.

'I don't know,' said Dina. 'It's worse because she's dressed up like that – you know – crying. Doesn't suit her.'

'Leave her alone,' repeated Haim.

Dina's replacement, Chava, hurried across the hall. She too was a pretty, sulky looking girl. Haim looked her over. She was fine, he thought, but he had a start with Dina.

As if confirming this, Dina put her hand on his arm: 'You were right, anyhow.'

Haim shrugged his shoulders. 'Just a technique,' he said. 'Most people are easy to understand.' He looked straight into Dina's eyes. 'You know what I mean? They want you to understand them, even if they argue.'

Dina fingered her gold chain. 'Right.'

'I'll give the doctor her handbag and he can check the details without disturbing her,' said Haim. 'Then I'll give you a lift home.'

Dina nodded. The hall was now so full of people, leaving and arriving, that the woman was almost hidden from sight. But as he chatted to Dina, Haim kept glancing at her through the crowd. It would be a nuisance if she bolted now.

SABBATICAL

I'D JUST COME back from seeing the Bernheims off at Ben-Gurion airport, which was an unnecessary gesture. If I hadn't taken them, I might have worked on my book, or taken the children swimming, or sorted the bills in the study desk. Not paid them, but put them in order. And I wouldn't have had the argument with my wife.

When I came in, she was taking a cake out of the oven. She had used my absence to show me just how much activity could be compressed into one morning: children taken to the pool, translation completed, cake baked. The Israeli female's rite of the Sabbath cake is anthropologists' material; Hanna seems to think her sexuality is in doubt if that hot, sweet-smelling mound doesn't appear on the table by sundown. And all I'd done with the day was to see off the Bernheims at the end of their sabbatical.

'Couldn't they have hired an Avis car and seen themselves off?' she asked. They could. 'And did they have to leave on a Friday morning, the hardest day of the week for us, when I need you around?' They did. 'And why did you lend them that suitcase when you know you'll never get it back?' 'I'll get it back,' I said, 'because they'll be here in a couple of years, and we won't be going anywhere before then.'

'You know quite well they won't be back,' she said, 'because Gail just couldn't wait to leave. I saw her throw out the Hebrew grammar she's been pretending to use all year, when she was packing. And she gave all her ordinary Israeli clothes to the maid and just kept the blouse with the Yemenite embroidery, and she'll probably pretend she bought *that* in Morocco.'

'They travel light,' I said, 'and they send books airmail. That was a terrible grammar, and if I remember right, you lent it to her.'

'And you insisted on lending them our subscription ticket to the Philharmonic, and they used it for the best concerts and left us the duds.'

'They'd do the same for us in the States,' I said.

'Yes, if we ever get there, which we won't,' said Hanna.

We sat and glowered at one another over the still steaming cake.

As Gail and Art had just left, I was feeling warmer towards them than I had for some time. 'Look,' I said, 'you know that Art really loved Israel. He was stimulated and contented and – do you know what I thought at the airport? I thought he looked healthy. I've never seen Art look healthy.'

'He can get the same tan in California,' said Hanna. 'All right, he had his students, and everyone made a fuss over him, but Gail complained non-stop: male chauvinism, no anti-nuclear movement, and why is the bread unwrapped?'

'We weren't trying to sell Israel to them,' I said, wondering uneasily whether we had been.

'And look what you did for him: intriguing, scheming, things you never do for yourself,' said Hanna.

We had now reached the point. Once more, without malice, Hanna was saying that I'm too unambitious, unaggressive, and un-Israeli too, though *that* she will never actually say.

So I got up and left the table and went into the study and slammed the door, or tried to, but since what we call the study is really an extension of the living room, and since we have the kind of sliding doors which don't quite fit – adapted from an American model, but probably with one page of instructions missing, like so many Israeli versions of American living – you can't really slam the study door. So I turned my back on the crack in the door, and pretended to work in the hour or so left before the Sabbath, and actually spent it thinking about Art and Gail Bernheim, who had taken up enough of my day already.

The previous evening they'd given us a present, a beautifully carved Italian wall cabinet which now stood in a corner of the study. Hanna had already put a plant on top to domesticate it, but that looked wrong, so I put the plant on the floor. They'd found the cabinet in the Tel Aviv flea market, and probably paid far too much for it. Art had always been generous, whatever Hanna said.

Hanna would tell everyone who had given us the cabinet, and it would be much admired, whereas if she were consistent she would chop it up and make a bonfire.

Art has left me with a problem.

I'd volunteered to be Art's man, when he had written to me that he and his wife were coming to Israel for a trial year, on sabbatical. Ah, that Israeli sabbatical, balm of hurt minds. The problem with living here is that I can't take an Israeli sabbatical myself. Actually, I'm not sure that he *wrote* 'trial year', but it was understood, because we'd been corresponding for years about this and other subjects, ever since we left college. I've kept all his letters, too, as if he were Oliver Wendell Holmes, though I'm quite sure he hasn't kept mine.

In the beginning, I was the free spirit, and Art was in a rut, or that was the game we played. I taught night school in Paris and Rome, wrote poetry, experienced life. He was working on extradition treaties for a government agency and had labelled himself junior lecturer in a university law department. Then he went briefly to Vietnam on an intelligence mission, and joined the anti-war brigade. I came to Israel just in time for the Six Day War, married Hanna, and remained.

By the time Art was ready to visit Israel, he was married too, the tone of his letters was less apologetic and the tone of mine, I supposed, was more harassed. But I still had the authentic edge on him. He wrote that he envied me Israel, where I was coping with the brutal realities that he had only glimpsed in Vietnam. Art was very good at defining moral and legal problems, but had difficulty in making personal decisions, such as which university appointment to choose, and where to send his parents, now senior citizens. He implied in his letters that I was lucky that both my parents were dead, as they no longer needed to worry about me, nor I about them.

Shortly after he married, I was surprised to read that Art, now a junior professor at Harvard, was taking an interest in the moral and legal aspects of birth-control campaigns sponsored by the US in the developing countries, an interest which had earned him a column or two in the weekly magazines. Both he and his wife, who had been in the Peace Corps, appeared on television and before congressional sub-committees. It was unlike Art to commit himself in this way, and it wasn't until I met Gail that I understood what had happened.

When Art wrote hinting that he would enjoy an Israeli sabbatical, and the department approved, I was slogging away at a draft of a book, long delayed. I was writing on a minor aspect of constitutional law, which I had chosen because it had philosophical ramifications, and yet seemed directly related to Israel's problems with politics and religion. I thought of myself as making some discreet, but fundamental contribution to Israel's future constitution. And I confided to Art, in my letters, what I would not have told Hanna: that the pressures of family life meant that I had to improve my position in the department, and needed desperately to publish.

Hanna had been very interested in my book at first, but now she wanted to know what people were going to do with it. She was comparing my work with Art's birth control campaign (and pro-abortion stance in the US), and as that is ever the interesting subject to women, Art was ahead of me.

I enjoyed being quizzed about Art, who had become famous. My colleagues, journalists, and anxious Foreign Ministry men were continuously on the telephone: was he pro-, anti-, left, right, Reform or totally secular? where did he stand on the Israel-Diaspora issue, the social gap, the Palestinians? 'Art doesn't believe in committing himself from a distance,' I said. 'Wait till he gets here.'

Hanna recognized Art at the airport, from a newspaper shot, before I did. He had become much fatter, and he had a library complexion, but he had the same deprecating grin. Gail made a good impression then. Perhaps she was a little too determined to ask informed questions all the way to Jerusalem: was that a kibbutz or a moshav, what system of irrigation were they using in those fields, how near were we to the old border? And so on. But, as Art commented, she'd been a reporter, and had the habit of asking questions – without necessarily listening to the answers, he added.

Art and I scarcely made contact in the first few weeks. He was, I thought, absurdly interested in college memories and old friends. I'm entirely without nostalgia for the old days, and Art is the only relic of that time for me. At first, moreover, I thought he had no awareness of Israel at all.

He was touchingly shy in the department, never tried to capitalise on his reputation. He gave his lectures diffidently, as though he expected to be criticised. He was not even roused when old Professor Altenhammer, for whom it was a point of honour to attack visitors, tried to find holes in Art's theories at a seminar, and was roundly defeated by his ambitious second-in-commend, Ben Ishai, with Art himself looking mildly on. He learned one all-purpose, beautifully worded phrase in Hebrew:

'I am not perfectly conversant with the language,' with which he fended off telephone callers.

But while he refused to be interviewed or lionised, Art made himself very popular in the department. He didn't mind the interminable committee meetings that he really was not obliged to attend; he never complained that the university had given him a windowless room in a noisy building; he didn't resent the way his schedules were suddenly changed, and he didn't lose his temper when someone else was found to be using his classroom. He seemed to enjoy everyone he met at work, from the janitor who never got his name right to the fussy German secretary they had given him, for whom he put on his Herr Professor act: 'Yes, Mrs Crechzner, I know that three of my five students at the six o'clock seminar are doing reserve duty and the fourth is working late in the office today, but I think I ought to come for that one righteous man, don't you?'

The Bernheims dutifully attended the department's social evenings. On these occasions, however, Art's silences irritated everyone. They would come in, Gail leading like an energetic tug guiding a sluggish liner through choppy waters, and Art would deposit himself in the most comfortable chair (Gail always sat on the floor) and make no effort to join in the conversation, which was held in English for the Bernheims' sake. Gail did all the talking, and after a while, as no one was interested in Art's wife, the conversation would revert to Hebrew, Gail would be relegated to the womens' corner, which she obviously resented, and I would have to talk to Art. After several such evenings, I began to notice that Art managed to chat with me (college reminiscences) and listen to the conversation around him at the same time. I also suspected that he knew more Hebrew than he let on; when I charged him with this, he just grinned.

After a few weeks we invited the Bernheims to a picnic in a forest near Jerusalem. It was mild late autumn weather, like a European summer, Gail remarked. (She was always comparing Israel with Europe, perhaps because for her the world was divided into three parts: the United States, Europe and the East). We drove up a winding road to a hilltop from which we could see the Mediterranean, a hazy blue line to the west, and the outline of Jerusalem on the eastern hills. It was one of our favourite places, but it did not have the effect on the Bernheims which we had expected. Gail began talking about Connecticut, and how beautiful it was at this season, and Art, who never noticed where he was, was more affected by the magnificent picnic spread Hanna had prepared. When we had eaten, Art lay on his back and closed his eyes. Gail was now talking of civil rights: she wanted to know why Hanna and I had no Arab friends.

'I had some Arab students who came round occasionally,' I said, 'but they weren't our age. Most students go to Haifa these days, it's nearer Galilee, where their homes are.'

'When those students of yours were in Jerusalem, where did they live?' asked Gail.

'I suppose in the university hostels,' I said. 'I didn't ask them.'

'I hear they can't find rooms in any private home in West Jerusalem,' said Gail, bright eyed, ferreting.

'I don't know,' I said lamely. 'No one's complained to me.'

'You never looked into the question yourself?'

'There was a seminar in Haifa last year about Arab students,' I said. 'Not just about accommodation. Job prospects, and so on. We didn't get too far. Politics.'

'I see,' said Gail. 'I guess not enough is being done on the integration issue. It's dangerous though, isn't it?'

Hanna glared at her. 'It isn't so simple,' she said. 'On the one hand they want to live apart, in different schools and neighbourhoods; they don't want to pay the same taxes either. To my opinion,' (Hanna's English tended to sag when she was angry and not too sure of her facts) 'you can't make comparisons with the American Negroes.'

'Blacks,' Gail corrected her.

'Blacks.' Hanna was sidetracked.

Art spoke with his eyes still shut. 'Let them be Negroes here, Gail, no one's listening.'

Gail tried to smile, but it didn't work. She stood up, brushing pine needles from her skirt. She wasn't relaxed, and she seemed angry with Art's listless position. His shirt was half out of his trousers, and he hadn't shaved. I suddenly remembered that Art never shaved on Saturdays; it was an echo of life in his Orthodox parents' home, like not eating ham or oysters. Art ate both, but he never shaved on Saturdays.

We had this kind of discussion many times subsequently with Art and Gail, or rather with Gail, because Art merely modified what Gail said. Gail was annoyed that the Israelis had no official birth control campaign; Hanna pointed out that official policy was to increase the birthrate, and that Israel needed more children. Gail couldn't understand why nuclear disarmament wasn't an issue in Israel; I pointed out that the fear of a nuclear holocaust was outclassed in Israel by more urgent concerns. Hanna had more trouble with Gail than I did, for Gail was attending a Hebrew language course at the university and after hours had time on her hands. She would drop in on Hanna for coffee, and Hanna, who had a part-time teaching job and also did translations at home, was furious at morning interruptions. 'The worst of it is,' she said, one lunchtime when I found her angrily stacking hamburgers for the children who were due in soon from their (according to Gail) 'ridiculously short' school day, 'she makes me say things I don't really mean, such as that the Israeli Arabs are better off economically than Arabs elsewhere, and abortions are cheaper than they are in the States, and kids are readier for serious study after army service. But she makes me so mad I turn into someone defensive and reactionary.'

'Just try and remember it's all personal,' I advised her. 'It's Gail versus Art, and since she can't rouse him, she scores with you.'

Meanwhile, Art and I were having different meetings. Over soggy meals in the campus cafeteria or on the long strolls that Art loved – he wouldn't stride, but moved along crabwise, talking – Art kept telling me how good, how very good he felt in Israel. He loved Tel Aviv, which Gail abhorred ('just like the Bronx'), the Orthodox quarters in Jerusalem, bargaining in street markets, talking to shopkeepers in the dingiest, ugliest little shops he could find. He was blind to the landscape, indifferent to Jerusalem monuments and to the Wall. But he liked to stand shyly in the doorway of some crowded little synagogue. It was Gail who was always exclaiming about the quality of the evening light on Jerusalem stone ('The only other place I know with that wonderful tone is Rome') or the way the hill terraces merged with the open desert, though she complained that the twilight was too short.

'We'll get it lengthened for you,' said Art.

Art also loved Hanna and her cooking. He used to come in and peer into the oven or the refrigerator, the way other guests look at books and pictures. He didn't need to actually eat her *burekas* or her potato salad. I told him he was a gastronomic voyeur.

'She makes all this stuff *and* she reads books,' Art would say. 'What a woman.'

It was difficult, therefore, for me to stay silent about Gail, but I discovered the perfect technique. I simply asked questions about her, which showed interest without actually involving me in lies.

One evening we were leaving the university together and were brought up short by a breathtaking downpour which suddenly hit Jerusalem after a cloudless winter day, and neither of us had an umbrella. We stood near the glass doors as hardier men pulled their sweaters over their heads and made a run for it. 'Has Gail joined that planned-parenthood organisation yet?' I asked. Art looked at me quizzically. 'They asked her if she had kids of her own, and she felt it was irrelevant.'

'Of course it was,' I said, pleased to be on Gail's side. '*And* personal.'

'Why not?' Art said. 'I like that about Israel. Everything's personal.'

'Isn't that claustrophobic?'

'No,' said Art. 'I like it. Hell,' he said suddenly, 'why shouldn't Israel be intrusive and personal and demanding, reactionary, militaristic, male-chauvinist, you name it. Why not?'

'That's disingenuous, Art, and you know it.'

'No I don't,' said Art. 'Everybody told me I'd be asked whether I was going to stay here, everybody warned me you'd try and recruit me. Why the hell are you all so delicate about it?'

I was taken aback. 'Does Gail—'

'Gail's a good kid, but she doesn't understand anything. You know she wanted to adopt a Vietnamese war orphan?'

He hadn't written about that.

'I wasn't against the idea at first,' said Art. 'Then I thought – why not a Jewish kid? So you know what she said? She said I was a racist.'

'Mm,' I said.

'So I'm a racist, fine. I wouldn't give way, so instead of adopting a kid, we went into the birth-control campaign.' This sounded bitter, and so unlike Art that I gave him a nervous look, and he laughed, relaxing.

'My guess is that she'll have a kid in the end,' he said.

'There's no reason why she shouldn't.' We stared at the rain. 'Anyway, I want to stay here; are you going to help me, or not?'

That was how it started. Art wanted a permanent job in the department, and no one had even guessed it. He was a distinguished visitor, disliked by Altenhammer, the department head, much admired by his deputy, Ben Ishai, and many others, popular with the students, whose opinion did not count. It is one thing, however, to like a man on sabbatical, especially the Israeli sabbatical, that intellectual equivalent of buying Israel Bonds, and another thing to want him with you on an everyday basis, disturbing the pecking order, complicating department intrigue.

Almost immediately, I was in trouble. I have never been particularly popular with my colleagues; I hate committee work and prefer to spend my free time with non-jurists, but the students liked me and I'd believed I was an acceptable, if eccentric, member of the department. But one day, when the reshuffling process following Art's candidacy was at its most intense, one of my colleagues did not respond to my smile in the library. Instead, he hissed: 'It's all very well for you, with that manuscript in that old briefcase of yours, but some of us want to get ahead, understand?' Then, perhaps horrified by what he had said, he shook my shoulder, smiled and left.

In that unpleasant moment, I saw myself afresh in my colleagues' eyes: not as a man quietly constructing his master-work, but as an employee, clocking in and out till pension day. And pushing old school friends ahead of colleagues.

'Should I get rid of this briefcase?' I asked Hanna. It was an old friend, dating back to college days, had been through Europe with me.

'I've been telling you to do that for years. Now I suppose someone else has said it.'

Ben Ishai was a diplomat. He decided to bring Art in as

deputy head of the department, his own post, thus avoiding a difficult choice between two other potential successors. The following year he himself was to succeed Altenhammer in the Chair. The crisis seemed over.

But Altenhammer had other ideas. He disliked Ben Ishai marginally more than Art. He had seen Ben Ishai hovering near him for years and it was Ben Ishai who would profit most from his retirement. He persuaded the university fathers to offer the Chair to Art.

On the night the news broke, Hanna and the children remained shut in the kitchen until after midnight, because the living room lies inconveniently between the kitchen and the bedrooms, and Hanna dared not open the kitchen door until Ben Ishai had left. It was useless for me to say that I had nothing to do with old Altenhammer's decision. It was hopeless to deny that powerful Baltimore donors had pressed Art on him initially, alerted by me. It was well known that Altenhammer liked me, but who was to know or believe that this was chiefly because of our discussions of walking tours in the Dordogne?

The next day Hanna and I had our worst argument in years. She said that she didn't want her home used as a department battleground. I said that she had always urged me to get more involved in department affairs; now that I had done so, she was turning on me. She said involved, yes, but not to the point of endangering my career for someone else. I said that since I had tenure I wasn't endangering anything. 'Yes, but what about promotion?' I shrugged my shoulders. She said I lacked the fighting instinct, and had passed this on to our oldest son. At this point Art phoned. Could we meet right away? Could he come over to my place, because Gail was resting? Hanna threw the dishes into the sink and marched out.

It is difficult to get angry with Art. He absorbs anger the way a tennis net takes a fast ball. But when he put his head round the door that morning, looking so pleased with himself, and puffing from the stairs – how can he get so overweight on Gail's cooking? – I just said, 'Sit down, there isn't any coffee left, and let's get it over with.'

He didn't even notice that I was annoyed. He just stood in the doorway, beaming, and I had to go round him to shut the door. 'Gail's pregnant,' he said.

He had told her about the offer of the chair the previous night, and she had responded with her own good news. You can't fault Gail's timing.

So I lost that first chance to be angry with Art. I brought out a bottle of Israeli champagne, sparkling wine as it is called, and we made all sorts of stupid jokes, like giving the child the name My Lai, and everything we said was in that vein. Show me the man who doesn't offend good taste when he is really moved. As far as I remember, we didn't even mention the department, or Art's future; it didn't seem relevant. We talked about our lives during the period we'd been out of contact – a time we'd scarcely touched on before – and for some reason Art filled me in about the other women in his life, and I told him about mine. We hadn't got to Gail and Hanna by the time Hanna came back in and, to give her credit, joined in the celebration with a will. She even said to me later that a child would make a lot of difference to Gail.

The four of us had never been more at ease than during the weeks that followed. Gail and Hanna suddenly found a subject they could discuss without friction, for Gail wanted to know all about pregnancy, and Hanna said that Gail was so anxious to make up for lost time, talking about the large family she intended to have, that you felt it was a mitzvah to explain things to her.

Art and I played chess; I usually won. We had discussions

about religion and Israeli law. He usually won. One day I told him that I thought marriage and divorce should be taken out of the jurisdiction of the rabbinical courts, and the Jewish laws which governed them modernised.

'Don't try to tidy up Jewish law,' he answered. 'Leave it as it is. You'll take the guts out of it. Either discard it altogether or accept the anomalies.'

I accused Art of sophistry. Would he advocate similar laws in the States?

He chuckled. 'That's what I'm coming to Israel for, to become a liberated reactionary.'

I couldn't shake Art on this or other issues. He was a political hardliner too. I told him he'd change his tune when he clashed with the real reactionaries, the nationalists and the clerics, when he found his freedoms menaced. He accused me of having come to Israel to escape my own Jewishness. We both enjoyed the fighting.

In the department, things were less easy. Art was holding an invisible umbrella over my head to protect me from the fallout of his appointment. I didn't like being Art's protégé. I looked forward to the time when he would become an Israeli and cease enjoying the privileges of an outsider.

Art and Gail went off to Galilee to see the spring before she turned green herself, as she put it. Art said that they'd have to go back to the States to have the baby, Gail wanted it to have American nationality by birth, and they wanted to be near both sets of grandparents. The following summer they'd return, in time to get settled before the academic year.

When they came back from the north Hanna asked Gail how she'd liked Galilee. Quite lovely, she said; in some places, with the spring flowers, it was almost like being in the Alps. Hanna and I exchanged a tolerant smile.

Art developed hay fever when the first dry hot weather of summer began, but bore it as stoically as he had the damp cold of winter. Department tempers had cooled over the Passover vacation, and Ben Ishai had been offered a visiting professorship at Chicago for the following year, so even he was polite when we met.

Then Art and I went for one of our Sabbath walks, like two old-age pensioners, I thought, given the pace he set. I reminded him of something I'd just remembered, that at college I had been the provocative isolationist, Art the committed liberal. I thought this was funny, but Art wasn't listening. He stopped under an overhanging tree in one of the placid avenues near our building, and with no preamble announced: 'I'm sorry, but I can't take the Chair, after all.'

I was surprised that I was not more surprised.

Art said, 'I don't know how to explain it to you, but maybe you've guessed.'

I said maybe I had.

'I want the job,' said Art. 'You know that. I wanted to stay. But in Galilee I saw how things were. I know what's going to happen when we get back to the States. And there's been an offer from Berkeley. She always wanted California. The money means nothing to me.'

'I believe you,' I said.

'You see,' he added, 'she'll need peace and quiet for a time, after the birth.' He talked as if Gail were a frail consumptive and Jerusalem Las Vegas. 'Later on,' he said, 'we'll be freer to decide.'

Here I disagreed, but said nothing. We strolled on, a couple of wise elders, with debris from the tree, dislodged by the hot *chamsin* wind, in our hair.

'I really like it here,' said Art. It was valedictory.

He was getting bald, I noticed.

Hanna thought I was making things too easy for Art. 'At least tell him the way you feel. Why is that so complicated?' Hanna likes to spell things out, mental springcleaning. I'm not like that, I can even see Art's point of view. Gail hasn't worn him down to the point where he resents it; not yet. Ought I to feel used and discarded? I don't think so. It has nothing to do with me. I feel sorry for Art.

However, I have bought a new briefcase.

OUT OF TUNE

IT NEVER OCCURRED to Mikael Lazarovitch that he would be troubled by the Israeli climate. He thought of himself in the sun, lightly dressed, with a sense of relief. He would throw off his heavy clothing with all the constraints of life in Russia. He did not reflect that he had always disliked torrid city heat, the mild, rainy summers in his Ukrainian home town. In such weather, he escaped after work to the river, to lonely walks in the fields and nearby villages, returning only late at night to the crowded family apartment.

For Mikael, the prospect of emigration meant that he would finally live apart from his family. He would not have to marry before setting up home on his own. He would no longer find his affection for them such a burden.

Hayuta, Mikael's mother, with her energy and moral passion – qualities Mikael knew he lacked – was the moving force in the family. It was she who had sustained them through years of social isolation and unemployment, from the moment that she submitted their request for an emigration permit until the moment they crossed the frontier into Hungary, on the way to Vienna and the plane for Israel. Without her, the family would have remained in Russia. To her husband, she had stressed family pride as a motive; to Sasha, Mikael's elder brother, she had held out promises of a career in the West. To Mikael she had promised a new piano.

Long ago, the family had decided that Mikael was to be a

musician; it was both a promise and an obligation. Hayuta was an engineer, her husband and elder son were biologists. In Hayuta's family – Latvian Jews, slaughtered in the Holocaust – there had been two musicians, and when Mikael showed talent for the piano, everyone exclaimed that he had inherited the family gift. But something went wrong. Unlike a real professional, Mikael proved unable to *memorise* music. He needed the sheets of notes in front of him. Sometimes he would forget the need, and his fingers would go on playing while he half closed his eyes; then he would suddenly stop. Hayuta said that he was nervous, that it would pass. But his playing was inexpressive; he played, literally, to himself. The feeling, the dynamics, he heard in his own head; his listeners heard only the notes.

He became an accountant in a factory office.

Hayuta bought him an upright piano, a Volga. When they all lost their jobs after applying for exit visas, Mikael had to sell it to a neighbour, who was not a real artist but a hack who played in parks and hotels. Hayuta wept, and said she felt guilty that Mikael had sacrificed his piano. But for Mikael it was no sacrifice. He played almost daily in the neighbour's home. People there talked through his playing, as they did through the new owner's music, and Mikael felt more at ease than in the respectful silence at home.

When Hayuta promised Mikael a new piano, as a bait to tempt him to Israel, he was doubtful whether he really wanted it. He was tempted, though, when he learned that it was a foreign make, a family piano, and she decribed it as a magnificent instrument. The trouble was that he would have to live up to this instrument, which Hayuta said he would do in a new country, beginning again, in a place which Hayuta promised would 'end all his problems'. He knew that she regarded him as a dreamer, only to be reclaimed by the touch of her firm, large hand on the back of his neck, her cheek nuzzling his. Mikael had a childish sweet tooth, and Hayuta had always bribed him with chocolate. He realised that she was afraid he might stay behind.

The piano had belonged to her grandmother. It had made almost as many forced journeys as Hayuta herself, and now it was back in Vienna, in the care of an old aunt. She promised her sons that they would visit the opera and reclaim the piano from Aunt Maya.

But it was August when they finally left the Soviet Union, and the opera house in Vienna was closed, and Aunt Maya did not want to part with the piano. It was, she said, the only souvenir of the old life. As Hayuta managed to persuade Maya to let the piano go, Mikael wondered at his mother's power of seduction. Whereas he would have tried rational arguments – a piano should not be unplayed, was no mere ornament – Hayuta charmed the instrument away from the old woman using Mikael's skills as the argument. She told Maya, quite untruthfully, that Mikael had been denied an artistic career by having to share a piano with a neighbour, that he had inherited the family gift, that he had always thought of the Vienna piano as in Maya's care until he could claim it. He blushed with shame at the lies, never having heard of the piano until two months earlier. The old lady thought his blush was modesty, and succumbed. Mikael was a handsome young man.

He could not deny that he coveted the piano. A small grand, a Vogel, as sleek as an antelope, so unlike the stocky Volga on which he had played at home, it looked coyly out at him from beneath an enormous shawl encrusted with embroidery and edged with a heavy silk fringe, and weighted with a load of vases, photographs in silver frames, and bowls of sweets (to which he surreptititously helped himself). To his surprise, his aunt had kept it tuned regularly; it had a beautiful, mellow tone, with a gentle female quality which Mikael liked.

Hayuta arranged for the piano to be crated and despatched by sea, paying for this by selling her jewellery. Mikael marvelled, in this Western city, at his mother's urban talents, kept unused for so long. She was exhilarated by Vienna, by her memory of the streets, by the shops, by her own skill in languages. She was a real cosmopolitan, thought Mikael, something he would never be, though his mother, in her imagination, already had him touring the West with her in tow as his manager. But Mikael was alarmed by the display of wealth in the city, by the street cafés and the shop windows. They made him feel provincial, and he was relieved to see at the airport that those bound for Israel were mostly as shabby as himself.

The piano took four months to arrive. During that time, the family lived in two tiny rooms in an immigration centre in a Tel Aviv suburb. It was then that Mikael Lazarovitch began to suffer from the heat.

'What does it matter?' said Hayuta, her face glistening with sweat, her thick black hair lank with it. The papers published the real news, she said, letters were not censored, there was fresh fruit in the shops and beautiful underwear, even for men, in bright colours (her men burst out laughing) and as soon as they mastered this terrible, terrible language they would all find work. Then they would buy furniture, a car, coloured under-wear! Mikael took a wet towel from the washbasin and knotted it round his neck like a scarf.

The immigration centre was a village stranded in a city, a group of prefabricated cottages in an old orange orchard, where a few trees, no longer cultivated, still remained, between high concrete buildings. At night, from within the windows of these buildings, the blue light of television screens glowed, and a metallic chorus of identical but incomprehensible talk echoed from the open windows. The screaming sirens of police cars which rang out almost every evening came, they soon discovered, not from the streets around but from some American city thousands of miles distant.

During the day, the light was blinding, yet hazy with city effluents. The air was as humid as if it was raining, or was about to rain, but it would not rain, Mikael learned, until October. The humidity accentuated family smells, odours never noticed till now, though Mikael and his family had always been cooped up together: his mother's rich, dark smell, the pungent brilliantine on his father's thinning hair, his brother's sweat (he had not yet adopted the Israeli habit of taking a daily shower), the herring left on the table from the previous evening's meal. Mikael fled outside, to the scent of those neglected orange trees which, in the autumn, were all blossom and no fruit, and the rampant bougainvillea which had no scent at all.

He hid behind sunglasses even when indoors. Tel Aviv with its traffic, posters and advertisements assaulted his eyes and ears. He admired the tanned, lithe youths and girls who moved freely in the heat, but felt closer to those clearly overwhelmed by it: dumpy housewives, straps of underwear escaping from their clothes, crescents of sweat beneath their arms, pulling toddlers along the pavements, or the paunchy older men leaning heavily on the counters of open snack bars as they snatched a drink or mopped their faces as they studied the menus. Noise, food and heat. Mikael had no appetite, but drank and sweated, sweated and drank again. He found an evil smelling backwater they called a river, but the fields around were all fenced in, either cultivated with crops under plastic, or high with thorns and rubble. The sea shore was tar-stained and crowded during the day, but there, in the earliest hours of the morning, he found a refuge, disturbed by no one but the occasional stringy, solemn old man jogging up and down on the sand.

He did not share his mother's sudden acquisitiveness. But he returned several times to a shop which sold chocolates and which had a large window display in the shape of a star of

David. One evening, after much hesitation, he spent what he thought was too great a part of the allowance his mother doled out on a small box of chocolates which he tore open as soon as he was out of sight of the shop. The chocolate was half melted, and left a sour deposit on his tongue.

The family made no friends at the immigration centre. The only other Russians were orthodox Jews on their way to the United States. It was a dead season for professionals from the Soviet Union, and the other tenants of the centre were South Americans. Mikael's parents and brother were the star pupils of the *ulpan*, the Hebrew language class. While he still struggled with the alphabet, they decided they would go on studying the language alone; it was more important to find work. They began a frenzied search, up before dawn every day and off to Jerusalem, Beersheba, Haifa. Mikael was disconcerted by their energy. He said that when he had mastered the language he would take any job that was offered him. Hayuta brought him hand outs from the conservatories, but he shook his head. He would work, he was not going to become a parasite, a student again, at his age.

Mikael rose every morning with a heavy head, worked steadily tracing the Hebrew letters, mouthing the words in his exercise book, hanging back in class, returning alone at midday to the small room he shared with Sasha. Then he slept – as he had never done in his life – till late afternoon, when a mild breeze filtered in from the sea. On one such evening, he woke to hear his mother and brother talking in low voices beyond the half opened door. He listened, eyes closed. Both, he learned, had found work in Haifa, and his first impulse was to rise and embrace them, congratulate them, but something held him back – perhaps his desire to find out more than they would tell him openly. From their talk he understood that his father would not find work easily. His qualifications were less impressive than Sasha's and he might have to work as a laboratory assistant. They spoke of him with compassion, which Mikael fiercely resented. He admired his father, and it had not occurred to him before that his status back home had been due to his being a party veteran, rather than to talent. Mikael still saw his father with a child's eyes, and he was angry to hear Sasha speak condescendingly of him, and Hayuta acquiesce. When they lowered their voices still further he guessed that they were talking about Mikael himself. All he could catch was the occasional word: 'fatigue . . . regret . . . no initiative . . .' He lay facing the wall, eyes open. When his brother left, his mother came over and placed her big, strong hand on his head, sighed. He turned and looked up at her, showing her he had been awake.

'Don't worry about me,' he said sharply. 'I shall find work on a settlement – agricultural work. It's the harvest season. I don't like the town and I need physical activity.'

His mother looked at him ironically, eyes twinkling, saying nothing.

'Yes, physical work,' he said angrily, and he sprang up, pushing her hand away. He was convinced by his own words. If his body rebelled, he would dominate it, push it to extremes. He would not follow his family to Haifa.

The woman from the Absorption Ministry tried to discourage him. It was simpler to deal with a family as a unit, she explained; Mikael, as he was unmarried, was not eligible for an apartment of his own. Volunteer work on the land would be a waste of time for him – it was for visitors from the West, not for immigrants. It was most unusual for a Soviet immigrant to want to join a collective. Mikael reassured her that he just wanted time to be alone, to feel the reality of the land – wasn't that the Zionism of which the books, the emissaries, had spoken? The woman – herself an immigrant from Odessa – suppressed a smile; clearly she had summed him up as the spoiled son of a successful mother.

Mikael signed on for a two-month stretch at a kibbutz in

Galilee. There he began work at dawn, encouraged by the early cool of the fields, but by nine each day he flagged. He watched the other volunteers, trying to find one whose rhythm he could follow, but they were students on holiday from Holland and Germany. They worked badly, complained, laughed and lazed; at night, they passed round fingers of hashish in the stuffy wooden huts where they slept. Mikael refused their offers; they laughed at him. He forced himself to work at twice their pace, and fainted one morning in the middle of a row of vegetables, slumping on to his half-filled sack.

The kibbutz organisers put him to work in the shade, in a banana grove. All he had to do was to raise the wooden gate which let a flow of water gather round the roots of the bushes, and wait until the field was full; then he was to lower the gate again, diverting the water to the next field. The first job had been too strenuous; this one was too leisurely, even hypnotic. Watching the water steal slowly between the roots of the trees, in the humid shade, Mikael felt his eyelids droop and a delicious weariness overpower him. He was suddenly back on a summer day near the river in his home town. In that second he realised his intense yearning for his birthplace, groaned aloud, and fell asleep.

This time they threw him out. He arrived back at the immigration centre on the day his family left for Haifa, mercifully missing them by an hour. The woman from Odessa greeted him indulgently. She had pulled strings, she said, and he could stay through the winter in the centre while he retrained for a job in an electronics factory. Unless, of course, he wanted to move to Haifa. It was blackmail. Very well, he agreed sulkily, he would retrain.

'I almost forgot,' she said, her eyes on his documents. 'A crate has arrived for you in Ashdod. I could send the forms to Haifa, but it is in fact in your name.' The Viennese piano had immigrated.

Mikael went to Ashdod himself in the cab of the agents' truck, though the man had told him there was no need for his presence; the agent cleared many goods every week. That day, Mikael saw clouds in the sky for the first time, and they appeared to him as a good omen.

In the customs shed all the immigrants' crates were being opened, their contents checked against lists. 'It's a piano,' explained Mikael, alarmed at the sight of the workmen's hammers and screwdrivers. 'You don't need to open the crate, it is carefully packed.'

'So *you* say,' said the customs man. 'How do I know what else you have in there?'

Mikael winced as the workmen began to wrench open the side of the crate, which fell apart, revealing a cave of straw and packing. The dismembered shape, shrouded in wrapping, was not that of the elegant instrument he remembered. Then he struck his head and laughed with relief; of course, the legs and lid had been removed for separate packing, the dislocation was temporary. The customs man looked at him suspiciously. He ordered the workmen to pull all the sections of the piano out of the crate and take off the wrapping.

'They'll damage it,' Mikael pleaded. 'Please be careful.'

'Do you think this is the first piano that's ever arrived here?' snapped the official. 'Open it up.'

Mikael was distraught. His mother would have known how to handle this situation, how to deflect hostility. He did not. The workmen began to pull out the straw and packing, throwing them on to the concrete floor of the warehouse; a gilt screw struck the floor and rolled away. Mikael lunged after it but lost it. The customs officer waited until the men were almost finished and then began groping inside the piano, peering; when his hands brushed the strings, strange, gentle sounds of complaint came from the truncated instrument. Mikael watched helplessly as the man pried and fingered and eventually, with the workmen's help, pushed the trunk of the piano, its gleaming black flanks now visible, back into the crate, throwing the packing after it. The workmen, unable to close the crate easily, gave the piano a final, impatient push that sent it flying roughly against the back of the crate.

'Stop! Moment!' Mikael shouted, searching vainly for other words in Hebrew. 'Murderers, assassins,' he cried in Russian. The official swung round angrily: 'Madman, take your piano and get out.' He tossed the documents on to the top of the crate and moved off. Mikael gathered them up with trembling hands. 'I'm sorry, I'm sorry,' he murmured to the piano.

When Mikael had uncrated the piano and set it up in his room (he had to climb over the piano to get into bed) he was able to assess the damage. There were a few splinters and scratches to the mahogany veneer, the gilt screw missing which he was obliged to replace with an ugly metal replacement from a local hardware shop, but when he sat down to play, it was like hearing the voice of someone loved and long dead.

He had been playing for only a few minutes when his Argentinian neighbours knocked on the door. The walls were too thin, they said, a child was ill, and anyway it was against the rules. So all winter the piano stood mute in Mikael's room while he learned a new skill no more interesting, no more boring, than the old one. The woman from Odessa then found him work at a factory in Jerusalem, at his request; he had read in the immigrants' paper that snow had fallen there, and that endeared the city to him immediately.

On one of his last weekends in the immigration centre his family came to visit him. Hayuta tried to persuade him to come to Haifa; she described their new apartment, the niche she had prepared for the piano. For the first time, Mikael lied to her. He said that he had enrolled in the Jerusalem conservatory to study with a Russian teacher. If Hayuta guessed that he was lying, she was too shrewd to press him. She only nuzzled him – he detected a foreign perfume – and commented that she was happy that he was planning for himself. Anyway, the country was so small that they could see each other every weekend if they pleased.

Mikael's father looked older, querulous. He was disappointed in his work. Sasha took Mikael aside while his mother made tea.

'You did right to stay behind,' he said. 'I'll spend a year or two in Haifa with them until they settle down. Hayuta has lost her head completely, she spends money like water and they have this mortgage on the apartment which will never be paid off.' He sighed. 'I don't understand this country. They encourage you to spend, to get into debt, to owe hundreds of thousands of dollars. It is frightening, immoral.'

'It is a different way of life,' said Mikael. He did not like the dismissive way Sasha was speaking of Hayuta. Perhaps here she did not know how to handle Sasha; she looked at him now almost apprehensively.

Sasha shrugged his shoulders. 'Yes, the whole country is in debt. I see no future here. In a couple of years I shall probably try America. They are interested in Soviet scientists. Then you could follow me, I would help you. We could send them money regularly, and they wouldn't be lonely. Hayuta has quite a little crowd of friends already – all Russians of course.'

Mikael shook his head. He suddenly understood that instead of achieving freedom from his parents, he was bound to them more closely than before. He had none of Sasha's ambition, nor his mother's energy, nor the heart to leave his parents in a strange society. When Sasha left, all his mother's ambition, his father's bitterness, would be reserved for him.

That night, when the family had returned to Haifa, Mikael looked at the piano with animosity. He had been bribed. The piano was his compensation for having been uprooted. Without checking to see if the Argentinians were at home, he rushed at the piano angrily. His fingers were stiff, the piano was out of tune, the false notes were like a reproach. He had neglected the piano all winter, betrayed his responsibility, had not noticed that, like him, it suffered from change.

In the spring, Mikael moved to Jerusalem. He found a room in the attic of a stone villa, whose owners told him that he could play whenever he pleased. For the first time in Israel he was happy. He liked the fresh, crystalline air, the pine trees heavy with recent rain, the chiselled stone houses. He breathed freely. He had the piano tuned by a blind man and he played four or five hours a day. It occurred to him that he might well find work in one of the little night clubs, or hotels where they needed a pianist for special occasions. Hayuta, of course, would be horrified; she might even try to reclaim the piano. But Jerusalem was the place to make his bid for freedom. There was more time in Jerusalem than anyone could possibly need.

No one troubled him save his landlords, who pestered him out of kindness. They said it was refreshing to meet a Russian who had no complaints. One evening they invited him to take tea with them.

'Is it what you expected? Do you like it here?' asked the woman.

'I expected nothing,' said Mikael truthfully. 'It is enough for me to be alone.'

He realised immediately that he had disconcerted them. He had been alone now for weeks, and had forgotten that these were secret thoughts.

'Well,' said the man, half smiling, 'You must have wanted

something you couldn't get in Russia. We hear that you couldn't speak freely, or lead a Jewish life, or go where you wanted. It sounded to us like a prison.'

Mikael considered. Hayuta had felt such things, but he had not. Now he could admit it.

'One accepts these things,' he said, noting their discomfiture.

The woman's next question was tinged with annoyance.

'What about the terrible things they said about Israel?' she asked. 'Didn't that trouble you?'

'But we didn't believe them,' said Mikael. 'It was like dogs barking.'

'Still, you must be glad to be out of there,' said the man, decisively.

Mikael did not answer. He thought of the river, and the fields; of city streets, trams, signposts. Every stone, fence, window and lamp in the street where he had grown up suddenly appeared to him and he had a great sense of pain and loss. His landlords were looking at him.

'Yes, of course,' he said, a stranger speaking in his voice.

It was the first warm night of spring. The next day, a hot wind blew from the desert, tickling his nostrils and making him sneeze. Odd, but not unpleasant. For five days the *chamsin* blew, and each day the heat in the little room under the tiled roof accumulated, until Mikael learned to close the warped green wooden shutters. On the sixth day the *chamsin* broke, its place taken by a wild, leaf-ridden west wind. He opened the window to let it in, and when he came home from work he found dry leaves and small brown spirals shed by the pine trees in the corner of his room. The piano was filled with white dust which settled again, like the finest of snow, each time he wiped it away.

It was during the second *chamsin*, two weeks later, that the piano began to complain. Mikael woke in the night without knowing what had woken him. Then he heard it – wood sighing, a hair's breadth sound of complaint. The next night it was more intense, or perhaps he was listening more intently. During the Sabbath morning which followed, he could hear nothing. But at night, it was clear; the wood was drying out, contracting, fibres were tearing apart in an audible process of suffering. He examined the piano for damage, but could see no change. When the *chamsin* ended, this time in a shower of rain, the sounds ceased.

That shower was the last rain of winter. From then on, the heat grew more intense, and Mikael developed stratagems to combat it. He wore his old cloth cap to work, took cool showers, closed his shutters every morning and opened them at night. These precautions amused his landlords as much as their fear of cold had amused him. But for the piano he could do nothing. At night he listened for its distress. Once he was jolted awake by a sound like the lash of a sleigh whip. He ran over and lifted the lid; one of the strings in the treble had tightened and finally torn free of the metal peg that held it taut.

The next afternoon the blind tuner came to repair it. 'Yes, it's having problems of adjustment; the wood is probably not very good.'

Mikael was offended. 'An excellent piano, a very good make, bought from a most reputable dealer.'

The tuner shrugged his shoulders. 'At all events,' he said 'not a Bechstein. Perhaps it should have remained in Europe. But don't worry, it will settle down.'

'Isn't there something I can do?'

'You could try to keep the floor tiles damp, wash the floor and don't mop it dry, or stand a bucket of water underneath. But I don't think it will make much difference.' He reanchored the string.

Mikael stayed awake at night listening for other strings to break their moorings, to lash out at the frame like mad horses loose in a stall, but they were quiet. Only the sound of the straining fibres continued.

The piano's ordeal began to obsess Mikael. He could not sleep, he fumbled at work. The piano seemed more out of tune every day, though the tuner, who had a better sense of pitch, told him it was his imagination. Now, however, the loud pedal had begun to creak in time with Mikael's playing. One morning the factory manager called him in and asked him whether some personal problem was troubling him. He was making allowances, but if Mikael had not been specially recommended, he would have fired him already. Was there something specific? Could he help?

Mikael stared at the man. Once more he knew that the truth was unacceptable.

'It is the heat,' was all that he could say. The manager sent him to the health officer who prescribed a sedative. That night Mikael took two pills and slept soundly. He woke with an uneasy sense that he had missed a night's watch, like a nurse who sleeps at the bedside of a dying patient. He switched on the light and looked at the piano, listened. Perfect silence. He raised the lid and propped it open. At first he saw no change. The strings were all in place, the carefully dusted gilt whorls which edged the soundboard glinted in the electric light. But on the varnished surface of the soundboard, which was decorated with two small painted cherubs cavorting inside a laurel wreath, was a long dark hair. Mikael put out his hand to remove it. But there was no hair; the board had cracked across half its breadth.

'It is the end,' said the blind tuner, his fingers reading the damage. 'Now nothing worse will happen.'

When Mikael played again, he tried to compare the sound, the resonance, with the piano's former voice. It was impossible. The creaking of the pedal, which had disturbed him at first, had become an almost imperceptible accompaniment to the music.

Soon he would not notice it at all. He would become deaf to the piano's deficiencies, just as he was not troubled by the inadequacies of his own playing. The music was in his head. Nothing worse would happen.

ELSIE'S CHOICE

AS MY AUNT Elsie walked home every afternoon from her office to her home near the sea, she would rehearse, in her head, a little guided tour for an imaginary guest, someone to whom she would introduce Tel Aviv: as it was now, and as she remembered it when she had first arrived in the city from London, so long ago; once she did the tour for me.

'There were none of these skyscrapers then, all the buildings were quite low, and rather scruffy, because the sea air made the plaster peel, but that was part of living at the seaside. The sand came up through the cracks in the pavement, and from my flat I had a marvellous view of the sea, a panorama, before they built that big hotel and blocked it out. Nobody had any money, there was nothing much to buy in the shops anyway, and I knew a girl who had just two sweaters to wear with her slacks, one in the wash and one she was wearing. A very pretty girl; she got married of course, good for her. She played the cello in a string quartet, and she always got the case caught in the doors of the bus – we took the same bus home. I prefer to walk now, because with all the traffic it's actually quicker. They still shut the doors on you if you don't look sharp.'

The total recall, the display of memories, was the clearest sign that Elsie was getting old. But although she talked to herself (or to the imaginary friend), she talked to other people as well, and like many solitary women, she was always busy, occupied with attendance at other people's celebrations, choir practice, exercise classes, office outings and exhibitions. As she said, she never had any time for herself.

Elsie had worked for twenty-five years as a clerk in the correspondence and invoicing office of a big firm which imported washing machines and refrigerators. The managing director was an American, Sam Berkowitz. He felt a special affection for Elsie, who had been with the firm longer than any other employee, from its very first year in business. Her salary was not particularly high, but when the matter of a pension, or severance pay was considered, special rules were made for Elsie. Berkowitz and his administration knew that she would never lie, never cheat, never ask for anything beyond what was offered her, never join an office workers' strike.

Pensioning Elsie off was always going to be a delicate matter, though, as neither Berkowitz nor anyone else in Israel knew Elsie's age; my mother, in England, said vaguely that she thought she was about sixty – my mother being the youngest in the family and having little memory of the infant Elsie beyond the stories she had been told – but she looked far younger than that. We worried about what would happen to her when she reached pensionable age, whenever that might be. She had not registered with National Insurance (who would have insisted on seeing her identity card) and for the same reason she did not belong to any health insurance scheme ('I'm never ill anyway,' she said). The firm, however, had its own private welfare schemes, and Elsie was not asked to fill in her age; she was promised a pension whenever she chose to retire.

Whatever her age, she did not seem to me to have changed much since my childhood. I don't know if Elsie had really been as pretty a girl as my mother remembered, though I believed that she had always been headstrong – 'We used to call her Spitfire,' said my mother – but she was still lively, and bright, and still had a youthful figure, long waisted and with long legs (there were photographs of her skiing in the Alps, many years ago), even if her nose was long, too, and seemed to grow even longer with age.

Elsie had never married; she was the only unmarried member in the family – according to my mother, for two reasons. In that generation, she said, either you 'brought something' with you to a marriage – or you had to 'compromise'. My mother had been an exception to this rule, as a wealthy man had fallen in love with her, but my grandparents had no dowry to give Elsie, and she was too 'fussy' to compromise. So she emigrated to Israel, where the family hoped she would find a man to marry her. Israel, from England, was imagined to be like Canada or Australia, a pioneering place, unspoiled, where you needed no dowry to be valued at your real worth. Also, like Australia, the depository for family problems.

But Elsie did not find her man, despite the sun and the sea and the simple pioneering life. Life in Israel became less simple and less pioneering as time passed, and it might indeed have helped had Elsie been able to 'bring something with her' to a marriage. But even apart from the money question, Elsie was not marriageable, not like other lonely women for whom someone, somehow, would arrange a match. There were no women like Elsie in Israel. There were widows: army widows, cancer and heart widows, and plain elderly widows. There were career women; there were single parents, recluses, babushkas and matriarchs. Elsie was none of these. She was an old-fashioned maiden aunt (a term for which there was no Hebrew translation, and no equivalent in England by this time, either): cheerful, quick to anger (Spitfire), good with children, and always busy – most recently at her art class.

Elsie went everywhere with her sketch book and her water-colours. Still-lives of flowers and fruit, and tiny portraits of beggars and pedlars decorated her home - one room, with two windows. One looked out at the shuttered windows of that hotel which had blocked her view of the sea, and past it to a tiny square of glittering water, all that was left of that view, and the other looked into the offices of a travel agency in the building next door. There was just enough space in Elsie's home for a bookcase, a dresser, a table which folded against the wall, two small armchairs, a rug and a sofa bed with a bright cover. The kitchenette was concealed behind a bamboo curtain, and there was a shower room just large enough to turn round in. The small balcony held a reclining chair with a parasol, where Elsie sat outside on summer afternoons after returning from work; with careful maneouvering, she could set up an easel in the parasol's shade.

Within this small compass, between office and home, Elsie's life chugged on, year after year. Sometimes she varied the walk home from the office in order to sit for a while in a scrubby little park with two palm trees and read the English language newspaper. Sometimes she went into an expensive grocer's shop and bought a few hundred grammes of salami, and jam in pots topped with little bonnets tied with gilt string, to entertain her friends – women from the art class, colleagues from the office – to a light supper. She spent two weeks each year in England with her brother's and her sisters' families, but was always pleased, she said, to come home; she wondered how she could ever have lived anywhere so cold and grey.

One spring a new teacher appeared at the art class, and Elsie began painting in oils and joined the life class. For the first time, in place of her small, precise brush strokes, she lobbed great splashes of colour on to the canvas; in place of the still-lives, there were lurid sunsets and nudes with their faces turned away, their bodies slack and flabby, with tanned arms and legs and white torsos showing nipples and patches of pubic hair. We were surprised by this work because Elsie had always been, if not actually prudish, certainly worried by naked bodies and bodily functions: in past conversations with me she had referred to her menstrual period coyly as 'my visitor' and when we went to the beach together, she preferred to go home in a wet, sandy costume rather than strip it off and dress under a towel.

The paintings were the first hint we had of a new turbulence in Elsie's life; the second hint was her sudden absent-mindedness. She often spent weekends with us and would help by taking the baby for a walk, feeding a child, reading a story, and would relax with us in the evenings. So it was disturbing when, in her new mood, she failed to return on time for the baby's feed, and seemed not to have noticed, when she did turn up, that he had screamed himself to sleep. 'I didn't hear him, there was a lot of traffic,' she said. She put chocolate spread on the children's hamburgers, and stopped in the middle of a sentence of a story she was reading them to gaze dreamily into space. Most surprisingly, when we pointed this out (cautiously, as if it were a joke), instead of taking offence (the Spitfire syndrome) she nodded and apologised. Such behaviour was so strange that at first we were worried that she might be ill; but she was still too young – we estimated – for the diseases we feared, and she was clearly not depressed. Her eyes shone, she always smiled, and when she turned up one weekend in a red jacket and with a new hairstyle, we thought that she had either fallen in love or won the lottery. But Elsie never gambled; she was very careful, even secretive, about her savings.

His name was Josef. Without explanation, as if we already knew this new person in her life, Elsie began referring to him casually: 'Josef doesn't like Francis Bacon'; 'Josef has a new commission to do a fresco at the Farmers' Union building'; 'Josef has a touch of the flu'. Josef was, we learned, the new teacher at Elsie's art class. He had recently arrived from Bukhara, she said, and had done well under Soviet auspices as a painter of commissioned work in factories, stadiums and lecture halls, though less well in the post-Soviet era. We could see that such a man might have scoffed at Elsie's watercolours and that he was the inspiration behind the giant figures and primary colours of her latest work. We assumed, patronizingly, that Elsie's infatuation was harmless, that it was giving her a new interest in life, and that it was good of Josef, whom we imagined as a kindly, avuncular person, to take so much trouble over a middle-aged amateur. So that when Elsie disappeared from sight for four weekends in a row, and then rang us to say that she would like us to meet Josef as he was going to marry her, we were quite shaken.

'He's never had a family life,' she explained. 'His parents died in an air raid and he was put in an orphanage. He never had anyone to look after him, and if he hadn't been so talented he would probably have ended up as a sign painter. One thing you can say for the Communists, they gave gifted people a chance. He was picked out at school and he always had work. But they exploited him terribly. He never even had time to get married.'

Primed by Elsie, we could soon recognise Josef's work – or work of the Josef school – at various sites all over town. He was frequently commissioned to decorate billboards when a site was blocked off for a high-rise building, and covered entire walls of public halls with processions of dancers, astronauts, or circuses – anything to entertain motorists caught in Tel Aviv's traffic jams and spare them the sight of a blank wall or the boredom of an over-familiar advertisement for cars or cosmetics. There was nothing very Soviet about these frescos, not a worker or a pickaxe to be seen, but the relentless cheerfulness was unmistakeable. To my mother's anxious long-distance enquiries, we could only respond that we hadn't met Josef yet, but that he must be making a good living out of all those acres of paint and that Elsie was clearly very much in love.

My mother snorted: 'The woman's a fool,' she said. 'She's making an idiot of herself and she ought to be discouraged. We don't know anything about this man. An artist! He may be amusing, but I shouldn't think he really wants to marry her.'

Although we were puzzled, too, if less worried about his intentions – we couldn't quite see Elsie as a sex object – we thought Elsie had the right to make her own choice at her age; what her family thought was unimportant. As for knowing nothing about Josef – well, in Israel a new immigrant was by definition someone you hadn't heard of, someone unverifiable. My mother, however, was determined to inspect her big sister's suitor herself and to protect Elsie from him if it came to that, and she booked a room in an hotel. It was there that we met Josef.

He was not at all as we had expected. In the first place, he was not from Bukhara but from Bucharest – Elsie's geography had always been shaky. (We weren't sure, either, whether Bucharest had actually been bombed during the Second World War, but we let that pass). Nor was he an uncle figure. Josef was well dressed, and had a silver cigarette case he brought out from time to time, and he paid exaggerated attention to Elsie, and held her hand in a demonstrative manner. None of my mother's questions about his background and his prospects – questions which were about half a century out of date and might have been directed to someone half his age – disconcerted him. He answered them all in an offhand way, and did not appear surprised that they were being asked. Perhaps this was the way things were still arranged in Eastern Europe, just as women from that region arrived in Israel wearing stiletto heels and with beehive hairstyles.

Not to be outdone, Josef asked a number of questions of his own. He glanced approvingly at my mother's jewellery and her handbag, asked her whether she had rented a car for her stay (he would be delighted, he said, to take her on a tour of the galleries) and surveyed the hotel lobby as if he intended to buy it, while Elsie – unusually silent – sat quietly admiring him.

We could see why she had been smitten; 'smitten' would

have been the right word, we thought, for her generation. Josef was handsome, tall, with hooded eyes and a fleshy mouth (though his teeth were like stained piano keys) and he spoke English reasonably well, peppered with French. He addressed us all by our first names, showing that he knew, had been told all about, our home life, our children, and our family jokes. He even called Elsie his little Spitfire. We disliked him immediately while allowing that it was unfair to decide that he could be up to no good with Elsie just because he looked, as my mother said later, like a drug smuggler without the dark glasses (but how many drug smugglers did my mother personally know, with or without dark glasses?). However, men who looked like Josef usually had sumptuous blondes on their arm, not ageing spinsters in mid-calf skirts, and I was disposed to stand up for Elsie's choice, while forced to agree that there was something odd about Josef's courtship.

'And where are you going to live?' asked my mother finally, her tone rather than the question implying that she was reconciled to the marriage in principle and could now move on to the details.

'In Elsie's flat, *entendu*, for the first few months,' answered Josef smoothly, 'until my Bucharest affairs are wound up. Then of course we shall move into a large apartment.'

'With a studio for Josef,' added Elsie, who until then had been silent.

'You'll be terribly cramped in Elsie's flat,' said my mother.

'I could never be too close to Elsie,' said Josef, and she blushed. We were all embarrassed.

When the two of them had gone, Elsie frogmarched off on Josef's arm, my mother said that she thought Josef could be bribed to leave Elsie alone. 'Did you notice the way he looked at my bracelet?'

'You couldn't do that to Elsie!' I protested. 'It would humiliate her; she'd never get over it.'

My mother retorted: 'He knows she comes from a warm loving family – she's told him that and far too many other things about us. What else can he be up to? He can't really be interested in Elsie.' She meant, of course, sexually attracted.

But we didn't actually know that. Odder things had happened. Even wanting to marry into our family because we looked prosperous wasn't a crime. If he was really going to live in that cramped room, he must have felt something for her.

So we reasoned, not wanting to deny Elsie her moment of romance. We suggested that my mother talk to Elsie, propose that she wait a little longer before committing herself, though we knew at heart that she was already committed. My mother insisted that I take part in the talk with Elsie, on the grounds that we knew her best now, that she had become part of our family, that we had more influence with her than her sisters, as we all lived in the same country and as she was so attached to our children. Yet this was no longer the case. Elsie had suddenly become remote, changed, no longer the maiden aunt but a girl buying her trousseau. She insisted on our going with her to buy new sheets, new towels, a new double bed that opened out from the wall, patterned curtains – 'Josef doesn't like shutters' – and she put up a new sign for her front door. Our eldest son, in his third year at school, had made Elsie a present: a thick piece of wood made to look as if cut from a tree, with her name arduously chiselled into it (thirty other children had made similar objects in the handicrafts class) which she had nailed to her door when still in her single state. But the new Elsie took it down and ordered a brass name plate which announced that Elsie and Josef Farquash, husband and wife, lived on the third floor, opposite the cut-price dentist, and next door to the woman whose queue of male visitors was absent only on Holocaust and Remembrance nights.

The wedding was to take place at the home of an aunt on my father's side, a wealthy old lady who lived on Mount Carmel in

Haifa in a villa with a garden and a grand piano. We had engraved invitations made. My parents headed the invitation on Elsie's side, and fifty guests were invited: a few family friends, Sam Berkowitz and Elsie's colleagues at work – she was to retire and draw her pension – and the entire art class and the head of the art school. Josef had no best man – he was giving himself away – and no guests of his own save for his 'business manager', a glum man who sometimes tailed after him and whom we had never heard utter a word.

The last invitation had been placed in its envelope when my mother said, trying to make it sound as if the thought had just occurred to her: 'Elsie, isn't it a pity – a shame that Josef hasn't any relations here, that he'll be all alone. We— you— don't you think you ought to know a little bit more about him?' here my mother's voice tailed off, as Elsie, without raising her head from the envelopes she was sealing, her long nose looking even longer with her head down, answered back, in her Spitfire mode.

'You think I don't know what you all think about Josef. You think I don't know how you hate him and think what a fool I am. You want me to stay alone for the rest of my life, that's what you think I should do, because Elsie's an old maid, Elsie doesn't have the right to get married like everybody else. You take it for granted. There are two of you, two of all of you, and I'm the only one alone. You think I can't have love, have someone to love, because I'm too old, well I'm *not*, and he knows I'm not, and I'm marrying him, good for me for a change, and that's all there is to it, and if you don't want to do the wedding we'll go off and do it alone,' – and here she ran out of breath and, still gasping, grabbed the invitations and rushed out of the room.

So Elsie married her artist and we all stood helplessly by. She wore a large hat which overshadowed her nose, and a cream wool suit, and Josef wore a black suit and a shirt with a starched collar which raised a red welt on his neck; they were married under a canopy in my other aunt's garden, and afterwards we all drank champagne. My mother went back to London, the newly-weds went to Eilat for a honeymoon, and for some weeks we heard nothing from them. I rang Elsie's number several times, but an answering machine had been installed, with Elsie's voice saying: 'This is the home of Elsie and Josef Farquash' and so on. She sounded very proud.

Two months passed, and on a heavy summer evening, curiosity drove me up the grimy flights of steps to Elsie's flat. I don't know quite what I expected to find: the two of them dancing the tango, or at easels face-to-face, or Josef cooking goulash while Elsie arranged tulips in a vase. What I did find was Elsie with a flushed and angry face, holding a wooden spoon with which she had been stirring tomato sauce, and Josef smoking on the little balcony. Elsie flung her arms round me and deluged me with questions about the family; but when I asked if she and Josef would like to come to dinner, she hesitated, with a worried glance at Josef's back. He hadn't much work at the moment, she said, things were not easy for him, he wasn't feeling very sociable. At that moment Josef tossed the cigarette butt over the balcony and came into the room. It took me several moments to recognise him, not because he looked very different physically – though he was unshaven, and wearing a singlet over his trousers – but because the former smooth and ingratiating manner had gone, as if he'd taken it off with the jacket and shirt on a chair in the corner. He glared at me for a moment and asked Elsie when dinner would be ready, as he had to go out. He might have been talking to a hotel waitress. They talked for a few minutes about arrangements for the evening: an ordinary domestic chat save that all the time we were talking he had his eyes on my legs. I wear shorts during the summer; not particularly brief or glamorous ones, half the women under fifty in this town wear shorts and no one gives them a second glance. But Josef's eyes never left my legs and I began to feel uncomfortable.

'Why don't *you* wear shorts?' he asked Elsie suddenly. 'You'd look good in them.'

'Better than I do,' I said, trying to make things easier, and indeed Elsie had long and graceful legs and my own are rather stubby.

Elsie had gone white. 'Come here with me,' she said, taking my hand, and – there was nowhere else to go – drawing me into the tiny bathroom. By forcing me down on the lavatory seat there was just room for her to stand and close the door.

'How could you?' she asked me, her face flaming now.

'What?' I said stupidly.

'Provoke a married man, coming here dressed like that,' said Elsie, gesturing with the hand that still held a wooden spoon dripping tomato sauce, and knocking over a plastic glass holding some toothbrushes.

'Elsie, dear,' I said, and put my arm on her shoulder; but she shook me off angrily.

'You ought to be ashamed,' she said. 'Go home!'

So I went. And for months more there was no contact between us.

One evening, about eight months after the wedding, we had a call from Sam Berkowitz. Elsie wanted her job back. Perhaps it had been a mistake for her to stop working, I told Sam: 'Even with her savings invested they weren't going to have enough to live on for long.'

'Josef's gone,' he said. 'Taken the savings and gone. She'd opened a joint account.' She was quite calm, he said. There had been no tears; she had just told him the score.

'He couldn't have done that,' I stammered; but as I said it, I realised that nothing was more likely. We had been absurdly certain that Elsie, always so careful with her savings, so secretive, had invested her money safely where Josef could not have touched it. Could she have been so blinded by love, so stupid, so reckless? It seemed that she could. We'd read stories like this in the newspapers, and we felt horror and shame that this had happened to Elsie. How would she survive?

I telephoned my mother, and we talked and commiserated and my mother said she had known it all along but what could you do, Elsie had always been headstrong, and of course they would take care of her financially if it became necessary, I promised we would keep a watching brief, and there was Sam Berkowitz who would let us know if there were any problems at work, and perhaps the best thing was to let her work it through herself, as it would be much more difficult if she had to cope with our sympathy as well.

We soon discovered that Josef Farquash had not only left Elsie but no longer taught at the art class; no new frescos of his adorned the building sites. Probably he had left the country. I did not intrude on Elsie's privacy, but one day when I was sure she was at work I passed by her flat. The new brass plate had gone, and the handicrafts class wooden sign with Elsie's maiden name was back on the door.

Eventually Elsie came round to see us of her own accord. She brought little gifts for the children, as she always did, and stayed to supper. Not a word was said about what had happened. If we had expected grief stricken accounts of her experience, or any sign that the experience had ravaged her, we were disappointed. Elsie never mentioned Josef's name again. She said nothing about what she had been through. It amazed us at first that she gave no sign of inner stress, no shame and no dismay. We found her more placid than she had been in the past, certainly calmer than during the Josef era. She was patient with the children, less of a Spitfire on occasions when we annoyed her. And because she behaved with perfect dignity – as we learned later – her colleagues at work and her friends at the art class welcomed her back willingly and without condescension. She resumed her old life, working and painting – no more nudes – and died of cancer a few years later in England, cared for by her brother and sisters, some months short of her seventieth birthday, it emerged, when we finally found her identity card. She was a good deal older than either we had suspected, or my mother remembered.

We puzzled over Elsie's marriage for years. Finally we concluded that Elsie had known, deep down, all along, what her lover was after. But she had wanted that love affair, wanted a man, even for a short time, wanted to be married, wanted to know what it was all about. She'd said so, hadn't she? loud and clear. And if the glimpse I had of her marriage was any indication, she had found the entire experience an intolerable strain. Sometimes, during sleepless nights, I wondered whether she had not in fact given him the money to go away and leave her alone. However it was – and we would never know – Josef came with a price, and Elsie settled the bill when the time came.

Good for her, as she might have said.

ELEPHANT RIDE

GERHARDT EPSTEIN (Gideon in his official life, now ended) was pleased to have been invited to a lunch party on Independence Day. Although he set little store by the day itself – he had stood on so many receiving lines as an ambassador that he was grateful not to have to play host – he did not want to be on his own, as he was so often these days, when other people were celebrating.

The atmosphere was far more subdued than he remembered. There were strollers, not crowds, in the streets, and few flags. There had been a time when the day was an occasion for military parades – those, thank God, were over – but he was surprised to see only small pennants fluttering on passing cars. It had worried him that he could not find his own flag, the family flag from days gone by (his tenants seemed to have hidden or lost it, as they had so many other objects in his flat) until he realised that putting out a flag was by now not obligatory, might indeed be a statement he did not intend to make. His old friend and colleague Hans (Hanan in his official life), wizened and immobilised in an old people's home, confirmed this: 'Flags? Of course not. Flags are for settlers, right-wing demonstrations. You really are out of date.'

He was. For over forty years, official briefings had taken up most of Gerhardt's visits to Jerusalem. He had faithfully represented a country where he had not grown up and which he did not really know. Retired now, on a small pension, and with the income from a few investments bought with restitution money from Germany, his wife dead, his children living abroad, Gerhardt planned to read the books he had put aside, listen to music, go walking in the hills around Jerusalem, stroll into the centre of town for coffee, tend the plants on the terrace of his flat. The Jerusalem of his memory was a city of golden light, hot sun and cool breezes, with tranquil alleys shaded by pines. Awaiting him, he thought, were days of work with his diaries and papers, evenings spent at lectures or concerts, dinners with old friends – halcyon days. The historians would want to hear whatever he could tell them, he thought, and he intended to write a memoir. Yet he put this off from day to day, affected despite himself by the long, slow passage of time without appointments, consultations, the discipline of work.

He was not disconcerted when, during his first winter in Jerusalem, the university did not contact him with the expected invitation to give lectures. Not everyone knew that he was back, he reminded himself. Nor were there any calls from the Peace Institutes, the geographical societies or the adult education departments, so many of whose members he had hosted at his embassies. He spoke to people in the faculty for Asian Studies, but the fact that he had been posted in the Far East did not qualify him, in their eyes, to lecture on its cultures. Only the head of one organisation, a German research institute, at a chance meeting at a concert, enquired whether he would like to give an informal talk, share his reminiscences, perhaps? These things, apparently, took time. Other people who nodded at him at lectures, at concerts recognised him, he was sure, though they hesitated to approach him. Perhaps they were not sure who he was, just as he could not place this face, that smile. At a certain social level, in this small city, every face was familiar, but the names had vanished from his memory.

Other aspects of his new life were troublesome, it had to be admitted: filling in forms, regularising his new status as householder and resident taxpayer. In the new municipal building, whose vast halls were crammed with scurrying, disputatious crowds – how did people like himself arrange their affairs? – he waited for his number to come up on a screen and then waited again while a bad tempered clerk, his attention continually distracted by people pushing forward with interruptions and appeals, turned up his file. Gerhardt took too long to explain what he wanted, and did not always understand what was said to him; his grammatical, academic Hebrew was innocent of current usage and slang. Later, buffeted to the head of the queue for his prescription medicines in the health fund pharmacy, where every patient demanded a special dispensation or argued over the fee, he was bewildered by people's aggressiveness and the clerks' indifference or hostility, but tried to take this, too, in his stride. He reminded himself that he was accustomed to being recognised and deferred to, and that others – a secretary, a driver, a junior, a messenger boy – had performed such chores for him for most of his life. In forty years he had not ridden on a bus, stood in a queue, shopped, been jostled in the street, shouted at in the market, hooted on the highway.

Nor was the city as he had expected. On leave between postings, Gerhardt had scarcely had the chance to inspect the 'united' Jerusalem whose indivisibility, as Gideon, he had pronounced in so many official speeches (one of the necessary fictions, he thought). Now he enjoyed walking beyond the Turkish walls of the Old City into the medieval Muslim town with its mosques and churches. Though he had been told that few Jews frequented the Old City any more – only the Orthodox Jews hurrying on their way to the Wall – he roamed the covered Arab markets to buy the spices he needed for his kitchen and ascended to the great platform where the domes and minarets rode above the walled city like ships at anchor. There he felt oddly at home. He had spent much of his life in ancient, alien cities.

Elsewhere, it was hard for him to find his way about. He was confused by the new bypass roads which sliced through the hills and changed every perspective; by the sprawling suburbs, Jewish and Arab, on the crowns and slopes of formerly bare hills, and by the new rabbinical seminaries at the entrance to the city, with the names of the religious sects they represented – names taken from small towns in Eastern Europe – written in giant black letters high on their façades. Black figures, too, the frock coated, bearded orthodox men and their families – once, as he recalled, confined to their own quarter, now everywhere. There was even a colony in his own district. They were odder to him now than the priests and tribesmen of the countries where he had served.

The city was also much noisier than he remembered it, whole streets in the jaws of bulldozers. Almost every district had its building sites with compressors, pneumatic drills and hammers going full blast. The ramshackle, intimate Jerusalem he had known as half a city, with the Arab town across the frontier, behind the walls and the barbed wire, the city to which he had first come as a young man forty years earlier, was gone. But change and growth were inevitable, he reminded himself. It was a sign of old age to resent change, and Gerhardt did not think of himself as old, despite his white hair; he refused the seats offered him on buses. He was fit, and that was what counted, surely. He was not like Hans, forced to confront real disability, and making up for it with searing sarcasm about everything and everybody.

On Independence Day, then, Gerhardt dressed for lunch in a safari suit made for him by a master tailor in a remote bazaar, and was pleased not to have to wear formal dress. A small gift would be in order, he thought, and he had boxes of small mementos which he had bought, during the last few months of his foreign life, with just such occasions in mind. He chose a little wooden elephant with tiny, sharp, ivory tusks, remembering Edouard, remembering the elephant rides; he sniffed it for the odour of the sandalwood, as a farewell – but in the dry air of Jerusalem it had lost its aroma.

His hosts were people he had met shortly after returning to Jerusalem, distant relations of his wife's and much younger than himself, both lawyers. He knew that he was invited as family, not for his personal distinction, but it was going to take time to build up a social circle of his own, and any opportunity to meet new people was welcome. Fond as he was of Hans and a few other old friends, he did not want to be confined to meeting pensioners. But Jerusalem was populated by cliques – professors, lawyers, politicians, journalists – and a retired diplomat was by definition an outsider. Hans was scathing about this, of course. 'Trained monkeys; that's how they see us, always have done. Bowing and scraping to the *goyim* and the blacks. No military experience – never in the country when there was a war on.'

Gerhardt had to admit that there was some truth in that last jibe. He had served in the army mainly for liaison and intelligence – a mascot rather than a soldier – and his reserve duty had been waived, then cancelled, as he passed the age of service. Hans, because of some obscure medical condition, had never served at all. But when Gerhardt reminded him, a little irritably, that everyone knew how essential the diplomats' work had been at moments of crisis, and that their skills had been crucial, Hans smiled sardonically. 'What skills? as messenger boys? Why do you think they took us on? We were hired for our manners and our tact, nothing more. Because we didn't slap men on the back and push past women; because we knew which forks to use and because we didn't raise our voices every time we wanted to make a point. You don't think they wanted you for anything else, surely. For your scholarship? For your intellectual ability? Did you really believe that?'

Poor Hans, Gerhardt thought, how bitter he is. The reason, in his view, was that Hans could not look back with the same satisfaction as Gerhardt on his professional life, for Hans had been unlucky. Despite his talents, he had several times been passed over as a candidate for prize postings in Europe in favour of politicians' friends, functionaries temporarily out of work, or the directors of newly bankrupt firms. Gerhardt had been content with more distant and obscure African and Asian countries. He had orchestrated agricultural aid to one African state, medical training schemes in another, and – his last achievement, perhaps the most important of all – the mining concession in the small East Asian state, Edouard's country, for which he was still nostalgic. Hundreds of villagers had worked in those mines, which had brought prosperity to a troublesome border region. On the political level, such schemes had won Israel UN votes. For Gerhardt personally they had been the purpose of his life, and if his own tact and knowledge had helped – long ago, in Heidelberg and Cambridge he had studied Far Eastern cultures – so much the better.

Before he left home for the lunch party, Gerhardt turned on the television to check on the news from London – a habit since his return to Jerusalem. He was bewildered by Israel's party politics, which had replaced the old dictatorial, crude power system by a host of squabbling factions. The morning paper took its brief international items from the agencies and syndicated columns, but Gerhardt was hungry for detailed news of the countries where he had served. The main items on the BBC news today were, sure enough, from Africa and Asia, but the images were almost interchangeable: running men with rifles, looters scampering out of burning buildings with crates, columns of refugees who tramped through the dust or lay starving in improvised camps, hollow eyes turned to the camera. It saddened Gerhardt that this was all that was known of the countries he had loved. One item in particular startled and dismayed him: in one East Asian state, 'According to unconfirmed reports,' said the announcer, 'rebel troops have seized the capital city. President Edouard and his family are said to have fled the country for an undisclosed destination and his home has been vandalised by the rebels.'

It had finally happened, then, despite our help, thought Gerhardt, as the cameras focused on the destruction of what had been a familiar, welcoming scene: the drawing room of a former French colonial mansion, but with its glass doors splintered, the wings of the great fans fractured, the silk curtains torn and trampled, the painted wood furniture peppered with bullet holes, and on the green and white tiled floor, the remains of the chess set over which he and the President had tried their skills. Edouard had been a friend, not only an ally; a fine, civilised man. They had discussed, many times, the possibility that he would have to end his life in exile, and before leaving, Gideon had made a well-disguised entry in a notebook now in his desk drawer: the telephone number and address where he could find him. He would do so now, as soon as possible; he might even pay his friend a visit, as soon as it was discreet to do so. Edouard's friendship was the closest he had formed, the most treasured, during all his years abroad. His signed photograph stood on Gerhardt's sideboard. Thank God, he thought, he had got away safely.

The television announcer glanced at a sheet of paper he had just been handed and added: 'Edouard's remaining supporters in the capital have told our correspondent that it was the help given the rebels by the Israeli Mossad which turned the tide against the President. That's all the news for now.'

Gerhardt laughed, then sighed, as he turned off the television. How absurd these journalists were, eavesdroppers to a man, what a talent they had for getting things wrong! The Mossad here, the Mossad there. If there was one posting where Gideon had had no trouble whatever with those people, it was in Edouard's country. Not that they hadn't sometimes caused him embarrassment. He had given them cover, as requested, which deceived no one; he had tried to limit the damage when they were caught or botched the assignment. Yet somehow they had kept their reputation for efficiency – especially, Gideon noticed, with the English, to whose adolescent love of spying they appealed. It was no accident that it was the British who were spreading this rumour. He wondered, as he double-locked his front door, who the 'remaining supporters' were who had sold the BBC correspondent this nonsense.

His hosts lived on the ground floor of a house in the German Colony, a quarter Gerhardt particularly liked, with its quiet lanes and old buildings, though today the lanes were clogged with cars. The front door stood open – Gerhardt had continually to remind himself that there were no servants – and guests milled about in the garden and blocked the door. It took him several minutes to locate his host's wife, a thin, energetic woman with protruding teeth, carrying a tray with glasses and bottles who, with her elbow, nudged him in the direction of a group of people, calling out: 'Hi Gidi, how good you came! This is Gidi, everyone,' (a diminutive he hated) and passed into the garden without stopping. Instinctively, Gerhardt put out his hand, but as rapidly withdrew it, since the men and women to whom he had been thus introduced were busy talking and eating, holding plates and glasses, and only one or two smiled vaguely at him and went on with their conversations. He stood still, the carved elephant in its wrapping paper in his left hand. No one spoke to him, but after a few moments, a woman who had noticed his indecision took him by the elbow and pulled him towards a table loaded with food, large chunks of food, from which guests were hacking portions (the quantities Israelis ate amazed him). Soon he too had a plate in one hand and was wondering what to do with the little parcel in the other. It was clear that he would not be introduced in the proper fashion, or recognised, or relieved of his gift. A little girl with long hair tied back with a ribbon and a pretty dress, perhaps his host's daughter, was watching him from a window seat; the formality of her appearance pleased him – he almost expected her to curtsey, as Edouard's daughters had done – and he went over and smiled at her. 'Are you the daughter of the house?' he asked pleasantly. She looked as if she did not understand the question, or perhaps the formal way in which it was asked, but when he handed her the parcel, her face brightened, and she took it and ran off.

Unencumbered now, Gerhardt strolled into the garden, looking round. Men and women clustered in separate groups, even where they sat at a table under a tree – a primitive arrangement, he thought – and he took a seat among the men. For a while, he listened, hoping to find a moment when he could join in, listening for a subject on which he could make some contribution, but the two men next to whom he was seated were arguing so hotly over local politics that no such moment occurred; he might have been invisible. So he was relieved when he was tapped on the shoulder by a man he recognised as his host, a burly, crew cut man in a linen suit, whose face, however, was anything but friendly.

'Did you give my daughter that?' he asked, tossing the elephant on to the table. Behind him stood the little girl, pouting, a rag wrapped round her finger. 'She cut her hand on it.'

Gerhardt tried to explain, but his host was not listening. The talk round the table stopped and everyone watched; from being totally ignored Gerhardt became a focus of interest and critical amusement. People asked one another, in his hearing, who the strange old man was and what the fuss was about. He was on the point of leaving when his hostess, who had been indoors, hurried over.

She hadn't had the time to explain, didn't her husband recognise Gidi, their great uncle? it was a very nice present, say thank you, they would just take the tusks out with the pliers and she'd be able to play with it, a little iodine on the wound and it was all over! She picked the elephant out of a hunk of salmon and hurried the little girl into the house.

'My mistake,' said his host, with a hint of sarcasm. 'Back here for good, are you?' Gerhardt said that he was, and that he would like to be introduced to his neighbours at the table. One man, it emerged, was a lecturer in information technology and the other worked in the Ministry of Finance. Gerhardt was introduced as, 'My wife's uncle Gideon, who's been in the Far East.' Both men nodded briefly at Gerhardt and went back to their conversation.

'Now you know,' said his host. 'Retired, aren't you? Must be great. I'd like a bit of a rest myself.'

'I intend to keep busy,' said Gerhardt rather frigidly. 'My memoirs will take up most of my time.'

'That's right, keep busy,' said his host vaguely, his eyes elsewhere, and went off to greet an arriving guest. Gerhardt's neighbours were talking about a television broadcast, so now he saw his chance to join in their conversation: 'I saw a very odd item this morning on the BBC – they've got hold of the idea that the Mossad's been giving support to the rebels who've driven out Edouard.' They both stared at him.

'Very likely,' said the information technology man, and the other nodded.

'Absolute nonsense,' said Gerhardt sharply. 'I know that country very well and everything that went on there. It's impossible.'

'Do you?' said the information technology man indifferently. 'I don't, but I know Gad Aloni, and his background, and he was involved in that mining business, wasn't he, and one thing leads to another,' and he went back to talking to his neighbour. Gerhardt made no further effort to interrupt and sat brooding.

Gerhardt's hostess reappeared with a huge salver of watermelon, from which people were taking slices with their fingers, and thrust it towards him with a warmly reassuring smile. He shook his head. Watermelon stains would be hard to remove from his safari suit. Unlike so many of the Europeans, Gerhardt had always eaten with chopsticks; like the Asians, he was skilled at lifting, wafting from plate to mouth grains of rice, meat rolls or other delicacies – pigeons' breasts, cockscombs, and miniature, transparent fish. In Edouard's house, watermelon had been offered the occasional visitor in the form of small cubes in a bowl, to be speared with tiny ivory forks.

The rumour was impossible, outrageous, he said to himself in the taxi on his way to the Ministry reception, at which he had promised to put in an appearance. He himself had handled the mining concession from beginning to end, until the vein of bauxite had been exhausted and the Israeli engineers had packed up and gone home. He had gone over all the supplies, all the budgets himself. Policy was to support Edouard, in line with the Americans and the Europeans. There was no question whatever of having dealings with the rebels, no political constellation which might have allowed for it. A certain number of officers in the local army had trained for a while in Israel, and the Presidential Guard had been supplied with sub-machine guns – a few crates, Gerhardt thought, not more, business handled by the military attaché, Ben Simon. Gerhardt could not understand why a piece of journalists' gossip, a stupid remark thrown out at a dull lunch party, by people not of his kind, had disturbed him so much. Or rather, he did know why: what troubled him was his memory of Aloni, a man he had detested, and whose fleshy face, insolent smile and narrow eyes he now recalled so vividly. The smile in particular.

He had not been requested to give cover to Aloni, whose position as head of a professional workforce was quite straightforward. Gerhardt had usually got on well with the various experts the Ministry had sent out to his postings in Africa and Asia. There was the eye man, bluff and short tempered, dedicated to his mission, curing trachoma and training local people to prevent its spread in the villages. There was the young water engineer, who, though too dismissive about the local people's ancient irrigation traditions (in which Gerhardt took an interest) was so conscientious that he camped near the reservoir under construction to make sure that no local people went off with his equipment. There was Gerhardt's old friend Wolf, like himself a German refugee from the thirties, a veteran kibbutznik. Wolf was supposed to teach the principles of kibbutz life to the tribesmen. The experiment had failed, but Wolf had made so many friends in the villages where he stayed that people would murmur his name as a talisman against bad luck. All these men had done good work, though policy had sometimes been short sighted, some of the regimes Israel supported had collapsed and some of the political support Israel received had been only temporary. Edouard himself had used the profits from the bauxite works wisely, on welfare and health.

But, yes, Aloni had been different from the other experts. Gerhardt was amazed at how much anger the mere mention of that name had caused him. There had been the incident during Gerhardt's unscheduled visit to the mining site; the door opened at the wrong moment in an Embassy office, that insolent smile. He had put Aloni out of his mind, avoided him, subsequently, as much as he could, left him to Ben Simon. None the less, an agreement between Aloni and the rebels was inconceivable. The man had not even learned a word of the local language.

The Foreign Ministry was a collection of fenced-off bungalows with paths winding between them, shoddy headquarters, though Gerhardt had always liked it, for it reminded him of the improvised character of the early days of the state. But as Hans had said recently: 'Just look round this city if you want to see what they think of us. Look at the other ministries, huge blocks with hundreds of offices, look at the banks, the hotels, the yeshivas, the synagogues where they've poured money into hundreds of thousands of tons of stone and concrete. Then look at where we are; still in a transit camp.' He had to admit, now, that there was something to Hans's criticism; it was time they moved to a more impressive building.

Once inside, however, Gerhardt felt at home, recognised, among his peers, people who knew and respected him. When he entered the low-ceilinged, crowded room, they turned to him, smiled and put out their hands. Hans, in a corner in his wheelchair, rolled towards him, and he heard his name – his full name – spoken on all sides. The Director-General, a new man whom Gerhardt scarcely knew, took time to say a few words in his honour. His acquaintances, his colleagues, had suddenly become old, frail looking, and the head of the East Asia desk, Abulafia, Gideon's superior for so many years, the man who had seen him through so many crises, his most reliable ally in the Ministry, had recently died. Still, the reception established who Gerhardt was and what he had done.

Hans was trying to reach him, manoeuvring his wheelchair from one point to another, but by sidestepping and continually changing his place in the room, keeping Hans just out of sight, Gerhardt held him off for as long as he could. Hans was the last person whom he wanted to know about the Aloni rumour and his growing worry, Hans with his need to reduce Gerhardt to the same state of bitterness, anger and self-flagellation as himself. Hans, with nothing else to occupy him, would remember everything, notice everything, and would make connections. Gerhardt fancied that he might even have confided his loathing of Aloni to Hans in a letter. But it was too late now to avoid him, Hans was beside him. Gerhardt saw from the grip of his hands on the arms of the wheelchair that he was excited, though he tried to make his voice sound casual.

'A great pity about Edouard, according to you the one man of integrity in that whole region,' he said. 'You must be very shocked.'

'I am.'

'We don't come out of it very well though, do we?'

'What do you mean?' asked Gerhardt, and drew up a chair; he did not like to stand looking down at Hans, who to talk to Gerhardt in this way had to squirm uncomfortably in his wheelchair, his head twisted to one side. There was no need to flaunt his own fitness.

'As long as we needed him, we protected him. Once he'd said his piece, we had no further interest in him.'

'You're quite wrong. We had no way of protecting Edouard if his army turned against him; all we did was to train and equip the Guard, but it was always a very small force.' Hans clearly had not seen the English broadcast – which was odd, because he was addicted to the foreign news' broadcasts; perhaps he had been on his way to the reception. Or had he heard it and was saying nothing?

'You'll be in touch with him, of course.'

'I thought of going to see him.'

'If *he* wants to see you now.'

Gerhardt hedged. 'It may not be advisable. He may be in danger until the rebels have established their regime and they feel there is no chance of his return. He was very popular among the people. I could be followed, they knew how close we were.'

'How much importance you give yourself, how naive you are, my friend Gerhardt!' said Hans, smiling and patting Gerhardt's arm to show he meant no real offence. 'That is not what I meant at all. Your friendship, your closeness as you call it, was part of the overall situation. I don't mean that Edouard wasn't your friend. But he's lost his country, and that is partly our doing, as usual, meddling for our own purposes in other countries' politics. Do you think he can separate that from your elephant rides and your chess games and your discussions of Proust?'

'We didn't meddle; we helped them as much as we could, we couldn't change their frontiers, there was that huge force waiting on the other side, and the gangs inside the country'—

'Freedom fighters against the ex-colonialists, some would say,' interrupted Hans.

'I know what some would say, and they are wrong. Edouard knows we supported him as well as we could, the Americans did nothing.' Gerhardt found to his annoyance that he was trembling. Hans had always had this power to irritate him, to shake his self-confidence.

'As you will say in your memoirs,' said Hans, smiling again. 'But surely you realise that what you remember isn't necessarily the whole story? If you really want to know how we diplomats are regarded, get yourself on to the board of censors and read a few files. It's quite an education. I recommend it.' With a nod, Hans released the brake on his wheelchair and rolled away to talk to another colleague. Their talk had obviously exhilarated him as much as it had depressed Gerhardt.

The state archives were housed no more grandly than the Ministry – in an office building down a side street, behind a garage and workshop area where mechanics, after servicing cars, raced them to test the engines. Gerhardt had intended to use the official files to amplify his own recollections and diaries. But the files he wanted were housed elsewhere, and would take time to retrieve. Meanwhile, he waited in the reading room and turned over his memories of Aloni.

Aloni had been very friendly with Ben Simon, Gerhardt remembered, but he had assumed that this was because they had served in the same regiment in the army in two or three wars, shared those experiences which he and Hans had never known. The camaraderie was there in the jostling he noticed when the two met in the Embassy corridors, a grip on the arm, a hand on the shoulder – something, Gerhardt thought, like a Masonic sign – and the terse, monosyllabic way they talked to one another. Formally speaking, as far as Gerhardt knew, the only link between the two had been Aloni's request for a security detail for the mining parties: the rebel guerrillas were active in the hills beyond the mine. Ben Simon had handled the request, with Gerhardt's knowledge, and had passed it on to the head of the Guard, who had supplied them with a party of overdressed young recruits with Israeli machine-guns – those guns whose dispatch Gerhardt had himself requested. There was nothing very suspect in that. But it was his own visit to the site, perhaps, that should have alerted him. The visit had been unscheduled, and there had been no specific reason why he had made it. Supplies of bauxite were regular, so Edouard's people told him, and Aloni had sent in periodic reports as requested, but Gerhardt thought he should see things for himself – particularly as the area was believed to be dangerous. It was the hallmark of his service in these distant and unstable countries that, in defiance of protocol and often of the security people, he had never remained locked up in the compound. He wanted to see whatever was done under his aegis.

The day of the visit had been overcast, and his driver was uneasy; the Embassy car, flying a small flag, was conspicuous on the lonely, badly-surfaced road which led across the plain and into the shallow, pebbled hills. Though they did not talk, Gerhardt sensed that the driver, too, was relieved when they arrived in sight of the camp, a huddle of tents and huts. Barbed wire trailed loosely between crooked poles, and a path led from the camp to the entrance to the mine, where men were loading open trucks from carts at the end of the conveyor belt which emerged from the mouth of the mine. It all looked neglected, open to attack, but as the car came to a stop at the gate to the enclosure, half a dozen men suddenly appeared from behind a hut. They wore no uniforms, and their long hair straggled from under headbands. Within seconds they had surrounded the car, and from all sides machine-guns were levelled at him and at the cowering driver. Yet almost as the guns appeared, they were lowered at a shout from Aloni, who now came loping towards him.

'What the hell are you doing here – sir?' – he added the last word with an insolent smile, an insult rather than a title. 'It's a good thing I wasn't down in the mine; they might have shot you.'

That was evident, Gerhardt had thought, as he climbed shakily out of the car and took Aloni's proffered hand – held out certainly not out of politeness, but as a sign to the toughs who now slung the guns over their shoulders and turned away. And toughs they certainly were, not the well-drilled dandies of the presidential Guard.

'Where are the Guardsmen?' Gerhardt enquired.

'I sent them back,' said Aloni; 'I needed reliable men who know what I want.'

They had toured the mine, Gerhardt had made notes under Aloni's sardonic eye, and before dark the driver and he were on his way back to the capital – one of the toughs riding a jeep ahead of them, gun cocked, till they were clear of the hills. Gerhardt had not pressed Aloni further about the new guards, accepting the brief explanation. Whatever his suspicions, he knew that he had only one alternative to ignoring what Aloni had done: to abort the mining project, and perhaps the mission. Besides, how could the rebels – if such they were – have overthrown Edouard's regime with a couple of crates of sub-machine guns? Unless, of course, he now realised, what he had seen was only the tip of the iceberg. Unless, to ensure the success of the mining operation, and perhaps Edouard's vote at that session of the Assembly, Aloni had delivered far more to the rebels than appeared. Perhaps he had worked through Ben Simon, who represented the Defence Ministry. If this were so, Gerhardt had been totally bypassed, totally ignored – even confidently ignored, 'sir'.

Then there had been the incident of the opened door. It had happened one morning – somehow the fact that it was morning, or midday, made it worse in Gerhardt's eyes – when he had gone to look for a member of his staff and opened a door and found Aloni with one of the telephone operators at the Embassy, a local woman. At first he did not understand what they were doing; a desk stood between them and the door, and Gideon thought that Aloni was whispering in the woman's ear, before the picture resolved itself: the back of the woman's head was towards him, her dark hair escaping from the knot which bound it, her whole body pinioned against the desk by the force of Aloni's thrusts. As he gave a final grunt and grimace, head thrown back, eyes open, he caught Gerhardt's eye, and smiled – that insolent smile Gerhardt still remembered with fury and with shame.

Gerhardt had backed out and closed the door. It had been rape, of that he was sure. The woman was respectable – he checked her file – with a husband and children, a temporary worker, who was gone a couple of weeks later. She had made no complaint – the risk was probably too great – though Gerhardt had promised himself that if she came to him, he would take action. To his own disgust, for he was an innocent in such matters, he found himself angrily wondering why Aloni had not gone to a brothel in the lower town, if such were his appetites, why he had risked the Embassy's reputation. He even contemplated sending the man home. But he waited too long, and such an action would have had to be taken immediately. When he passed Aloni in the corridors, sat with him at meetings, he saw that the man knew this. Gerhardt had hesitated not only because of his natural reserve, his fastidiousness, but because he feared an inevitable breach with Edouard and his country; exposing Aloni, he had thought, would cause more harm than good. So it had seemed at the time.

Besides, the mining job was completed successfully, Edouard's envoy had cast a supporting vote at the Assembly. Who cared now how Aloni had defended the mining camp, who cared about a temporary employee raped at midday behind an unlocked door? And was Gerhardt now making an issue of Edouard's fall and its cause out of nothing more than his own aversion to a man who had defied him? It was this question that he had to answer, and it was becoming an obsession.

A set of files was delivered to Gerhardt's desk in the archive, containing the careful, learned dispatches he had sent back to Jerusalem from earlier postings, full of comments on the culture and folklore of distant peoples. Scarcely any, he noticed, had been minuted or annotated, save when he reported on the success or failure of aid projects.

When he mentioned this later to Hans, the answer was predictable: 'As I told you: they never read your little essays, and why should they have done? You weren't sent out there to study local customs.'

The files on Edouard's country and Gerhardt's mission there were closed for many years more. He wrote to Edouard – a long, intimate letter of commiseration – at the secret address in Switzerland, and received no reply. He considered travelling there, appearing suddenly – Edouard would surely not have the heart to close the door in his face – but what Hans had said deterred him. Edouard might be thinking even now that whatever Aloni had done had been with Gerhardt's knowledge and consent. The thought became unbearable. He considered writing to the BBC, making contact with the correspondent who had picked up the rumour, but dismissed the idea almost as it occurred; a former ambassador could not go running after journalists. Instead, he wrote to the Director-General, saying that he needed access to the files on his last posting in order to check details for his memoir. He was fobbed off by a junior in the man's absence and asked to wait for his return. But then, without any action on Gerhardt's part, the chance to find out more about Aloni and his actions suddenly presented itself.

Gerhardt had turned up to give his talk – on the remains of ancient cultures in some of the countries where he had served – to the German research institution which had pursued him. He insisted that his talk be given in English. Though he spoke German with Hans and other old friends, and felt comfortable doing so, with German diplomats and envoys he had always preferred a neutral language, as if to stress that, despite his origins, he was not of their number. On this occasion there was an audience of a dozen people, all pensioners save one, and most from Hans's old people's home. The odd man out, he learned, was a young historian, also a journalist and columnist for the morning paper, who listened gravely and intently, nodding now and then. Gerhardt found himself, during the lecture, repeatedly addressing this young man, catching his eye. He was grateful for the attention of someone of this age and of this background. It reassured him that he was not yet obsolete, that his experience still had some relevance for the young, and he was pleased that after questions had been asked and answered, the young man was waiting for him at the door.

'That was a pleasure,' said the young man warmly. 'I hope you're going to publish your experiences.'

Gerhardt beamed. 'If you think a publisher would be interested,' he said. 'I'm not an expert like yourself, I abandoned my academic life so long ago.'

'Oh, that's not what I meant,' said the young man. 'The stuff about irrigation practices and what's left of the old temples is all very interesting, but my field is the politics. You didn't say much about your political experiences. I'm sure they'd be well worth reading. So few of our diplomats ever write their memoirs; not that they're too discreet, it's just that most of them wouldn't know how to put two words together. You're different. And you were there, you saw it all happen. For one thing, you must be pleased they finally ran Edouard out of town.'

Gerhardt's expression changed so suddenly that the young man put out his hand as if to steady him, as if he thought he had suffered an attack.

'Edouard was one of my closest friends,' Gerhardt said stiffly.

The young historian frowned, began to say something, and stopped. Then he said: 'I think you should see Abulafia's papers; his children have just deposited them with the Institute, and I saw some of them last week.'

'Aren't they classified?'

The young man shrugged. 'Well, perhaps they should have been, but he wasn't that well known, no one's likely to be interested.' Something in Gerhardt's face told him that this remark, like the previous one, had been tactless. He looked at his watch, muttered, 'Well, it's been great, thank you, and if you'd like to talk about it, here's my number,' extracted a card from an inside pocket, handed it to Gerhardt, and hurried out.

The hour was too late, that evening, to visit the Institute, but Gerhardt was there at opening time the next morning – to the annoyance of the archivist, who said that the Abulafia papers had not yet been sorted or catalogued and were not yet open to the public. It was only after a sharp argument – Gerhardt, in an uncharacteristically aggressive mood, citing his veteran status, his close relationship with Abulafia, his research partnership with the young historian, and even his own failing health – the last flagrant lies inspired by his white hot need to see the papers, that he was finally seated in a corner with a stack of files in front of him.

The answers were all there.

As he read, Gerhardt, conscientious as ever, found himself absurdly dismayed that papers which should surely remain classified material for thirty years or more were now in the public domain. But even as this occurred to him, he realised that no historian would be able to use them without a knowledge of the context, or his own cooperation (was this why the young man had approached him? very probably). For the papers which concerned him in particular were notes, with no official headings, and the people they referred to were identified only by their initials or by a nickname: Edouard as E, Aloni as A, Ben Simon as Buma and Gerhardt – to his chagrin, for Abulafia had been at least the same age as himself – as 'the old man'.

The papers, verbatim notes of Ministry meetings, were in the wrong order. The first note that met his eye was the copy of an instruction he himself had received, in code, regarding the UN vote, asking him to 'express satisfaction to the President on the fulfilment of his assurance regarding the Assembly resolution'. But there was also a rough draft of a dispatch telling 'Buma' that the time had come to present 'E' with his 'gift crates', clearly cash payments. Each December they had sent Edouard gift-packed grapefruit, oranges, fine wine and liqueur chocolates. But the message had been drafted in February, well after the President's birthday and more significantly, two weeks before the assembly vote. The defence attaché had obviously been cued to play a part, with Aloni, in some operation of which Gerhardt knew nothing. The message did not refer to the guns, for these had been supplied six months earlier, with the relevant instructions to Ben Simon copied to the ambassador.

All other copies of messages to 'A' remaining in Abulafia's papers, messages drawn up at the end of office meetings in Jerusalem, had been sent to Aloni via 'Buma', and Gerhardt had never seen them. Very few were in code; it was clear that Abulafia knew of Aloni's mission, which had been decided on well before, between Aloni and his Mossad bosses, at meetings in Tel Aviv (such meetings were referred to, with their dates) and there had been no need for more than a trigger word or phrase to put the plan into action. Gerhardt, on the other hand, had been left completely in the dark.

Worst of all: from the references to E, and his part in an agreement, it was quite clear that it was Edouard, not the rebels, who had been in the Mossad's pay. Edouard had been bankrupt, and the Guard as corrupt as he was himself. The bauxite reserves had been negligible (so said an expert report commissioned by the Mossad, another document Gerhardt had never been shown). The mine was little more than a stage set, then, designed to keep the President popular until his usefulness was past. The rebels, fanatics as they might be, were the real incorruptibles; they had not needed the Mossad's assistance, and they were no more stoppable, as the Mossad had realised, than a force of nature. They were referred to, in the messages, as the monsoons, the rains which would soon flood the northern part of the country, and then reach the capital itself. Aloni's guards, it seemed, who Gerhardt thought were rebels, were Mossad men too. Gerhardt suddenly recalled that the shouted order on his arrival at the camp had probably been in Hebrew – though words he had not recognised – army slang.

As for his own part in all this, the role of 'the old man': Gerhardt was wryly pleased that he had obviously been expected to oppose the entire operation, on moral grounds. Why, otherwise, had every detail been kept from him? Almost every message contained a reference to him: 'essential that the old man have no word of this'; 'the old man may object'; 'try and keep the old man out of it'; 'make sure the old man makes no further visits to the camp'. They need not have troubled to deceive him, Gerhardt reflected bitterly; he and Edouard had spent so much time discussing Proust, talking about Jungian theory and Buddhism, that he had never questioned Edouard's integrity. He had assumed that Edouard, with his European education and tastes, served his own priests and tribesmen with the same devotion with which he himself served a country he did not know, and where perhaps he did not quite belong. He recalled what Hans had once said to him: 'People like ourselves not only are obedient servants, whatever the regime. We also attribute our own standards to every rascal we encounter.'

Time passed. Gerhardt set aside the idea of writing his memoirs and no longer offered to talk about his experiences in the Far East. The thought that worried him more than all else was that Hans, with whom he now spent most of his time, might find out the truth about Edouard. But, given both friends' increasing frailty, and the time the young historian – or his successors – would take to publish, this was very improbable indeed.

NO PROBLEM

YOU KNOW HOW it is: you begin to see your parents as people, and it's great, and it's uncomfortable. You feel superior but you also feel less secure. That was what made David so jumpy when Abu Abed started working for the family. It didn't affect me the same way, because I'm naturally a more secure sort of person, girls usually are; that's why I can talk about it to you, and David can't. I don't think I have a problem about this whole business, but I'm the only one in the family who doesn't, I can tell you that.

I'm a couple of years younger than David and we've never really got on together, which I think is fairly normal. Because our parents are both professionals they think everything should be working perfectly, if you make a joke and say we're a typical dysfunctional family, they take it personally. What can you expect when your father's a psychologist and your mother's a sociologist.? What made it even more difficult for David and me to to fight in peace and quiet was that the grandparents – Dad's side – are so totally primitive. When we were kids, they wanted David to play with guns and me to wear skirts and for both of us to smile for photographs and stay in on Friday nights when they come round for the Sabbath, you know the sort of thing. They hated us to quarrel, too, they were unbelievably uptight and because they came from such a repressive back-ground they'd actually *say* things like children, you have to love one another, you are all we have in the world. Don't get me wrong, I feel fine with the grandparents. But David said, in their hearing, that he couldn't be such a hypocrite as to pretend he wanted to go with the school group to Auschwitz. The grandparents lost *their* parents there, have a heart. David said that if Dad didn't understand that those visits were a kind of tribal ritual, what was all his training for? What *I* thought was that it wasn't worth upsetting people just to prove how unhypocritical you are. I was always a lot more tolerant of parents, or perhaps it was because I was younger and hadn't started criticising yet, I don't know, it's your job to explain, isn't it? No? Oh, OK, I know, your job is to wait and see how I explain it myself.

The first difficult question that David asked was: why did Abu Abed speak Hebrew, while Dad and Mum couldn't talk to him in Arabic? Simple enough, you'd think, and I'm not sure that David didn't ask it quite innocently; he was only about twelve at the time. We both realised it was a difficult question, though, because Dad got so hot and bothered about it, and said that with all his seminars and lectures and congresses how on earth would he have had time to study Arabic? Then he added that he *had* actually started learning Arabic after the Six Day War, as some of his friends did, when it looked as if there was going to be a lot of contact with the Palestinians, but had given up because the only people who wanted to talk to us, he found, were the collaborationist type who were just out to make money. And then he got married and didn't have any spare time, he said, looking at Mum, and then there was the Yom Kippur war, and then we were born. David was right, he said, in thinking that we (meaning everyone) ought to speak Arabic, if we and the Palestinians were really going to live together. David said: 'I didn't say you ought to I only asked why you didn't.' Then Mum, who is often much more forthright in her quiet way, told Dad the kid deserved a real answer (she's always into treating you like an adult even when you may not want it) and said: 'The real reason is that Abu Abed *has* to speak Hebrew and we don't have to speak Arabic.'

David nodded as if he understood, but at that time, he says now, he didn't realise what Mum meant, which was that Abu Abed was working for us and other Jews and not the other way round.

We didn't find out what Abu Abed's real name was until everything was over; so you'll have to wait for it too, till I finish telling you the whole story. Abu Abed, of course, just means the father of Abed, and Abed himself was a young man with the shadow of a moustache who went everywhere with his father. Sometimes Abu Abed brought a much younger child of about eight or nine who we thought was a grandchild but who was just his youngest; he had a lot of children, ten or twelve, I think.

At that time, which was round about the beginning of the eighties, almost everyone I knew had an Abu somebody working for them. Dad didn't have much contact with Arab psychologists, colleagues I mean, except when he met one abroad – they only started talking to one another much later, during the *intifada* – but absolutely everyone recommended an Arab housepainter or an Arab car mechanic or an Arab gardener to friends. Abus charged much less and their work was better. All the Abus were more or less alike. They all looked very dignified and elderly, about the age of our grandparents, who are late fifties, and they all were very quiet and very polite, and they all came to work with food tied up in headcloths, and they all brought prayer mats. At midday, wherever they were, on a roof if they were mending it, or in the garden or even inside the flat, they'd unroll the mats and face eastwards and drop to their knees and start praying.

David and I used to watch Abu Abed praying, when we were home for the school holidays. At that age, when David was really asking for information and not asking questions just to provoke, he asked why Jews needed books to pray from, while Abu Abed knew the prayers by heart. Our relations didn't do any praying, and the only time we saw people praying was at the Wall or on television, or once or twice when the grandparents took us to a synagogue, where people always seemed to have prayer books to read from. Neither Mum nor Dad knew much about the way Arabs prayed, they just said vaguely that he'd been brought up to pray like that three times a day, and that religious Jews did so too. When David started being critical, he said that they were trying to give us the idea that we had something in common with the Palestinians, though we knew quite well we had nothing at all. He said that what Abu Abed was probably praying for was for Allah to come and drive the Jews away once and for all, how did we know what he was asking for? Mum said that was a very racist remark and David said on the contrary, if he'd been in Abu Abed's place that was what he would have prayed for. I remember that Dad and Mum just looked at one another and had no answer for David, and found some excuse to end the conversation.

They didn't really know too much about Abu Abed. He was recommended to them by a friend who'd told them about this marvellous painter who was so quiet, such a good worker, and completely trustworthy, you could leave him in the house and go to work. If he said the whitewashing or painting would take four days, it took four days. He didn't start one job and then go to another on the same day like our painters and builders did. He cleaned up every day after work, he took exactly the price he'd quoted at the beginning and didn't add on all kinds of things which hadn't been foreseen, like the only piece of piping in the shops which was that bit more expensive, or a different kind of spray paint which he'd just tried himself in his own flat.

David says – we've talked about Abu Abed a lot recently – he remembers the first time they got hold of him. Mum went to a friend's house to meet him and thought he was a university professor having tea in the friend's garden; they were all sitting together and the real university professor looked a mess while Abu Abed had his beard neatly trimmed and wore a well-ironed white shirt, as he always did. The friend who'd recommended him said Mum would have to come and drive him to our place, because he didn't like asking the way to a new address from strangers, people were getting suspicious. There had been a few incidents. On the other hand, we didn't know where Abu Abed lived (somewhere near Hebron, he said) or even what his real name was, then. If he rang up he just said 'Abu Abed speaking' so we called him Abu Abed too, and although it seems funny, we never asked what his full name was. Of course Dad paid him in cash, so that he didn't have to go to a bank to present a cheque, so he never wrote a name on a cheque. Mum said they could be really nasty to an Arab who came with a cheque, asking where he got it, and so on, and we assumed he didn't have a bank account of his own. Actually *he* never asked to be paid in cash, Dad just thought that was what he preferred. We found out later that he did have a bank account, and a cheque book, and why not? Maybe Mum and Dad thought he kept the cash under a tile in the floor.

I remember the first real argument at home over Abu Abed. David was sixteen by then, and he had been in this civics class at school, learning about trade unions and labour laws, and at dinner one evening he asked Dad how much we were paying Abu Abed per day, and Dad said Abu Abed was paid for a specific amount of money per job, and he didn't know how it worked out per day. David worked it out and said on a daily basis they were paying Abu Abed too much, was it because he was an Arab? Dad was nettled and said he wasn't going to make money out of Abu Abed, he paid him well because his work was excellent, and he finished a job very rapidly. David asked how many hours a day he worked and then told Mum and Dad that on an *hourly* basis they were paying him too little. That made them even more annoyed and Dad said that Abu Abed didn't pay tax on what he earned and got paid in cash and didn't give receipts so that he was doing very well indeed. He fixed his own hours and sometimes he went earlier and sometimes later. So, of course, David made a face and asked whether Dad and Mum knew they were breaking the law? I remember that Dad got up, waving some food on his fork, he was so agitated, and said that this was a temporary situation, the main thing was that we were pleased with the work and Abu Abed was pleased with the pay, he had a huge family to support. When the Palestinians had their own country they'd make their own laws. Some temporary situation, said David, it's been going on for twenty years now.

That certainly isn't your father's fault, said Mum, you know we're both in favour of leaving the Territories, but we can't leave a vacuum behind. David said he wasn't interested in politics anyway, but the whole thing stank, didn't they notice that Abu Abed brought his ten-year-old son to work with him when he ought to be at school? It went on and on like that and they were all shouting in the end, I didn't take part because I wasn't sure whose side I was on. I'm still not sure.

Afterwards I went to David's room where he was doing his homework and told him to shut up about Abu Abed. If he was going to be completely honest, I said, he'd say he just didn't want an Arab in the house, and David didn't like him because he was so polite; it was easier with people who were rude so you could be rude back. By now, Abu Abed was around a lot of the time, there were always odd jobs to be done like fixing the drains or even insulating the walls; the old Arab houses in Jerusalem are beautiful to look at but they need a lot of maintenance. Abu Abed always knew what to do, because ours was the kind of house, he told us, that he had built himself. David said that personally, he would have preferred to live in a modern block and wasn't it extraordinary that Dad and Mum, with their liberal views, didn't mind living in what after all had been an Arab family's house. I told David everyone lives in what was once someone else's house, unless you buy a brand new flat in a brand new housing block. Mind you, I did ask Mum about our house once, because there was this article in the paper about rich Arabs abroad who were asking for compensation for the houses they'd owned. She said they'd bought it from a friend who had bought it from another friend, who had bought it from Arabs before the War of Independence. Personally I don't believe that, perhaps Mum believed it, or wanted to, but I bet the friend was just trying to make a quick sale and knew Mum's views. The house was probably what they call abandoned property.

I think there was something else that annoyed David about having Abu Abed around. He'd come, as I've said, with two of his sons, and they were incredibly respectful to their father. He gave orders, usually in a quiet voice, sometimes a bit sharply, and they jumped to it, whatever he'd asked them to do. Not only the little boy, but the big one, Abed, with the shadow of a moustache, as well. As Abu Abed brought food for them, Mum couldn't offer them anything to eat, but in the hot weather she always provided water and Coca-Cola. The little boy would look at her rather fearfully and then go and ask his father if it was all right to accept. He'd never do anything without his father's permission. It was rather funny to compare them with Dad and David. When Dad came home, if he asked David to do anything it would take half an hour with lots of excuses and grumbles and in the end Dad would lose his temper and say, 'I'll do it myself then,' and David would say something like, 'Oof, you get on my nerves,' as he clattered through the house on his way to do whatever it was, badly of course and Abu Abed would look up from his plastering or tiling or whatever he was doing and just *look* at David very briefly. He didn't actually say anything, of course, but he looked at him. That got under David's skin.

Abu Abed had lots of problems, his wife was ill and he had to take her for treatment to Ramallah and to Hadassah hospital to our doctors, and sometimes even to Amman where he had a brother, and he was involved in a law suit about a patch of land, against an ex-villager who now lived in America. He used to tell Mum about these problems and she always asked him how things were going when he arrived to do some work, so he shouldn't feel she wasn't relating to him as a human being. Or that was what she told David, when he was in a hurry and wanted her attention, if she was listening to Abu Abed's problems at the time.

The intifada made things difficult for everybody. Abu Abed lived near Hebron, which meant that on the way to Jerusalem he was stuck in road blocks for document checks and got to work very late, and wasn't so reliable any more, and many people went back to employing Jewish builders and plumbers. Mum and Dad didn't blame him, but even so it was a nuisance. Since he never came on time, or came just when he could, and not at a time we'd fixed, he was around when we were all out, and there was this problem about the key. Mum always boasted about having an Arab whom she could leave in the house on his own, he'd never touch anything, and she'd go to work and leave him plastering or whatever, and then she'd come back before he left. But she never actually *gave* him a key, though of course she gave our weekly cleaning woman a key. She said someone might notice that he was letting himself into the house, and make trouble for him. David told me that he thought she meant someone might make trouble for *us*, because when there were bombs on buses and stuff, any Arab seen around was suspect, and not everyone liked neighbours employing Arabs, and especially letting himself in with a key. Once, when Abu Abed put a plastic bag with his pitta and olives and his best pants, which he changed out of to do the painting, next to our gas canisters, some busybody went and called the police who called the sabotage squad. Fortunately the man in charge was sensible, otherwise they'd have blown up the canisters together with Abu Abed's pitta and pants.

Abu Abed was too old, or looked too old, to be suspect to the soldiers checking documents at the roadblocks, but Abed with his little moustache was just the age of men they were looking for, and sometimes he was turned back and they never arrived at all. In the end Dad spoke to some people he knew in the Civil Rights, and one of them had a cousin who knew one of the Civil Administration people in Abu Abed's area. Dad asked Abu Abed for his identity number and got him a piece of paper which whizzed him through the roadblock with however many kids he was bringing with him. After that Abu Abed thought Dad was God or someone, and every time he came, he brought us a plastic bag with figs or apricots from a tree in his garden, or the apricot toffee he made himself and put out to dry, as they do, on his roof, and Abu Abed's *leder* and his figs were served up at Mum and Dad's Friday evenings, introduced by the story of how the figs got to be there in the first place. So David told me, he's a terrible eavesdropper, hangs around at home too much if you ask me.

The figs nearly got us into trouble with the grandparents on Mum's side. One weekend they came round and we were sitting in the garden and they said what delicious figs, but they did hope Mum hadn't got them off one of those Arab women sitting on the pavement outside the post office, they're cheaper than the ones you get at the greengrocers, but at least in the shops they come in boxes with plastic wrap, which means they've been properly checked out, you know where they come from; did Mum and Dad realise that most of the West Bank Arabs still irrigated with sewage water? Remember the cholera scare in the seventies? Mum said hastily that there was no danger with fruit off the trees, only with lettuce and stuff. She didn't want Dad to tell them about Abu Abed, because her father really hates Arabs, wouldn't have one in the house, because of his war history, and she kept talking so that Dad wouldn't be able to say, as he did to friends, that these figs came from someone's garden, an Arab we know personally. Those were personal figs, David went round muttering sarcastically for days, not just any old figs.

Spring came round, and one day Abu Abed didn't turn up. It was annoying because we'd begun to depend on him, and it had been a bad winter, and there was a damp patch on one of the walls, where there's a drain outside. The sort of thing he always knew how to fix. His phone wasn't working either. He'd said that so often that Dad said he probably hadn't paid the bill and the phone had been cut off. David said that if he hadn't been living in the Territories, someone could have taken the car and gone round to see where he was – that was the problem with employing West Bank Arabs, you had no real address. All we knew was that he lived next door to a carpenter who worked for a friend, so we rang her, but she was unhelpful; she said the carpenter hadn't done a good job but she had no idea of how to get in touch with him either.

Mum found someone else to insulate the wall, and weeks went by, and then one day Abed turned up on his own, which had never happened before, with a sack on his shoulder. David and I were pitching a ball into the net on the garage wall – it was holiday time – and Dad was out, and Mum was working at her computer. She was rather annoyed at being disturbed, but Abed insisted on seeing her, not rudely but in a wheedling sort of way. His father was in Amman with his mother, he said, and he'd come along to see if there was anything that needed repairing. There wasn't. But he didn't go away, just looked round as if willing bricks to fall out or drains to burst, just to give him something to do. He pointed out that the stones in the garden path were working loose, but Mum said they could be fixed another time, she was busy, and then she added that we kids would fix them, all it needed was some more sand and earth underneath the stones. Abed looked at us and the very faintest smile appeared under the smudge of his moustache, and that annoyed David, who said, 'Yeh, we'll fix it,' though he never fixed anything. 'Sorry,' Mum said, 'tell your father we wish your mother better,' but Abed went on standing there, and it suddenly occurred to me that he really needed the work badly, or the family did, and I followed Mum into the house and told her so.

'I can't *invent* work for him, can I?' she said annoyedly, but we went back outside because David was calling. Abed was walking round the garden looking up at the trees. There had been a violent storm and a couple of branches on the pine tree between our house and the neighbours' had snapped and splintered; they were hanging by the splinters at odd angles, one of them resting on the telephone line. The branches were about twenty feet up or more, and Dad had said we'd wait for the neighbours' gardeners, who owned a proper ladder and an electric saw. But there was Abed taking a handsaw out of his sack and before we could stop him, he was half way up the tree, agile as anything, finding footholds on the stumps of other branches we'd had cut during other winters, and when there were no more of those, wedging his foot on any small growth on the trunk, or even on branches which looked much too slight to bear his weight.

'Abed, don't!' said my mother, but she didn't sound very convincing, and I knew she really did want the snapped branches cut down, she'd been nagging my father about them for days because they looked really heavy, with other smaller branches on top of them, and she'd told us not to go underneath the tree because one more gust of wind and they'd come toppling down on us. And Abed was already up there, half sitting half lying in a narrow fork between the trunk and one of the snapped branches and sawing away at the splintered wood. The handsaw made an old fashioned sort of rasping noise, unlike the shriek of the electric saws which had been busy in the road all that week, but it was enough to bring out the neighbour who looked on, as there was just a chance that one of the branches might fall into his yard.

'He'll fall,' said my mother with a little catch in her voice.

'No he won't,' said the neighbour. 'They never do.'

'Gravity doesn't apply to Arabs,' said David under his breath. 'Mum, get him down.'

One branch loosened and fell, Abed flinging an arm round the trunk just in time.

'Abed, leave the other branch,' my mother called up to him. 'Enough. The other branch can wait.'

But Abed was already higher up in the tree, almost hidden by branches and foliage; we could just see his arm with the saw going backwards and forwards across the second, splintered branch. Then the saw caught in the wood and as he leaned forward to free it, saw, branch and Abed slowly fell. Abed, who was heavier, was underneath, but luckily he fell on to the earth, which was soft from the rain, not on to the wall, made of concrete, which divided our garden from the neighbours'.

He was just a bit shaken, to our relief, or – as Mum said – his whole clan would have been after us, though it was his idea to climb up there in the first place, not ours, we hadn't even asked him to saw the branches off. Mum and Dad talked that evening about how grandpa (Mum's side) had accidentally knocked down an Arab kid driving through East Jerusalem, he wasn't really hurt, grandpa drives so slowly, but people called an ambulance and police wouldn't let the Arab witnesses have grandpa's address; they said 'you never know.' This time no one called the police. The only witness was the neighbour, who said maybe Abed should go and have an x-ray, but he laughed, and Mum gave him some mint tea with a lot of sugar, and then he got paid and went, limping a bit but apparently all right.

That weekend Uncle Ron from Tel Aviv, who's a lawyer, incidentally, came to dinner and heard the whole story and asked Dad if he had third party insurance for people working in the house, and Dad said sure, of course, so Ron said just as well, because you never know. Mum said – rather nervously, I thought – that Abu Abed wasn't that sort of person, he knew exactly what had happened and wouldn't have blamed us. Ron said sure, but repeated that you never knew, and though Abu Abed might not want to make anything of it, his lawyer might, there were plenty of West Bank lawyers who would have jumped at something like this as a test case. David said Abu Abed did have a lawyer, because didn't Mum remember Abu Abed telling her he had a law suit about some land with a neighbour of his? There you are, said Uncle Ron. What do you mean, a test case? Dad asked. I wouldn't worry, said Ron, but I don't suppose you've been paying National Insurance for him, have you? And what about VAT? I don't suppose he charges VAT either, does he? Dad laughed and said this isn't north Tel Aviv, I don't ask for receipts from Abu Abed, he doesn't keep books.

All right, said Ron, but just be careful. Your Abu Abed may be dumb but there are plenty of wise guys out there ready to make something of an accident like that. You were lucky.

Ron had everyone worried, and we were very pleased when Abu Abed and Abed turned up two weeks later, ready for work. This time they fixed the garden path and whitewashed the garage, which didn't really need whitewashing, but it was Pesach time anyway, and only David noticed that Abed still had a bit of a limp, and after the first day's work he told Dad he ought to insist that Abed have an x-ray. Mum said that David was right, that if it had been one of us she'd have had an x-ray done straight away.

'He isn't one of us,' said David caustically, 'they have plastic bones, don't they?' Dad told David to shut up; no one could walk around with a broken bone, Abed would have been in hellish pain, it was probably just a bruise which could make him limp for weeks.

'Never realised you were a doctor as well,' said David, and Mum told him, as she always did, not to speak to his father like that, which made no impression whatever.

Dad appeared to be right, as Abed's limp grew less, and everything returned to normal, although we noticed that Mum hovered a bit when Abu Abed came to work. Not that she had to worry, as he really never did anything dangerous, he wasn't a carpenter or an electrician and never pretended to know anything at all about mending machines, and you can't get into much trouble fixing a drain. But then the two of them, Mum and Dad, made their biggest mistake.

We had this old car, a Fiat, which Dad called a 'carthorse' though by this time it couldn't really have pulled a pram, let alone a cart. It stood outside the house most of the time as Dad had a newish Renault and Mum took taxis when she was in a hurry, but she used the Fiat for local shopping for a while before giving up on it completely. The engine was all right, and so were the brakes and the steering, it had passed the test, but the rest of it was a disaster. It had been broken into so many times that the driver's door didn't close properly and the others were jammed; passengers had to crawl in over the driver's seat, under the steering wheel and over the gear stick, the carburettor made a noise like Judgement Day and it wasn't worth mechanics fees. No one even tried to steal it any more, or to raid it for spare parts. Every time we took it to the filling station – we never put in more than a quarter of a tank – one of the Arab attendants asked how much we wanted for it. It was a favourite Arab car, the Fiat – there were plenty of stolen spare parts in the West Bank to fix it with, people said – and David stopped driving it because the police pulled him up so often and then – because he wasn't an Arab – let him go even without questioning him. That made David so angry that I asked him whether he'd rather have been charged with handling stolen cars. I don't remember whose idea it was to give the Fiat to Abed.

Abed was over the moon, I've never seen anyone made so happy just because of getting an old wreck of a car. It made Mum and Dad feel gratified that it was going to change Abed's life, that for the first time he was going to have wheels. Remembering Ron's warnings, they gave him the car documents, and explained about renewing the compulsory insurance in his own name in case he hit someone. That didn't look likely as he drove off, carefully, not flooding the engine or burning the brakes as David always did. We all felt very pleased about having made the Abu Abed family mobile, more or less, and Dad said they could always find a local mechanic to patch the car up. As the neighbour said, 'they'll mend it with string'.

Everything that happened afterwards we learned from the newspaper, and the police who came round to ask questions. It was on the television news too, but so briefly that we missed it and they didn't repeat the item, and it was just lucky the TV journalists didn't bother to interview us, though they might have done. Our name wasn't in the paper either. Some people will do anything to get on to TV, but it was the last thing our parents wanted, I'll say that for them.

What happened was this: a few days after we gave Abed the Fiat, there was an ambush on one of the roads leading from the

Hebron road to a settlement, and one of the settlers was killed. The army set up a road block to trap the killers, and Abed ran into it. In the ordinary way this wouldn't have been a problem for Abed; all he had to do was to slow down, stop and present his papers and those of Abu Abed, who was with him in the Fiat. All the papers were in order except for one thing: Abed didn't have a driving licence, it turned out, and he panicked. God knows what he thought would happen to him, he'd have been fined, of course, and banned from driving, but he hadn't hurt anyone, so they wouldn't have jailed him, or at least that's what Ron said. Anyway, he panicked. So instead of slowing down and stopping, he turned the car right round on two wheels and drove back the way he had come, stepping on the accelerator, and a soldier had to jump out of the way. The soldiers fired in the air and yelled at him to stop, but he didn't. So they assumed he and his father were the killers and fired again, first at the tyres and then into the car, and they killed Abu Abed straight off and wounded Abed.

A day or so later, as I said, the army sent the police round to ask Mum and Dad about the car and how it had come into Abed's possession. They thought it might have been stolen, together with the documents, but Dad assured them it was all above board, that he'd given Abed the car as a present (prompted by Ron, he didn't say it was in part payment for re-laying the garden path, which it was) and that squared with what Abed had told them in the hospital, and in jail. The enquiry was no big deal, they just took a statement from Dad; there had been plenty of incidents like this in the past. The important thing was to investigate whether the soldiers who killed Abu Abed had acted 'according to the rule book', which apparently they had. After all, there had been a murder a couple of days earlier on that road, and Abed's behaviour had been suspicious.

I think my parents were pretty shaken. Mum and Dad had

thought they were doing Abed a favour and instead it had ended with his father getting killed. But – since this is where you come into it – and since I'm supposed to tell you anything I like, Dad said, and whatever comes into my head, I don't think it's Abu Abed's death that's upset us all so much, as what went on afterwards between David and Dad.

David came home from school, with the evening paper in his hand, and without even taking his satchel off his back he began attacking Dad.

'Why didn't you check that Abed had a driving licence? You checked everything else, didn't you? You made sure *we* were in the clear.'

Dad made the mistake of arguing with him, of defending himself.

'When you sell a car,' he said, 'you don't check if the buyer has a *driving* licence; that's *his* responsibility.'

'This wasn't an ordinary sale,' said David, 'nothing else between you and Abu Abed was legal, you can't be so holy now about it, he didn't give you receipts and you didn't pay VAT or insurance while he was working for you, as you ought to have done, even for one day's work you pay insurance, that's what you do with the cleaning woman, because she's Jewish and she knows her rights.'

'We were doing him a favour,' said Mum.

'No you weren't,' said David, turning on her, 'you were just getting the car off the road, you know you'd wanted to for ages, and you'd have had to pay to have it taken away.'

'Don't talk to your mother like that,' said Dad, righteous all of a sudden.

'And you don't change the subject,' answered David, 'bunch of hypocrites,' and he actually had tears in his eyes, not for Abu Abed I think but maybe for himself, because we'd never had a row like this, and it was getting dangerous. Which is why, of course, Dad rang you up and asked me to talk to you, because

I'm the only one in the family who's calm and detached about the whole business.

What do *I* think about it? Well, I think the main thing is that we all feel guilty and that makes us angry but there really isn't any reason to feel guilty, we didn't create this situation. Oh, and something else. I said I'd tell you Abu Abed's real name. It was Muhammed Deir Yassin, he's the son of one of those refugees from the village where we slaughtered about a hundred people in the pre-State period. Well, the killers weren't people like us, they were rightists, but it sticks to us too. His name was written on all the documents which the policemen brought, and it's funny as I said that we never knew it before, probably because Dad never put the whole thing on a legal footing. But maybe that's another reason Abu Abed never demanded his rights, never showed us any document with his whole name, I mean, who would have employed him, with a name like that?

FAMILY TREE

ELIE AVRAHAMI WAS a Sefardi, sixth generation in the country. The pedigree defined him, elevated him to the highest rank this irreverent country was likely to grant anyone: a gentleman, as he was always described, using the English word. He spoke softly, and people instinctively lowered their voices when talking to him. His great grandfather had worn the Ottoman fez, and on the walls of his law office were photographs of his grandfather wearing the horsehair wig of a British Mandate judge, and of his father, newly graduated from Oxford – wearing the gown and holding the mortarboard, but with the black velvet skullcap proudly visible. His family belonged in this part of the world, had been here, naturally and inevitably, as far back as anyone could remember. Those who had ruled the country had known that, and had honoured and promoted its members, who had been judges, mayors – notables, in a word – long before the upstart Eastern Europeans, the socialists and their rivals, had battled for control of the community.

The socialists had gone now, and there were other Sefardi Jews, north Africans, most of them, factory workers and lorry drivers, bank clerks and policemen and the seminarists who wore the black frock coats of the orthodox Polish Jews and had rabbis whose hands they kissed; but these Sefardis had no kinship with the Avrahamis, were even more remote from them than the European Jews. The origins of the Avrahamis and their peers were in the Levant. They wrote unpublished memoirs, nursed their grievances, and – like Elie – they became the guardians of their history and prestige. Their power was concentrated in banking and in real estate and consolidated by dynastic intermarriage. Sometimes the clans could be seen, formally dressed, at charitable events for unlike the intellectual elite of the city who cultivated their friendship, their status depended on their generosity – or grouped round the table at very expensive restaurants where old women sometimes ate alone and visiting American philanthropists were taken on official expense accounts. They played bridge.

Elie Avrahami lived with his wife in a magnificent but dilapidated mansion in what had once been the thriving centre of a much smaller city, and still carried on his working life behind his grandfather's old brass plate over the battered door in a neglected building in a grimy side street behind the main post office. His office was furnished with a threadbare Persian carpet, two or three chairs, and a plant which had not been wiped or dusted in years but had grown so high that it folded back against the ceiling and towards the window, as if hoping one day to escape from the world of fading paper which surrounded it to the trees in the park outside. His desk was covered with files piled so high that his head, over his stiff wing collar – something hardly anyone wore these days – was only just visible beyond them. Friends who dropped in to consult him wondered whether he even knew the identity or vintage of the files on the lower levels of this pyramid, and how he might extract one without the whole structure toppling to the floor, though frequent visitors noted that while its height never varied, the files were regularly consulted and rearranged. The disregard for show, the overloaded desk over which Elie's taut, enquiring face peered at his clients, had its own subtle theatricality, unlike the ostentatious busyness of the humming, thick-carpeted offices of some of his colleagues. He had never agreed to be interviewed on television, like so many of the ambitious lawyers and doctors of the city. He also refused the appeals of rival politicians and squabbling neighbours to represent them.

Elie Avrahami was one of the best lawyers in the city, learned beyond compare, respected even in the Supreme Court, but he was a specialist. His field was property law, and in particular, the laws governing the acquisition and sale of that section of central city land still in private hands – buildings and plots belonging to old families like his own, to Arabs and to the churches. No one knew better than he the intricacies of Ottoman property and land law, the records of the Tapu land registry, the yellowed, indistinct handwriting of its deceased clerks. As most of his clients were wealthy, he did not need more than a few cases a year to keep him and his wife in modest comfort, while a hardworking junior handled the notarial business of the firm, which paid his own salary and the rental of the premises.

It was through his work in the files of the land registry that Elie had first traced the origins of his family; locating one branch after another, disentangling the in-laws from the outlaws, the rabbis from the rentiers, the dependants from the poor relations, in what became the passion and eventually the main occupation of his life. For nearly thirty years he had followed the Avrahamis down every alley of the last three centuries, collected their marriage and their death certificates, their commercial charters and correspondences in several languages. Their portraits – from a great oil painting of his grandfather to the small daguerreotypes and tiny oval watercolours in lockets – decorated his house or were laid neatly in the drawers of an old trousseau chest. It grieved him that he could not visit Syria, where he suspected the family had still deeper roots, but an Arab client of his had visited archives and antique shops in Damascus and unearthed a menorah with the family name engraved beneath it, invisible until the plinth it stood on was unscrewed. In an Istanbul library he had found a book annotated by his maternal great-grandfather, and in the Turkish archives, details of a law suit conducted by a great uncle against a distant cousin.

The Avrahami home stood just off the main Jaffa Road, once the commercial centre of the Jewish part of the city, the 'triangle' of three main roads with cafés, shops, banks and cinemas. The banks were still there, but commerce and recreation in the city had migrated: to the huge shopping mall in the suburbs, to multiple cinema halls in the industrial zone, to what one mayor had dubbed the 'Cultural Mile' stretching from a gentrified quarter facing the old city walls to the theatre, a concrete bastion near the Presidential residence.

The most expensive streets were shaded by trees and dotted with European-style gardens with their intensive-care drippers and sprinklers. The Avrahami mansion, at the centre of a stone patio with palms and urns of geraniums, lay in a dusty, deserted wasteland of car parks and empty lots, with hoardings carrying advertisements for rock concerts and rabbinical edicts, and at the corner of the main street, the only public lavatory in the area. Despite its surroundings, the house, like Elie Avrahami, had a noble pedigree: each generation since its construction in 1870 had confirmed in legal documents its founder's wish that the house was to remain within the family, never to be sold.

But the mansion was under invisible siege. For years the city's bureaucrats, the building contractors, the industrialists busily converting western Jerusalem into a modern, ring-roaded, multi-storeyed, high-rise centre, had been trying to persuade Elie Avrahami to sell up and move out. For he owned not only the house and its garden, but the car park and the empty lots around it. He was not the only private owner of property in this central, and valuable, area of town; but the others, while living elsewhere, held on to the land because it was constantly rising in price. Rather than exchange real estate for cash, they yielded parcels of land or old buildings to the builders and the contractors only when sons and daughters and their families needed ready money. But Elie Avrahami had no children. He resisted the developers because the house, with its lonely backyards, was his heritage. He and his sister, who was also childless, were agreed that the house was to go to the Israel Museum, as an annexe, and the land to the Municipality, as a park in their name. They were the last surviving Avrahamis.

Until one evening he answered the telephone in his study and was told by a cheery American stranger that he was talking to his cousin Joe from Minneapolis.

'I am desolate that you have the wrong person,' he said in his Gallic English. 'I have no relations in the United States.'

'That's what you think,' said Joe with a laugh. 'We never doubted we had relatives in Israel. I'm only sorry I can't talk to you in Hebrew, but we're working on it.'

'Who gave you my phone number?' Elie demanded, less courteous now. He made a mental note to reprimand his clerk.

Joe sounded only slightly disconcerted. 'You know your grandfather – my great-grandfather – had a brother called Menashe.'

'How is that?' Elie had a moment of mental dizziness. The communal records which had perpetuated that phase of the family history had, he knew, been destroyed in the earthquake of 1927. Only his grandfather's private papers, preserved by the family, bore Menashe's name. How would such information have fallen into the hands of this American stranger?

'I can hear this is a bad moment,' said Joe. 'Just tell me when I can come round. We have to talk. I've got the whole family tree from 1890. You can fill me in on the Middle East side.'

'The Middle East *side*? But all the Avrahami family are from the Levant. With a very short period in Salonika,' he corrected himself, 'but that branch returned to Safed in 1880.'

'Have I got news for you!' said Joe. 'I told them you'd be surprised. I'm learning more about our family every day. And today you can do it all from your own home; we might even get some more details about the Latvian branch, we've just opened a web site. Of course, they might have all been wiped out in the Shoah, but you never know. Now the Communists have gone we might even find out.'

Elie was even more alert. 'Whom did you tell?' he asked. 'Who are you working for?'

There was a puzzled silence. 'Working for? The family at home, of course,' said Joe. 'We're all into this; aunts in Florida, the New York family, my kids — we're all hooked on this thing. We've been everywhere. On the net, that is. I've worked on it day and night for six months now. This is my first actual visit here.'

'How do you come to have the name of Menashe Avrahami? Who told you about him?'

'Why, Mr Avrahami, what a question! You did yourself.'

'*I* did?'

'In your monograph, of course. That was really a great piece of research. For the 1970s, that is.'

'That monograph was read to the Oriental Society in Paris which is open only to members. I don't think that you belong to this society.'

Joe Abrams laughed long and loudly, as if appreciating a very subtle joke. 'I do not, you're right. But anything in print finds its way on to the net eventually.'

'The net?'

'Internet, Mr Avrahami, don't tell me you aren't on it yourself.'

'I am not. But why are you collecting this information?'

'Like I told you, I'm drawing up a family tree. It takes up ten square feet in my apartment now, on the wall. How many Jewish families can go this far back, if they're not Rothschilds? Not that we've done badly.'

Elie nodded grimly to himself, as if confirming a suspicion, and took up his pen. 'I should like you to give me your name and address, and other details.'

'Sure. Joe Abrams. I'll give you my card. The family shortened the name when they arrived in the States from Latvia. But there are plenty of original Avrahamis elsewhere.'

'No doubt,' said Elie, coolly. 'Please come to see me in my office on Thursday at five in the evening, and we can discuss this further. But let me make things absolutely clear at the outset, so that we do not waste your time. I have no intention whatsoever of selling.'

'Selling what?'

'Thursday evening, Mr Abrams. The office address is in the book, as you probably already know.' And he put down the telephone.

At dinner that night he told his wife his suspicions. 'At first I was completely puzzled, but now it's clear. Since they can't get us to sell, they're plotting to challenge our ownership. They have a branch in the States of course, and they've found someone who will claim a share in the property – as a family inheritance, through Menashe and his children.'

His wife looked at him wonderingly – touchingly so in his eyes.

Aviva Avrahami trusted her husband to solve all the practical problems of their joint existence; she was a woman who had gone straight from her father's care to that of her husband, and knew no more of the world than they had allowed her to know – which was the limit of possible expenditure on their household economy, the charities to whose work she contributed, her own elegant clothing. As a consequence, she had an unlined face but also an overly docile temperament; sometimes Elie

wished that she could contribute rather more to their occasional
discussions than the kind of question she now asked.

'But surely, Elie, with all your knowledge, you can contradict
them?'

He answered, with a trace of irritation: 'Of course, but do
you realise the annoyance, the waste of time, the interminable
formalities, the postponements, the time in court.'

'So what advantage is it to them? You've always said they
wanted a quick sale so they could start building.'

The innocent logic of the question annoyed him even more.
'They're hoping to wear me down, of course. So that I'll sell
now, to prevent all the inconvenience and the waste of time.'

'Well,' said Aviva placidly, 'You'll just have to make it clear
to Mr Abrams that it isn't worth *his* time and trouble either.
You can be very hard when you want to be.'

The American, Elie noticed immediately with satisfaction,
could not have looked less like an Avrahami. He had reddish
sparse hair, fair skin, a plump face and blunt features. He was
not wearing the kind of clothes Elie regarded as suitable for a
business interview, but a sunhat — which he removed — an
open-necked short-sleeved shirt, and shorts, and all that was
visible of him was covered with freckles: his face, his balding
head, his forearms, and his round, shiny knees. 'Hot day,' he
remarked, after offering a damp hand for Elie to shake.

'Well, better get down to business,' he added, and from
under his left arm he extracted an enormous roll of stiff paper.
'This is the shorter version,' he said with a wink. 'Now, where
do I put it?' He looked at the wall of files on Elie's desk, and
recognised that dismantling it was impossible. 'How about the
floor?' But one look at Elie's face indicated that there was no
way this erect figure in the stiff collar was going to get down on
hands and knees.

Elie asked his clerk to prepare a table in the next room – the one he used for architects' plans, he specified. While the clerk was doing so, and without any invitation from Elie who sat silently watching him, Joe Abrams explained his mission.

'I guess you're wondering how I got into this. I ask myself that all the time. It takes up most of my spare time, and my wife keeps telling me it's bad for the eyes, for the back. All the peering into screens; not just the PC, but the microfilm. Everyone else is playing golf or working out in the gym, she says, and what are you doing? Putting together a jigsaw puzzle – that's not exercise. My partners have been complaining too. I put in less overtime than I used to – I'm in real estate, you see' – at this a flicker of interest passed over Elie's face, which Joe noticed: 'What's your speciality as an attorney?'

'Property,' said Elie drily, and Joe's face lit up. 'Well, that's good to hear, I'd thought I was the only one in the whole family with an interest in real estate – we're all doctor this and professor that in the States, we need some practical sense. How is it with the Middle East branch?'

Elie answered only with reluctance. However, he had agreed to see the man; he had to respond, had to keep the man in his office long enough to find out what precisely was his strategy, even if it meant listening to this nonsense.

'The Avrahamis were traditionally dealers in jewels.' Abrams nodded. 'They were always skilled in commerce, and for the last few generations, they have been active in the law. My sister is also a lawyer, though of course no longer an Avrahami. She is married to a Valero.'

'Well, you know we don't have to go along with that any more, women can keep the name going these days.'

'Impossible,' said Elie curtly.

'You'd accept an Avrahami woman who remarried into the clan the second time round, wouldn't you?' said Abrams cunningly.

'Sarita Zacuto Avrahami,' replied Elie, automatically.

'That's the lady!' said Joe triumphantly, 'I can see we're going to have a lot to talk about,' and Elie wished he had not answered. He wanted nothing to do with this man; he hated the intimacy that was being forced on him. He got up abruptly and went to assist his clerk, who was stacking papers and files neatly on the floor. 'This won't take long,' he assured him. But when Joe had unrolled his chart, which immediately coiled up at both ends, and manoeuvred one section into the centre of the desk, Elie was disconcerted.

It was like looking at the familiar map of the world and seeing that a whole new continent had been added, a new shape which altered and deformed the original. The genealogical chart which Elie knew so well, the tree with its particular configurations, linkages and dead ends, its prolific and its withered branches, was pushed to one side; headed 'Middle East' and spattered with question marks in red ink, it hung down over the edge of the table. Only an outlying arm of the eighteenth-century Istanbul branch, which after settling in the Holy Land came to a full stop in Jerusalem with Elie and his sister Shoshana, was fully visible; Europe had shrunken to a dot in Latvia, but America – a formidable size – was densely populated with Avrahamis.

According to Elie's research, Yehoshua Avrahami, jeweller to one of the later Sultans, had married twice (it was unclear whether the second marriage was bigamous or had taken place shortly after his first wife's death) and the only child of this late marriage was Menashe, who had made off first to Greece and then, as testified by a solitary letter home which it had taken Elie years to locate, to the Baltic. Whether he had married, and to whom, and whether he had any children at all, was unknown to Elie, and had never interested him. Having left the Levant, abandoned his family, for Elie he had become an outcast. But here, on Joe Abrams' chart, was a Menashe

Avramovich of Dvinsk, married to Marya (question mark, though whether the question applied to the marriage or the name was unclear) whose nine sons and daughters had all emigrated to the United States in the 1880s and spawned the whole new continent, an immense tree of Abramoviches and Abramses, including the freckled intruder now looking expectantly at Elie for his reaction.

'Avramovich is not Avrahami,' Elie objected.

Abrams looked at him pityingly. 'Sure,' he said. 'I checked that out. Avrahami was his original name, it's in all the sources. And there's another thing; I haven't been there myself, but there's a website for people finding out about roots in Eastern Europe – ancestors dot com – and they find photographers to go round the old Jewish quarters and take pictures. We got lucky. There was an old building – it's gone now – with a jeweller's shop, as you said, Avramovich Rings Bought and Sold, with the name Avrahami in brackets. Must be the same guy.' And he produced a photocopy of an old photograph from his folder in which all this was indistinctly visible. There was also a shadowy figure near the door who might or might not have been the proprietor.

'That is not evidence. It wouldn't stand up in court,' said Elie, allowing himself a smile. 'Such things can be easily fabricated.'

'Court?' said Abrams, amazed. 'Who said anything about a court?'

'Please,' said Elie, indicating that they should return to his office. Abrams, discomfited, rolled up his chart and followed the older man.

When they were both seated, Abrams clutching the roll awkwardly on his knees, Elie said, 'I think I told you on the telephone that I do not wish to sell any portion of the property, whatever you may have heard. I don't want to bore you with the details, but there have been many attempts to persuade me to sell. You may have been told that things are otherwise, but I am simply not interested. It is a great pity that you should waste your time on this' – he gestured to the chart – 'this *game* and these fictitious relatives.'

Abrams face flamed. 'Hey, that is *really* insulting,' he said, clutching his roll of paper even tighter.

Elie looked at him coolly, but the man did not avert his eyes, and Elie had a moment of doubt. 'God,' said Abrams angrily, 'I thought, I thought I was going to meet someone who was just as deep into this as I am. I thought you'd be *pleased* to find out more about our family, and I want to tell you, I don't know anything about any property and I wouldn't give a shit if I did, I'm doing well enough, I don't want anything that belongs to you, Mr Avrahami, I wanted to know more about this great family of ours, but if you want to disown your own ancestors, that's your business, I guess. They weren't just jewellers, we had great thinkers, great architects, great writers; nothing to be ashamed of. I've traced them all back to Menashe.' He got up.

'Wait,' said Elie, holding out his hand 'Perhaps we could go into this further—'

'No way,' said Abrams, still angry, 'You think I'm after money, we can't work together. I'll carry on by myself.' And he stalked out of the office.

'You're still worried about that ridiculous man, aren't you?' Aviva Avrahami was alert to her husband's moods, but knew no better than to state the problem without suggesting a remedy. This only annoyed him.

'Of course not,' he lied. In fact he had spent the weeks since Abrams' visit reading about those named Abramovich (or Abrahamowitz, Abramovitz, or Abramovicz) who had emigrated to the United States from the Baltic during the last two decades of the nineteenth century, or rather, since there were so many sons of Abraham, in different permutations, of those who were the most distinguished, those who appeared in encyclopaedias and anthologies. One had indeed been called Avrahami, one of a number of pseudonyms; he was a maverick Zionist, who had supported the idea of a Jewish state in Uganda and ended his life as a publisher in England. There was an Abramovitz who had revolutionised the use of concrete in building, another who had made his name in American journalism criticising abuses of the law in real estate, and a third – a rabbi – who had given evidence about the Talmud in a famous libel case. None of them resembled Elie's family, which had always been well assimilated, conservative, living and worshipping quietly, indistinguishable in most ways from their Arab neighbours. Elie spent hours in the Diaspora museum in Tel Aviv consulting print-outs about Dvinsk, tapping slowly on computers, which he had never used before; it was all very alien to his own archival knowledge of the Avrahami family. How had Abrams traced all these noisy radicals back to Yehoshua the jeweller? There was a sole possible link: the letter Menashe had sent to his father, the one letter he ever had sent home, one of Elie's most prized finds, discovered in the pages of an old book, locked away in the trousseau chest together with the daguerreotypes and the lockets. But there was no document to prove the connection between Menashe and the Americans.

Since his meeting with Abrams, Elie had had qualms, worried that he had acted too hastily. The man's anger, he thought, might have been genuine. Confronted with an accusation, caught out in a lie, some men might react with anger, but Joe Abrams did not seem to Elie to be such a man.

But then the surveyors arrived.

At first they came without equipment. Aviva noticed them – two men who were pacing slowly between the noticeboard on the far side of the car park and the fence enclosing the patio, measuring the distance with their feet. By the time she went out of the house to question them, they had gone. She did not mention the visit to her husband. These days everything made him nervous.

The second time it was Elie who spotted them from his study, one passing a measuring tape to the other, as they calculated the length of the waste lot adjoining one wall of the house. He opened the window and asked who had sent them.

'The contractors,' one said.

'Who? Which contractors?'

The two men looked at one another, and shrugged their shoulders. 'They didn't tell us,' they said, and turned away.

'You have no right to be here,' he called out to them. 'This is private property.' But they ignored him. He rang the municipality and spoke to clerks in the town engineer's office, but none knew of any contractor who could have sent surveyors. The men were nothing to do with them. His suspicions of Abrams revived.

He took his sister, Shoshana, who was a criminal lawyer, into his confidence. Their childlessness had kept them very close, and she was Elie's partner in the inheritance, and his confidante in a way that his wife was not. Aviva could commiserate, but Shoshana would advise. Brother and sister met in a garden café near Elie's house. Shoshana carried her black gown slung over one shoulder; she was between hearings.

'Neither one nor the other,' she said when she had heard the story.

'What do you mean?'

'Abrams is no innocent. But you've brought this on yourself. On us, that is.'

'How?'

'Your monograph set him off on this search, which may have been genuine. But now he knows that there is money involved – because you've told him – he'll try even harder to prove he is a joint heir. Meanwhile he is assessing how much the property can be worth.'

'The surveyors,' muttered Elie, aghast.

'Exactly.' Shoshana looked at her watch. 'I have to be in court.'

'So what do you suggest I do now?' Elie's clients would scarcely have recognised their severe lawyer in the man who now looked appealingly at his sister. He had always thought of her as harder headed than himself.

'I'll think of something. If Abrams gets in touch again, send him to me.'

But Abrams did not ring. Instead, a letter arrived in Elie's office one day from a lawyers' firm in Tel Aviv – a firm with ten partners and an envelope with a logo in the shape of a crown, no less – informing him that Joseph Abrams of Minneapolis, USA, representing eighteen other residents of that city, of Baltimore and of New York, intended to contest the ownership registered in the Jerusalem Tapu by which Elie Avrahami and Shoshana Valero were declared to be joint heirs to several parcels of land (and here an exact description was given), on the grounds of their direct descent from a common ancestor. While they were not desirous of occupying any buildings on the site, or of themselves making use of the property, they would expect to be compensated at such a time as the property changed hands. Documentation was attached.

When Elie and Shoshana next conferred together – in Elie's office, this time, with the desk for architect's plans once more cleared, and all the documents spread out, compared, and studied – they looked at one another with consternation. There were some twenty photocopies of documents. Some were taken from a Latvian archive, with translations, such translations duly notarised and confirmed as accurate by another notary public in New York, of the date of Menashe Avrahami's naturalisation as a Russian citizen; of the name-change from

Avrahami to Avramovich in Dvinsk; of the death certificate of the same Menashe Avramovich, of the birth certificates of his children, and of their naturalisation as American citizens; and all subsequent certificates in the American archives.

'Extraordinary,' muttered Elie, painfully admiring. 'I've never seen such complete documentation going so far back.'

'He's trumped us, hasn't he, with his Internet?' said Shoshana angrily, bent like Elie over the documents. But then a thought struck her, and she straightened up 'But he's forgotten something. All this proves is that there was a Menashe Avrahami who changed his name in Dvinsk, and who his descendants were. But who was this Menashe Avrahami?'

'What do you mean who was he? He was our grandfather's brother.'

'We know that; but he can't be sure. These documents show *us* that it's the same Menashe, but *they* have no evidence. There are thousands of Avrahamis, as you say, and Avramovichs, all over the world. The only document to link him with us and our property in Jerusalem is that letter in your possession, telling your grandfather that he'd arrived in the Baltic and the date when he became a Russian citizen – the same date as the one on Abrams' document. You mentioned in your article that there was a Menashe, but you said nothing about the letter. From their point of view the link is missing.'

'In any case,' said Elie, only half listening to her, 'They realise that for as long as I'm alive they have no chance of getting hold of the house or the grounds. Property which is occupied can never be contested successfully.' He drew a deep breath.

'But there *is* a problem, Elie,' said Shoshana. 'They're all much younger than we are. You said yourself that Abrams isn't more than forty. They'll fight it after we go. They might find the letter.'

'Never,' said Elie, furiously. 'They'll never get our property, not an inch of it.'

'There's only one way of making absolutely sure,' said his sister, and after a moment's hesitation, since she knew her brother: 'Destroy the letter.'

Elie sat late that night in his study, looking round at his possessions: the ormolu clock with a pendulum, presented to his father by an Armenian client, the beautiful Persian carpets, the porcelain and the glass. He had willed all this to the Museum, so that a part of the house should be kept as it had always been, with a plaque at the entrance explaining the family's history. Other rooms would hold minor collections of nineteenth-century art, of which a few watercolours of the Holy Land by foreign visitors were his own. For the first time he imagined all this disintegrated, sold off to different bidders, lodged apart. He knew what happened after death. His own body would be washed by strangers' hands, and if the property was divided, the buyers would come, each turning away finally with one object in their hands, divorcing it from the others.

He wrote out the first draft of what was to be the best, the most closely reasoned legal paper of his life, arguing that whatever the claims put forward by the Abrams and other families of the United States, there was absolutely no evidence to support their assertion that they were descendants of Yehoshua Avrahami of Istanbul and Jerusalem, who had built the house to which he and his sister were the last heirs.

The next day, he decided, he would check his sources and write a final draft, to be lodged with the legal adviser to the Museum with precise instructions.

And then Elie Avrahami rummaged in the trousseau chest for Menashe's letter, and – without re-reading it – tore it neatly into pieces, as if it were a bill settled long ago, and not one of the final pieces in the structure he himself had built, with so much care, over so many years. As he did so, he recalled, without quite knowing why, that in many of the oldest Jewish houses in Jerusalem one corner, one lintel, was deliberately left unfinished as a reminder of the destruction of the Temple. Abrams might do his worst now, might assemble a whole host of new inheritors with his modern expertise; there was virtue, still, in imperfection.

MOBILE SERVICES
01633 256550

716104 W

12/04

MAINDEE

MALPAS

13.7.05